Girls Can't Hit

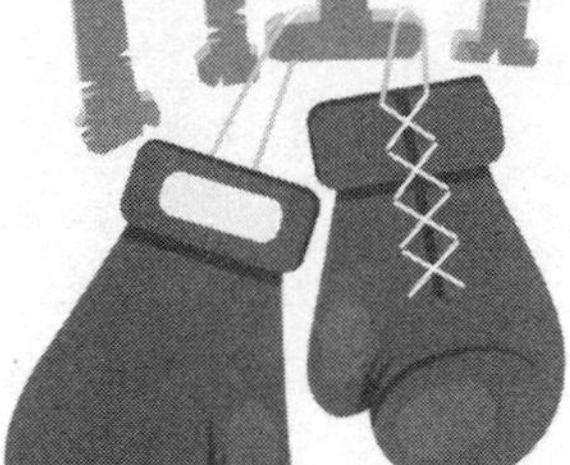

Girls Can't Hit

T. S. EASTON

FEIWEL AND FRIENDS
NEW YORK

A FEIWEL AND FRIENDS BOOK
An imprint of Macmillan Publishing Group, LLC
175 Fifth Avenue, New York, NY 10010

Our books may be purchased in bulk for promotional, educational, or
business use. Please contact your local bookseller or the Macmillan
Corporate and Premium Sales Department at (800) 221-7945 ext. 5442
or by e-mail at MacmillanSpecialMarkets@macmillan.com.

Library of Congress Cataloging-in-Publication Data is available.
ISBN 978-1-250-10232-4 (hardcover) / ISBN 978-1-250-10233-1 (ebook)

Book design by April Ward
Feiwel and Friends logo designed by Filomena Tuosto
First edition, 2018

1 3 5 7 9 10 8 6 4 2

fiercereads.com

For my daughters. Who can.

With special thanks to Alice and Rikke and everyone at Farnham Boxing Club—Where Champions Are Made!

GiRLS CAN'T HIT

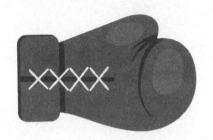

PART ONE

THE
CONTENDER

THE DISHWASHER

I groaned inwardly. It was a cold Tuesday morning in May and my parents were arguing about the dishwasher again.

"Honestly, Liz," Dad said, "you don't need to rinse the plates before putting them in. That's the whole point of a dishwasher."

"If you rinse the plates," Mum said patiently, "then the dishwasher is more effective. Otherwise, you get potato starch streaking the glasses."

"Look," Dad said, "why don't you go and sit down and let me do this?"

"Oh no," Mum said. "I'm not falling for that. You'll start putting wooden spoons in."

"You CAN put wooden spoons in," Dad said. "That's why we bought the German one."

"If you two don't stop arguing about the dishwasher," I butted in, "I will throw it into a quarry."

"We're not arguing, darling," Mum said brightly. "We're just discussing."

Other unimportant things my parents ~~argue about~~ just discuss include:

- Whether to butter both pieces of bread in a sandwich, or leave one side for condiments only.

- Whether to put your coat on a few minutes before leaving in order to "get toasty" or just as you leave so you "feel the benefit."

- Whether jam or cream goes first on a scone.

- Whether Jaffa Cakes are cookies or cakes. ("There's a clue in the name, Liz!")

- Whether you're allowed to fold the corners of book pages over to keep your place.

None of these issues will ever be resolved. Ever.

I love my parents dearly, but they drive me crazy sometimes. Aside from her dishwasher obsession, my mother is possibly the most terrified person on the planet. She panics over the tiniest things and she won't let me do anything that she considers even remotely dangerous. She made me wear a neon vest on my walk to school right up to eighth grade before I rebelled and threw it into a duck pond. Even now she insists I wear a blinking light on my backpack. Last month I asked her if I could go to London with my friend Blossom to attend a Knitters Against War protest march and she immediately had palpitations and got a migraine.

"A march? There might be terrorists!"

"Mum, they're knitters."

"There'll be an extremist wing. Don't you know how dangerous London is? A man knocked me over on a tube platform once."

"By accident," I reminded her. I'd heard the story before.

"I could have fallen in front of a TRAIN," she said dramatically. "My life would have been snuffed out in a moment."

"Dad would have found someone else," I said. "He's resilient."

My father drives me mad, too. He's one of life's fence-sitters. To Dad, there are always two ways of looking at things. "Faults on both sides," he says about the conflict in Israel and Palestine. "Both candidates make good points," he says whenever two lunatic politicians argue with each other on the radio. "There are two schools of thought," he explains when I ask him what he thinks about the death penalty. Apparently there are two schools of thought about the death penalty, but only one about rinsing plates before loading the dishwasher.

I watched the two of them edging around each other in the narrow kitchen. One would put something in the machine, only for the other to reposition it, or take it out altogether.

"You CERTAINLY can't put that knife in," Mum said.

"Why not?" Dad asked.

"That's a paring knife. It's vital that it remains sharp. The water will blunt it."

"So how would you suggest I wash it?"

"In the sink!"

"Using what? Sand?"

They drove my sister, Verity, batty, too, which is why she moved to New Zealand a year ago, along with Rafe, my two-year-old nephew. I missed Verity and Rafe dreadfully, but I didn't miss the arguments. Mum and Verity fought like stoats in a sock.

"Fleur? Fleur?" I realized my father was trying to get my attention.

"Yes?"

"What do you think?" he asked.

"I think you are both insane," I replied.

"Yes, but what do you think about putting paring knives in the dishwasher?"

"I think," I said, getting up from the table and grabbing my schoolbag, "that there are two schools of thought on the issue."

IAN BEALE

Ian Beale intercepted me as I reached the door. "Don't let him out!" Mum yelled. "He's on antibiotics." Ian Beale is our old dog. We got him when the last dog died, maybe ten years ago. The last dog's name was Patch, which I thought quite dull. I was so upset when he died that Mum made the mistake of letting me choose the new dog's name. I was a big *EastEnders* fan back then. Even now one of my favorite things is when Mum calls him in for tea. "Ian Beale! Ian Beale!"

Not a lot happens in our village.

Ian Beale suffers from any number of chronic ailments

and I believe may be Britain's most medicated dog. He has to take so many potions and remedies that he sometimes can't manage his dinner. I feel very sorry for him and wonder sometimes if he wouldn't be better off being allowed to run wild, even if it means he goes to the big kennel in the sky a little sooner. But that sort of thinking isn't allowed in our house. I dropped to one knee and gave him a big hug, holding my breath as I did so. Ian Beale is rather whiffy. As I opened the door narrowly and squeezed through, he watched me go, a slight look of betrayal in his bloodshot eyes.

It was early to be leaving, but I needed to escape. After all, better to arrive early at school than to be sent to prison for stabbing your parents with a paring knife. We live in a village about two miles outside the town of Bosford, sort of between Hastings and Brighton, about an hour and a half from London.

School is in Bosford, and I usually walk with my friend Blossom, who also lives in the village. Sometimes we get a lift with another friend, Pip, who has a car but shouldn't be allowed to have a tricycle in my opinion. He is a terrible driver. He doesn't go fast, and I suspect he's never even broken the speed limit. But unfortunately driving slowly doesn't stop you from hitting things, or crossing the white line into oncoming traffic. When he parks he creeps incredibly slowly into the space, showing brilliant clutch control, then invariably, at the speed of an exhausted snail, he'll hit the wall with a soft crunch.

I ran into Blossom by the church. I've known Blossom forever and she is the best person in the world. She has mad curly hair and twinkling green eyes. She's a bit taller than me, but most people are.

"All right, Fleur?" she asked.

"All right, Blossom?" I replied. She fell into step beside me and we strolled down the Bosford Road.

"So are you going to Battle on Saturday?" I asked. Going to Battle was a thing we did. Battle is a small town near Hastings and the place where the actual Battle of Hastings was fought in 1066. When I was a child I used to think that battles were called battles because the first one had been fought in Battle.

But of course Battle is called Battle because it was named after the battle. There wasn't anything there before the battle except some cows in a field and, I guess, a really rubbish gift shop. English Heritage is always looking for people to work there, and we take the bus down on a Saturday morning to earn money dressing as Saxon peasants and relating the details of the battle to jet-lagged American tourists. We know a LOT about the Battle of Hastings, although we may have made some of it up. Like once I told some lovely people from Iowa that William of Normandy had married his own horse. Also I have to admit our accents are a bit hit-and-miss. I do a sort of West Country pirate accent; Pip does Scouser because that's the only one he can do. Blossom usually ends up doing a sort of *Mary Poppins* cheeky, chirpy Cockney thing.

I love going to Battle, but the only problem is you have to dress up in period costume and you get funny looks on the bus when you're wearing a wimple. Since Pip got his car he usually drives us down, which is a lot easier because it means he doesn't have to argue with the bus driver about whether he can put his halberd in the luggage rack. Blossom and I mostly do crafts with the kids, and sometimes she helps out with the ghost walk through the abbey. Pip is a guard. He wears leather armor and tries to scare the children, but they just laugh at him. We're very much Team Harold when it comes to the battle; Saxon blood courses through our veins. In my opinion, there are two types of people in the world: Normans and Saxons. And there are two types of Saxons: the noble thanes and the peasant churls. I'm definitely a Saxon churl. A defender. Minding my own business. Keeping myself to myself, not sailing about the world conquering people and marrying horses.

PIP

As we walked down the narrow lane, fat bees lurching drunkenly from poppy to cowslip, Blossom was moaning about her boyfriend. He comes from Glasgow, calls himself Magnet and works in a tattoo shop as an assistant piercer. I quite like him, but Blossom finds him irritating. Also he's never around. He's a total hippie and wants to live off-grid, but all that means is he sometimes turns off his iPhone.

"For someone who is all about peace and harmony in nature, he's often really grumpy," Blossom said.

"He's not grumpy," I replied. "He's just Scottish."

"He's got himself involved in something called the Project," Blossom went on. "It's an experimental, self-sufficient community that he and his friends from the

Socialist Action Group are trying to set up in a thistle-strewn field in Essex."

"Why?" I asked.

"They're all convinced that capitalism is about to implode and society will crumble into anarchy," she said. "They're basically left-wing survivalists. It sounds pretty grim, and apparently when you're in the field you can't get a phone signal."

I shuddered.

"He told me he wants me to move there and live with him when it's finished."

"What?! What did you say to that?"

"I told him that if the apocalypse comes," she said, "and capitalism does crumble, then I'm determined to go down with the sinking ship, clutching my lifeless iPad."

"Shush a minute," I said. "Can you hear something . . . ?"

We stopped walking and held our heads at a slight angle in that way you do when you want to make it clear you're listening really hard. I could hear a blackbird shouting madly at us, and the sound of our neighbor Mr. Palmer's tractor in a nearby field, but those weren't the sounds that worried me. It was a clunking, roaring sound of a badly tuned engine chugging through the hedgerows.

"Is that . . . ?" Blossom began just as the car came trundling slowly around the tight corner of the narrow lane. At the speed it was going there should have been ample time to stop. The driver saw us, and his eyes widened in alarm, but the car carried on coming, heading right for us. We squealed and leaped into the hazel hedge as it missed us by inches. I heard a scraping thump. Blossom groaned underneath me and I peered out of the hedge to see the little white Clio had crashed into the hedge on the other side of the lane. We got to our feet and I emerged from the scratchy branches. I stepped toward the car, brushing myself off, as the driver's-side door opened and a long leg emerged. That long leg was followed by a succession of other long limbs and necks and heads and all the other bits you'd expect to see attached to an extremely tall human male. Atop all this gangliness was a grinning, pale face under a shock of bright red hair.

"Pip!" Blossom yelled. "Why didn't you stop?"

"My foot missed the brake," he said.

"You nearly killed us!"

Pip blinked at us in surprise. "You were walking in the middle of the road," he said. "To be fair." If I was asked to describe Pip in two words, I would probably choose "drunk giraffe." Watching him walk, I sometimes wondered if his joints had been put on backward because everything seemed to bend the wrong way.

"You need to work on your braking skill set," Blossom said.

"Would you like a lift to school?" Pip asked.

"Yes, please," Blossom said.

"Magnet wouldn't approve," I told her. "After all, when capitalism crumbles there'll be no more cars and we'll walk everywhere."

"I know," she agreed. "But let's cross that bridge when we come to it."

"If we come to a bridge, Pip will drive off it and we'll drown," I pointed out.

"I'll take my chances," she said. "I have a blister." She got into the backseat of Pip's Clio.

"Is your car okay?" I asked him.

"Yes, think so," he replied. "Why?"

"It's just that you crashed into the hedge," I explained.

"I didn't crash," he said. "I parked. Are you getting in?"

Deciding I was probably slightly safer as a passenger inside Pip's car than a pedestrian out of it, I got into the back with Blossom. Pip folded himself back into the driver's seat with difficulty before puttering off down the lane, blowing black smoke, me calling out directions. I always feel like the navigator for the world's slowest rally driver when I'm in a car with Pip. "Right-hand coming up in twenty . . . fifteen, ten . . . eight . . . five . . . three . . . one . . . TURN . . . TURN FOR THE LOVE OF GOD . . . left-hand sharp . . . keep going . . . now straighten the wheel . . . mind that horse . . . red light . . . red light . . . RED LIGHT!"

I'm only sixteen and have never so much as depressed a clutch, but I'm still a better driver than Pip. I've broached the subject with Mum of driving lessons when I turn seventeen, but just the thought brings her out in a cold sweat. She showed me a very long and unnecessarily detailed article she'd found featuring statistics that said there was a much lower mortality rate for people who waited until they were nineteen before taking their test. I didn't push it. It's pointless to argue with her when she's made up her mind.

OH, FLEUR

Pip dropped us at the school gates and drove off to find a parking space somewhere in the side streets. The school is quite modern. It was built about ten years ago and is starting to look tatty. It's all wooden clapboard and brick and floor-to-ceiling windows that never get cleaned. Originally there were going to be loads of playing fields, but half of them got sold off for affordable housing and now there is an entire community of people right behind the school with dozens of tiny children who spend the whole day peering through the fence calling you rude names. It's quite disconcerting when you're trying to eat your lunch in the sunshine and a six-year-old is calling you a cockwomble.

As Blossom and I headed toward the main entrance I sensed someone charging up behind me. I turned and my heart sank to see it was Bonita Clark. Bonita doesn't suit her name in any way. She should be petite and balletic and smiley, but Bonita is none of those things. She is strong and stomping and sweary. And here she was, almost sprinting as she tried to get ahead of me and through the door first. The thing about Bonita is that she is the most extraordinarily competitive person on the planet. She's captain of the netball team and the field hockey team. She runs cross-country and plays soccer with the boys, and she's good. There is much to be admired in Bonita.

I'm afraid to say that Bonita doesn't feel the same way about me. Our difficulties started a couple years ago when I ~~was forced into the field hockey team against my will~~

eagerly seized my opportunity for sporting glory. Bonita was captain and tried to explain the rules and tactics to me before our first game. She put me at fullback. It didn't end well. I let my attention wander, and the other team scored a goal while I was texting.

Bonita was furious. "It's not that I expected you to be the best of the best," she said. "But I thought you'd at least watch the game." It wasn't much better when I *was* paying attention, to be honest. I got overexcited at one point and I took out one of my own teammates with a wild swing of the stick that a Saxon yeoman would have been proud of. Anyway, after that I somehow found myself off Bonita's team and onto Holly Frobisher's, though what poor Holly had done to deserve that I really don't know. Now I often have to play *against* Bonita, and she's always knocking me over, or running rings around me, trying to humiliate me, which isn't difficult, I have to admit. After all, I have as much sporting endeavor as Kanye West has humility. Bonita thinks sports are important, competing is important, winning is important. I don't. We're just different. What I don't understand is why it bothers her so much.

Most upperclassmen aren't required to take any kind of sporting activity. But Bosford is an exception. Our glorious motto is *Mens sana in corpore sano*. A healthy mind in a healthy body. The theory goes that only by exercising the body and the mind together can true excellence be reached. "Try telling that to Stephen Hawking," I said to Miss Collins, my advisor, when she told me I had to sign up for field hockey again this semester.

"When you're as brilliant as Stephen Hawking, you can stop playing competitive sports," she said, handing me a field hockey stick and a pair of shin pads. "Until then you're at fullback."

So that's Bonita; she just has to be best at everything. At netball, at field hockey, at soccer, at running. And now she wanted to be first through the school door. It was a double door, but only one door was ever open. The other was bolted shut. Now, what I should have done, of course, was just stop and let her go by. Who cared who went through the door first? I didn't care if she scored a dozen goals against me in field hockey, so why should it matter if she got through the doorway into the school before me? But I was feeling mischievous today.

I think sometimes I just get bored with doing the sensible thing and so I end up doing something idiotic just to see what happens. Like the time I took up the sousaphone. The teachers had told us all we needed to choose an instrument. Most people were sensible and went with flute or clarinet. The boys all chose guitar or drums. But because I thought it would be funny, I went with the most bloody inconvenient instrument I could think of, which is a brass monster so huge you have to wear it. I could hardly lift the thing, let alone get a noise out of it, and of course I gave up after a few weeks. Anyway, today was one of those days, and I pretended I was going to let Bonita pass through the doors first, but at the last second I lunged forward and got there at exactly the same time as her. We got stuck like two corks in the same bottle. She glared at me.

"Sorry," I said. "So sorry. My bad."

But as she pushed forward, I pushed forward, too, ensuring she couldn't go through.

"Sorry," I said again as other students stopped to watch the fun.

Then Blossom, who had already gone through, reached up and released the bolt holding the other door closed. It flew open with a ping. Bonita and I sprang forward, sprawling on the hallway floor, schoolbags flying. A huge cheer rose from the students who'd had their Tuesday morning brightened enormously. Bonita got to her feet first and glared at me.

"Seriously?" Bonita snapped. "This is the thing you choose to get competitive about? Going through a door? Why don't you push this hard on the field hockey pitch?"

"I don't care about field hockey," I replied. "But doors are important to me."

"You'd better watch yourself, Waters," she snarled, and I realized I'd crossed the line. My heart pounded and I kept my mouth shut. Luckily, Blossom stepped in between me and Bonita. She's completely fearless.

"What are you doing, guys?" she asked, pleading. "We're never going to bring down the patriarchal edifice if we're fighting each other."

Bonita stepped forward, fuming. But my edifice was saved by the patriarchy in the form of Mr. Singh, who came along and told us all to get to class. "This isn't over, Petal," Bonita called as a parting shot. She thinks it's funny to get my name wrong. She does it to Blossom, too, and calls her Flower. It's an irritating coincidence that Blossom and I do have botanical-sounding names. Throw Pip into the mix and we sound like the panel of *Gardeners' Question Time*.

I felt shaken after the incident. Honestly, why do I do these things to myself? In third grade, Mrs. Fowler told me I was an attention-seeker. All the jokes and mucking around were just ways of seeking acceptance. A defense mechanism. I'm not sure if that's true. When Verity lived at home, and she and Mum would fight all the time, I think I tried to play the clown to ease the tension. I don't like it when people fight. Unfortunately, cracking a dumb joke at times of high drama often just makes things worse.

I was relieved when Pip joined us just before we went into the LRC for English. Pip, for all his oddness, is a quietly reassuring figure. If people like him can exist and function in society, then there's hope for all of us. If that sounds horrible, then I don't mean it that way. He's an intensely warm and caring person, and I don't know what I'd do without him. Blossom told him what had happened with Bonita, and he wrapped his spindly arms around me, like a ginger Groot. "Remember the old saying," he muttered. "Tricky days make us stronger."

"Thanks, Pip," I said.

"Or they kill us," Pip added. "Tricky days can also kill us."

BLOSSOM PANKHURST

At lunch I went looking for Blossom. It didn't take me long to find her. She was standing in the main foyer, holding a piece of paper and remonstrating with Mrs. Turvey, the PE teacher.

"Who do they think we are?" she was saying. "Second-class citizens? What did the suffragettes fight and die for?"

Mrs. Turvey frowned. "I think they fought and died for votes for women. I don't know if they had strong feelings about the membership policies of community sports clubs." I snatched the paper out of Blossom's hand and inspected what turned out to be a cheaply produced flyer.

Bosford Boxing Club

Did you know boxing is a great way to keep fit?
Now signing up new members.

Wednesday
Adult sessions: 8:00–9:00 p.m.

Saturday
Junior session: 9:00–9:45 a.m.
Adult sessions: 10:00–11:15 a.m.

Thursday
Ladies session: 8:00–9:00 p.m.

Whether you're looking to spar, compete in tournaments or just lose some weight, boxing is for you!

"I know, right?" Blossom said to me. I noticed Mrs. Turvey sneak off while Blossom's attention was diverted.

"What," I said. "You don't like boxing?"

"You can't see what's wrong with that flyer?" she asked. I read it again.

"Is it the missing apostrophe in 'Ladies'?" I asked. I've inherited my mum's obsession with punctuation.

"It's not the missing apostrophe," Blossom replied. "It's the missing chromosome. Why should women be forced to attend on a different night than men?"

"That's what this is about? You want to hit men?"

"Maybe, but that's not the point!" Blossom snatched the flyer back from me and held it up. "Fleur, this kind of segregation is illegal under the Equality Act 2010. Clubs can't stop people from joining on sex grounds."

"So what are you going to do about it?"

"I'm going to go down there on Saturday and tell them they have to change their policy. Then a letter to the council, copying in my MP, then if they still refuse, direct action. Like the suffragettes." She smiled grimly, her eyes lighting up at the prospect of a fight to the death.

"Do we have to go on a hunger strike?" I asked. "It's just that Mum's doing roast beef on Sunday. With Yorkshire pudding."

"Fleur!" Blossom snapped. "This is serious. Are you going to support me in this?"

I sighed. "Yes, of course I am."

Blossom smiled with satisfaction. She knew I'd give in. I always do.

PRINCE GEORGE

On Wednesday after school my boyfriend George came to pick me up. George is the exact opposite of Magnet in every respect except one, which is that he's usually absent. Wednesdays and Sundays are the only days I see George. He's a few years older than me, is at

Hove Naval Academy doing officer training and has a very busy schedule. Wednesday is Date Night. He also comes up for Sunday lunch with my family and sometimes Blossom. I'm not really sure how that started, but start it did, and George isn't the sort to change tradition. It's a tidy arrangement, George keeps telling me. He gets on very well with my parents and they talk about things like the economy and the situation in the Middle East. Mum is happy for me to go out with George, even though he's nineteen, because he's a military man, and Mum thinks I'm safe.

As it happens, I am safe with George, though not necessarily in the way Mum thinks. Sometimes I wonder if he couldn't be slightly more daring in that regard, if you get my drift. I suppose that's another point of difference between George and Magnet; George doesn't seem to be into piercing things. He's old-fashioned. Not particularly religious, just very, very proper.

"I have firm ideas about things," he says.

There's lots about George I love. He's hot, for a start, and he has a car and money, which is nice. He has quite a plummy accent, at least in comparison to the rest of us yokels. I secretly find posh boys a bit sexy, which is not something I would ever admit to Blossom, but hey, we all have our weaknesses.

Most important, though, George makes me laugh. Which sounds like such a cliché, but it's a true cliché. I met him at school when he was an upperclassman. He was confident and charming and handsome. He was known around the school as Prince George, which isn't very original but suited him. Even then he was in the

Naval Cadets. I used to watch him across the playground until one day he just came over and started talking to me.

"You're Fleur Waters, aren't you?"

I nodded. "How do you know my name?"

"I asked around," he said.

"You asked around?" I replied. "Like a cop, knocking on doors?"

"Um . . . well, I actually had to ask a few people because at first no one seemed to know who you were. Someone thought your name was Fiona."

"I clearly make a big impression on people," I said.

"You made an impression on me," he said. Then he laughed and looked embarrassed.

I wonder if that's what made me fall for him. His admission that I'd made an impression. The first boy to notice me. Maybe that's all it took, for someone to notice me and to take the time to find out my name wasn't Fiona. He asked me if I wanted to have lunch with him in the cafeteria the next day, and I said yes straightaway and that was sort of that.

Blossom was unsure about him, though. "Are you sure he's right for you?" she asked one day when he wasn't around. "I bet he votes Conservative."

"He's just different," I replied, shrugging. "I thought you were all about the diversity."

"Hmm . . . he's not the MOST diverse person on the planet," she pointed out diplomatically.

"Did you ever stop to think that maybe he's the person everyone else is diverse *from*," I suggested. "Without George, NO ONE would be diverse, and who wants to live in that world?"

"I like him," Pip said. "I didn't have any money yesterday, and he bought me a cheese roll."

Being bought a cheese roll was enough for Pip, and we could all learn a lot from him. So George was made a permanent fixture. Before he went off to the academy that September he came around to my house for "a talk." I wondered if he was going to break it off. I remember that night very clearly. It was still just about warm enough to sit out, and we walked down through the large rear garden that overlooks Mr. Palmer's wheat field. Early windfall apples dotted the lawn. We sat at the old picnic table at the foot of the garden and watched the swallows swooping, plucking evening bugs from midair. "I think we can make this work," he said after quite a lot of preamble. "I'll see you twice a week at least. And maybe you can come down to Hove for weekends sometimes."

"Weekends in Hove," I said. "Living the dream." I felt I should say more, but, rather like my dad, I was of two minds. George was safe, and lovely, and I quite liked the idea of seeing him just twice a week, knowing when, and for how long. So that all that side of things, the romance-y, emotion-y side of life, was taken care of and kept in the proper box. I wouldn't have to worry about it. *Why not give it a try?* I thought. I know what's behind Door Number One. From where I was sitting I couldn't even see Door Number Two.

So that's how I ended up at Chickos on this Date Night. Chickos wasn't our normal sort of place; we usually went to a little Italian restaurant he knew or a great Thai pop-up a friend had recommended or an intriguing new Lebanese café that had opened up in someone's front room near the Lewes roundabout. We take it in turns to choose, and he always pays. But sometimes you don't want fancy food and World Music. Sometimes you just want greasy chips and cheesy tunes. So tonight I'd chosen Bosford Chickos, which I quickly realized he wasn't happy about.

"So explain the ordering system again?" he said, for the third time.

"It's not as complicated as you're making it," I said. "You just go up to the bar and order your meal, and they give you a little rubber chicken with a numbered wooden spoon shoved up its bum so the waiter knows where to bring your food."

He turned in his seat and looked over at the bar. "But there's a queue."

"Do you want me to go?"

"No, it's just that we already queued to get the table. Now we have to queue again to order the food? This is really inefficient."

"Yeah, but the chicken's delicious."

"What about drinks?"

"Same system, you queue up," I said.

"Another queue?!"

"To maximize efficiency," I suggested, "you could order the drinks at the same time as the food?"

"I like to have a drink while I inspect the menu," he complained. I kicked him under the table and he yelped.

"Remember you asked me to tell you when you were being whiny?" I said.

"I never said that."

"Didn't you? Well, anyway, you're being whiny now." George laughed like I knew he would and went off to stand in the queue. I shook my head and smiled at the same time. He was nineteen going on thirty-nine, but he didn't lack for self-awareness and he always took it the right way when I teased him. That was a side of him that Blossom just didn't see.

He came back after a while carrying a rubber chicken with a wooden spoon up its bottom.

"See?" I said.

"And you come here often?" he asked.

"No," I lied. Pip, Blossom and I ate here quite a lot on Saturdays after we got back from Battle. It's not everyone's cup of tea, of course, but they let Pip store his halberd in the umbrella stand. Mum doesn't like Chickos because (A) it's in rough West Bosford and (B) she suspects there should be an apostrophe in the name but isn't quite sure, and that unsettles her.

"Just thought it was something a bit different," I said.

"It certainly is," he said, looking around. He wasn't really dressed for Chickos, in his jacket and pointy shoes.

"Maybe we could go to a club afterward," I said. "Do some dancing?"

"You're only sixteen," he pointed out. "And also you hate dancing."

"I don't hate it. I'm just really bad at it," I said. "But it doesn't matter at Lick'd because it's so dark no one will see me. And they never check your ID either."

He frowned. "I don't know. I have an early start tomorrow. We have Navigation with Major Horton."

"So what about Saturday night?" I asked. "Come up on Saturday. Take me dancing."

"But I'm coming up on Sunday," he pointed out. "For lunch, like always."

"So come up on Saturday and stay over?" I suggested,

rolling my eyes. He stared at me, wide-eyed, as if I'd suggested he throw me onto the table and ravish me then and there. "I'm sure Mum wouldn't mind." Actually I'm sure she would mind very much. She'd definitely put George in the spare room, but that was fine with me. If nothing else it would be nice if George and I could sleep under the same roof for once. Even sleeping in the same county would be an improvement.

The food arrived. We'd both asked for a quarter of a chicken. I'd ordered chips and coleslaw. George had gone for a baked potato and sweetcorn. He tries to keep the fats to a minimum because there are constant fitness tests at his college and he has to go for ten-mile runs every couple of days. It doesn't sound like very good training for a war to me. If the Russians attack, our junior naval officers will be starved of calories and exhausted from ten-mile runs.

"Here are your meals," the waiter said quickly before turning to go.

"Excuse me," George said. "I ordered some drinks? Two Diet Cokes?"

"You'll need to wait for the drinks guy," the waiter said abruptly. "I don't do drinks on Wednesdays. Monday night and Sunday lunchtime I do drinks, but never Wednesdays."

"Never Wednesdays," I repeated solemnly to George. "Still think Wednesday is best for Date Night?" George sighed, and started picking the skin off his chicken. "That's the best bit," I protested. "That's where all the flavor is."

"A hundred and fifty calories per thirty-five grams," George said automatically. "I'm running tomorrow."

"Well, you need some flavor," I said, reaching across to the next table and swiping two bottles of peri-peri sauce. I inspected the labels. "Medium and . . . ooh, extra hot. Wanna try?"

"No," George said. "I'll try some of the medium."

I splashed some onto his chicken. "Whoah whoa!" he cried.

"Don't be a wuss," I said. He took a tiny morsel on his fork and tasted it gingerly.

"Oh, that's quite hot," he said. As I went to splash some on my own food he shook his head. "Don't give yourself as much as you gave me. You won't like it."

I narrowed my eyes. "Is it . . . is it because I'm a girl? You think I can't handle spicy foods?"

"No," he said hurriedly. "I just think medium is quite hot enough for . . . for anyone."

"It *is* because I'm a girl," I said.

"It's not," he protested. "Honestly."

"If you were with one of your navy chums, you'd be egging him on right now," I said. I was looking for an excuse to have some fun, but at the same time I was a little cross at his casual misogyny. "You'd probably be pantsing each other and pouring extra-hot peri-peri sauce over your genitals."

"I really don't think you've got a good idea of what goes on at college," he said, frowning. "Look, just put a bit of the medium on and leave it at that." But it was too late. I grabbed the extra-hot sauce and splashed it on, laughing like a maniac. Two splashes, three.

"That's enough," he said, looking anxious.

"Hahaha!" I cried. Four splashes. Five. George tried to snatch the bottle from me, but I was too quick, holding it out of his reach. We glared at each other. He held out a hand. "Give me the peri-peri sauce, Fleur."

"Shan't," I said.

"Please, Fleur. Give me the peri-peri sauce." We sat for a while, watching each other, trying not to laugh.

"Fine," I said. "Here you go." I held out the bottle, but as he tried to take it from me I quickly turned it upside down and splashed more sauce onto his chicken. He finally got a hand to it and we struggled over it, snorting with laughter. Eventually he got it away and hid it under his chair.

"Now," he said. "Eat your chicken."

"You eat yours first," I said.

He reached over and took my hand in his. "We'll do it together," he said. And so we did. Together we picked up our knives and forks, together we cut off a piece of chicken, together we ate, chewed and swallowed. Together we looked into each other's eyes.

"It's not so bad," he said.

"I don't think it's kicked in yet," I replied, just as I felt the beginnings of a tickling, burning sensation in my mouth.

"I think it might be kicking in now," he said, his face suddenly crumpling. I wanted to agree but couldn't speak. I knew if I opened my mouth fire would shoot out and turn my boyfriend into a flaming ball. And then who would protect us from the Russians? The burning sensation had by now become a raging fire. It felt as though dystopian overlord fire imps were roving around in my mouth burning rebels with flamethrowers. George didn't seem to be coping any better. Sweat poured down his forehead, making him blink furiously. He'd gone deathly pale and was clutching his knife and fork so hard it looked like they might snap. As I snatched up a napkin and started dabbing my swollen tongue in a vain attempt to scrape off the residue, I saw, through streaming eyes, George stand and wave furiously toward the bar before gasping, "Where's the drinks guy? Where's the flipping drinks guy?"

BOUDICCA

George wasn't the only one who had to undergo grueling physical training the next day. Thursday was PE with Bonita, specifically field hockey. There were other girls playing, too, I think, but Bonita was the only one who paid any attention to me. If it weren't for her I could happily spend the game sitting in a corner making daisy chains and thinking about death. The other girls knew I was a slacker and just ignored me, but Bonita made it her mission to drag the game in my direction and make sure I had to get involved and try to stop her from scoring, which I was never able to do, of course.

I hadn't slept well after Date Night. The chili sauce had wreaked such destruction across my ravaged mouth parts that they continued throbbing all night, and not in a good way. George and I had joked about it afterward, but neither of us really felt like kissing when he dropped me off at home, and I was regretting what I'd done. I lay in bed and thought about George. *We do have fun. He makes me laugh and I make him laugh. And I like that we see such different things in each other and appreciate them.*

George would never have gone to Chickos if it weren't for me. I would never go to Akvars on the Hastings Bypass if it weren't for George. But as the clock ticked over past one a.m. and I still couldn't find sleep, I lay in the dark and wondered if the only reason I was with George was *because* he was different. Was I just doing it for a laugh? Was he just another sousaphone?

So I wasn't entirely match-fit the following afternoon, and when I saw Bonita and her pals thundering toward me like Boudicca and her Iceni warriors, my heart sank. I groaned and held up my field hockey stick like a Roman legionnaire with a short-sword. Needless to say, I was trampled and went down heavily, my skirt flying up around my ears. Someone, probably Bonita, stood on my wrist as she charged through. I lay there in darkness with my skirt over my face, rubbing my wrist furiously, listening to the guttural whoops of the Iceni tribe celebrating the scoring of another goal.

I'm not competitive at heart, but it would be nice, just once, to get the better of Bonita.

RICKY

On Saturday, Pip and Blossom picked me up early in Pip's car. It was overcast and I'd worn a coat and comfortable shoes, suspecting that Blossom might make us stand outside the boxing club for most of the morning. I was hoping I might be able to pop off to Superdrug at some point, because I needed some face wipes and tampons. Maybe I could even sneak into Accessorize to buy something for Blossom's birthday. Pip was wearing a long black coat over black trousers and a sweater. He had wraparound shades and would have looked like Neo from *The Matrix* if it hadn't been for the stovepipe hat. Blossom was in full protest regalia. Her black jacket was covered with little badges, from Save the Whales through Campaign for Nuclear Disarmament to a picture of Jeremy Corbyn made to look like Che Guevara.

Pip's driving seemed even more erratic than usual. He never stopped to let oncoming cars go by, even on the narrowest lanes. They'd flash their lights and beep their horns, but Pip would just trundle on through, oblivious, sending them swerving up onto the pavement or sometimes into fields. Because we were going so slowly, there was usually someone right behind us, flashing their lights in annoyance or roaring past. It was never very peaceful driving in Pip's car.

The boxing club was in the Bosford Memorial Hall, near Saint Peter's Church, not far from the train station and in a slightly disheveled part of town. Just by the church was the boundary of the largest public housing project in Bosford, the Gladwell Estate. Pip parked and we walked down the street toward the hall.

"What did the club organizers say?" I asked Blossom.

"I haven't spoken to them," Blossom said.

"You didn't phone them?"

"I find it's always better to talk to someone face-to-face," she said confidently. We stopped in front of the church and I swallowed nervously.

"It's just that . . ." I began.

"It's just that what?" Blossom asked impatiently.

"Well, they're boxers. What if it's full of men with tattoos on their faces and no teeth?"

"Come on, you two. Where's your backbone?" Blossom said as she turned and marched straight in. Pip and I looked at each other, shrugged and followed, more hesitantly. A lady with gray hair sat at a trestle table just inside the door. She wore a tracksuit and had a ledger open in front of her along with a little box of coins. Blossom frowned at the woman.

"Hello," she said. "Can I help you?"

I peered past the table. Beyond the woman, in the main part of the hall, about two dozen children of various ages were skipping rope, or at least trying to skip. A very large, stocky man with a shaved head was glaring at them. Most of the children looked about as coordinated as Pip. The oldest looked to be in his early teens, the youngest maybe five or six. They were mostly boys, but there were a few girls. I wanted to point this out to Blossom, but she was busy talking to the lady at the trestle table.

"I've come to talk to you about this," Blossom began, holding up the flyer.

"Yes, dear," the lady said. "Are you interested in our Thursday session?"

"Why can't I come to the Saturday session?"

"Well," the lady said. "Thursdays might be more suitable."

"Why?" Blossom asked politely. "Are Saturdays men-only?"

"You'd better talk to Coach Ricky," the lady said. I turned to see the huge man approaching, his brow furrowed.

"Can I help you?" he asked.

"Are you in charge?" Blossom asked.

"This is my club, yes," Coach Ricky said. He had a deep voice and a South London accent.

"Are you aware it's an offense under Section 4 of the Equality Act 2010 to deny membership of a club on sex grounds?"

"What?" Ricky said, looking confused. "Sex what?"

"You can't stop someone joining your club just because they are a girl."

Ricky turned to the children who'd all stopped to watch the exchange. "SKIP!" he roared. They all leaped to it. "You're a boxer?" Ricky asked, turning back to Blossom.

"No," she said. "I think sports are patriarchal, especially martial arts."

"So what's the problem then?"

"Just because I don't want to box doesn't mean you're allowed to exclude me."

"Look," Ricky said. "The women we get coming to the club are just doing it for conditioning. Y'know? To get fit? It takes commitment and focus to be a proper boxer, and when you tell me that you don't like sports, then I'm wondering why you're even here." I looked around the hall as they argued. It looked a little shabby, to be honest. I saw a couple of ancient punching bags hanging from racks. The lady with the gray hair smiled at me.

"Are you a boxing coach, too?" I asked.

"Yes," she said. "I run the ladies' session. We do boxercise, no pads or sparring. I'm Coach Sharon, that's Coach Joe." She pointed to a grizzled old man in tracksuit bottoms who'd taken over leading the skipping exercise. He hardly looked able to walk, let alone skip, but he leaned over slowly, grunting with the effort, and got his fingertips to the skipping rope Ricky had left behind. Then he raised himself with difficulty. He flipped the plastic rope over his head and, almost without seeming to move, hopped his feet over it.

Pip and I watched, fascinated, as the old man started skipping. Slowly at first, then gradually quicker as the kids shouted at him to hurry up. His hands twirled faster and faster, becoming a blur as his gnarled old frame bopped up and down steadily, bouncing like a twisted spring. Then he did that odd flipping thing that fit people do with skipping ropes where they seem to twist the rope back and forth. Joe closed his eyes and concentrated as the rope became a whistling blur, his feet seeming to move in slow-motion, lifting just high enough to let the rope hiss by underneath.

"He's amazing," Pip said breathlessly.

"Would you two like a cup of tea?" Sharon asked. I think she could tell our hearts weren't in Blossom's protest. Sharon led us to a trestle table and went to an urn to make our drinks. Blossom was still remonstrating with Ricky. I could see her pointing to something on the flyer.

Sharon came back with two cups of tea and some papers. She placed them down in front of us. "Have you ever thought you might like to box?" she asked kindly. Pip looked up at her in alarm.

"Not really," he said.

"We're a bit short of numbers, you see," Sharon said hopefully. "What about you, dear?" she asked, turning to me.

"Me?" I asked.

"Yes, why not?" she said. "You could come on Thursday, that's ladies-only boxercise. It's quite gentle." Boxercise and nattering with a bunch of old women? I might as well be at Mum's Pilates class.

"Hmm," I said.

"What about Wednesday nights?"

"Can't do Wednesdays," I said. "Date night." Blossom came over then, having finished with Ricky, or having been dismissed by him perhaps; I'd missed the end of their discussion. She looked cross.

"Would you like a cookie?" Sharon asked. "While you read through the forms?"

"No, we wouldn't," Blossom said. "Thank you very much."

"I'd like a cookie," Pip said.

Sharon brought a selection over on a plate and Pip grabbed one gratefully. Blossom shot him a look. "Don't tell me you're going to sign up?"

"No," Pip said.

"Then why are you taking a cookie?" Blossom hissed. "You take their cookies and then they've got you."

"It's not some gateway drug to the patriarchy," I said. "It's a custard cream."

"I'm just saying that maybe it's a bit rude to be taking cookies when you have no intention of signing up," Blossom said impatiently. "Now can we go? We've made our point."

"What's the hurry?" I asked. "Haven't finished my tea yet."

Blossom sighed and took out her phone. I looked at the forms. There were a lot of them. None were particularly reassuring. Health warnings, disclaimers, statutory obligations, next-of-kin, a list of local osteopaths. Even if I had wanted to take up boxing, I wasn't sure I wanted to sign my name at the bottom of a set of documents that seemed to give someone the authority to inflict hideous damage upon my person. I wasn't Anastasia Steele.

Coach Ricky had taken over the training session again, and Joe limped gratefully off for a sit-down. "All right, my little champions," Ricky roared. "Are we going to train hard today?" The kids screamed a big YES. "We're a team, here," Ricky said. "We don't poke fun at each other. If you see someone else struggling, you help them. Give them encouragement, all right? Show them how to do it better. And finally, what we learn here today stays in the club, got it?" The kids nodded solemnly. "I say this every week, every session, because it's important," Ricky went on, waggling a finger. "If I hear any of you have used your boxing skills out there on the street to hurt someone else, you're out of the club. Understand?"

The kids mumbled general agreement. I saw one little lad at the side looking a bit guilty. "UNDERSTAND?" Ricky roared.

"YES, COACH RICKY," the kids yelled in unison, even the guilty-looking one, who I suspected might be resolving to lift his game in the future.

"I wish Coach Ricky was my dad," Pip said unexpectedly. I knew what he meant about Coach Ricky, though. He was gruff and unsmiling, but he was one of those people you just know you can totally trust just by looking at them. The sort of person you were desperate to please. The kids seemed to agree. They watched him constantly, followed him around, listened when he spoke and jumped when he said jump. We drank our tea and watched the kids leaping up and down. At one point some of them put gloves on and took turns tapping two big pads Ricky wore on his hands. "One, two, duck," Ricky would say. "One two, one two, duck." Whenever he said "duck," he'd reach out with the pads and they were supposed to duck underneath, but they couldn't ever time it right and he kept tapping them on the side of the head.

"Keep your guard up," he said to the guilty-looking boy, who nodded and punched himself in the head to help the new information sink in. I liked Guilty Boy. He seemed the sort of person who was constantly striving to improve himself without ever quite managing it. Pip eyed the kids as they waved their massive gloves around unconvincingly. "I reckon I could take some of these guys down," he said.

"Not that one," Blossom said, pointing to a mean-looking boy with close-cropped hair and an earring. He looked about eight.

"No," Pip agreed. "Not him." I was enjoying myself. It felt restful there, sipping tea while fifteen mad children leaped about taking swings at one another.

"Are you going to fill it out, then?" Coach Sharon asked, appearing behind us.

"Oh, yes," I said, sitting upright. "Just reading through the fine print."

"Okay, let me know if you need anything. Another cup of tea? Another cookie?"

"No thanks," I said.

"I'd like another cookie, please," Pip said. Blossom stared at him darkly. Just then a young man walked in through the door. Late teens, a little older than me.

He had olive skin and dark hair and eyes. He looked Mediterranean, or maybe Middle Eastern. He wore a loose T-shirt but even so I could see he was ripped.

"Tarik!" Ricky called to the new arrival. "Nice of you to show up."

Tarik. *That's a nice name*, I thought as I watched him stretch. He was lithe and muscular. He turned and of course caught me staring and I quickly pretended I was inspecting an interesting light fixture just behind him.

Pip brought another cookie to his mouth and was about to bite down when Sharon said, "So, are you going to fill out these forms or not?" Pip looked panicked.

"You did take two cookies," I reminded him. Pip shrugged. Then he reached over and grabbed one of the forms and the pen and signed his name. Blossom sighed.

"And what about you?" Sharon asked me.

"Me?" I watched the boy as he put on a pair of boxing gloves.

"Yes, dear, what about you?" Sharon said, slightly impatiently.

The boy stepped up to a hanging punching bag and started hitting it. He was fast, two quick jabs with his left hand then a big whack with his right. He hit the bag so hard I heard the bolts creak where it was attached to the ceiling. He dropped back, his guard up, and I saw him grin, exposing perfect white teeth.

"Maybe," I said. "I might come next Saturday."

"Stop being passive-aggressive," I said in the car on the way to Battle.

"I'm not being passive-aggressive," Blossom replied primly. "I just find it really interesting that you decided to join the very club we were protesting against."

"We were taking direct action," I said. "While you were arguing about apostrophes on a flyer, we slipped behind enemy lines to bring them down from within. I'm like Charlotte Gray. Pip's like . . . um . . ."

"Frodo," Pip suggested. I couldn't think of anyone Pip was less like than Frodo, but I let it go. As we parked the car, Garnet Pitman came hurrying over to meet us. Garnet was one of the chief volunteers at Battle and had very strong opinions. He ran walking tours for people who were terribly serious about history and organized archaeological digs and got excited about misshapen lumps of rock that he claimed were arrowheads. Ignoring me and Blossom, he spoke to Pip.

"What's your name?"

Pip looked panicked. But he stuttered out his name, somehow.

"Right, Pip, we're a bit short on numbers for the battle reenactment today."

"You're having a reenactment today?" Blossom asked.

"Just a practice, really," Garnet said dismissively. "The big one's in October, obviously."

"Why October?" I asked.

He turned slowly to look at me with contempt.

"Because that's the anniversary of the battle itself. The fourteenth of October."

"Really? I've been telling everyone it was the twentieth of March." I got my phone out to check.

Garnet glared at me, tutted and looked back at Pip. "Can you help us out? Harold will give you a shield and tell you what to do."

"King Harold?"

"Yes, King Harold, leader of the Saxon army. Ruler of Britain. He's in the café having a mochaccino."

"You're absolutely right," I said, looking up from my phone. "The battle was on the fourteenth of October."

"I KNOW," Garnet snapped.

"Twentieth of March is actually World Oral Health Day," I said. "How could I have gotten those confused?"

"Can we be in it?" Blossom asked, ignoring me. "The reenactment?" Garnet looked at her as if she'd just asked for permission to set fire to the abbey.

"I'm afraid there were no women at the Battle of Hastings, my dear," he said coolly.

"I don't believe you," Blossom said. "There must have been SOME women at the battle."

"Yeah, who ran the tea shop?" I asked.

"There were certainly no girls," Garnet said firmly.

Blossom bristled. "There weren't any iPhones, either," she said, pointing to the one in his hand.

"I need that to coordinate with the Saxons. I have an app. And no one will notice a phone."

"No one's going to notice that we're girls either," Blossom said, refusing to let it go. I would have given up by this point, but Blossom never did. She would have held out longer than Harold and his mochaccino.

"Of course they'll notice you're girls."

"We're going to be swishing swords," Blossom said. "Not twirling tampons."

Garnet drew himself up to his full height. "There's no need for talk like that. It's very important to our visitors that we put on a realistic demonstration of what the battle would have looked like. And I'm afraid that means men only."

"There was another young woman who the men tried to stop from fighting," Blossom growled. "An ordinary, devout girl who went on to conquer half the French-speaking world."

"She's talking about Celine Dion," I said.

"I'm talking about Joan of Arc," she corrected.

"I don't have time for this," Garnet huffed. He turned and led a terrified-looking Pip off, leaving Blossom fuming.

"Garnet thinks he's such a thane," I said.

"This must be illegal," Blossom said. "I'm getting out my human rights law book as soon as we get home."

"Come on," I said. "Let's go for a coffee. I'll buy you a Bakewell tart."

"What are you doing?" a small boy asked once I had taken up my post.

"Whittling," I explained. "I'm using a sharp knife to fashion useful tools from wood." I was sitting in a hovel that we'd constructed a few weeks before. I was dressed in my Saxon finery, which was not great because the weather was warming up and the tunic was hot and scratchy. Blossom was off doing one of her ghost walks. She plays the madwoman who leaps out from behind a gravestone and stabs the tour guide. Sometimes people think it's real and faint with the shock, but mostly they just laugh.

"Can I have a go with the knife?" the small boy said as more children came into the hovel to poke about.

"No," I said.

"What are you carving?" a little girl asked.

"Whittling, not carving," I said. "It's a spoon."

The children leaned forward to inspect my work. "It doesn't look like a spoon," the little girl said. I peered at it; she was right.

"It looks more like a willy," the small boy said. They screamed with laughter.

"Excuse me?" I said, outraged. "I haven't finished yet." I looked closer and they were right; it did look like a big wooden willy. A sort of medieval marital aid.

"How come you're not going in the battle?" the little girl asked.

"Because girls don't fight," the small boy said. "They just stay in the house and do cooking and willy-whittling."

"Girls do more than that," I said. "Nowadays at least."

"Not really," the boy said. I was about to retort when one of the dads poked his head through the door.

"Come on, kids, the battle's about to start."

I put the knife safely away and followed them out of the hovel. The air was a bit cooler outside, and I was pleased to see Blossom come strolling along. We joined the crowd assembling on the concourse just below the abbey: from there you could get a great view of the whole battlefield.

"There he is," cried Blossom, pointing Pip out to me. He was wearing a helmet and carried, or rather dragged, a sword and shield. He stumbled along behind the other Saxons as they formed a raggedy line at the top of the slope.

"There are the Normans," Blossom cried, pointing to a group at the bottom of the slope wearing armor and adjusting one another's helmet straps.

"Boo," I said.

"Boo," everyone cried. Technically you weren't supposed to take sides, but no one liked the Normans, with their horses and fancy armor. There was only one horse today, a small pony struggling under the weight of Garnet Pitman, who was looking at his phone. Garnet was playing William, of course. With a hoarse shout he lifted his sword and dug his heels into the pony's flank. It trotted slowly up the slope toward the Saxons.

The fickle crowd gave a cheer as the Normans charged. "William! William!"

"Who wins?" the little girl asked.

"You'll just have to wait and see," I said.

"I hope it's the Saxons," she said.

"I hope so, too," I said. I always hoped the Saxons would win, but they never did. We watched four Saxon archers fire blunt arrows over the heads of the approaching Normans.

"The Saxon archers had a problem," I explained to the little girl and boy who were standing beside us. I knew the details of the battle very well, even if I was hazy on the date. "It was common practice to collect the arrows your enemies fired at you and fire them back. But the

Normans didn't have archers, so the Saxons quickly ran out of ammunition."

"They are so dumb," the little boy said. "No wonder they lost."

"Spoilers," Blossom said.

"They lost?" the little girl cried, bereft.

"We don't know that yet," I said, glaring at the boy.

Eventually the Norman charge reached the Saxon shield wall. I could see Pip, crouched down, watching the line of knights approach.

"The Normans charged and charged again," I said. "But they couldn't break the Saxon shield wall, the stout English yeomen stood firm against the French." But then we heard a high-pitched shriek from the battlefield. Pip dropped his shield and ran helter-skelter away from the battle toward a stand of trees, disappearing from view. The Norman knights seemed surprised by this development and stopped in their tracks. No one had ever run off before, not at this point in the battle anyway.

"Oh, Pip," Blossom muttered. "It's not real." The Saxon line shuffled across to plug the gap, and the battle continued.

"Why did that soldier run away?" the little girl asked.

"Because he's sensible," I said. "And he didn't want to get killed."

"He's a wuss," the boy said.

"Yeah, that too," I agreed. I wasn't convinced Pip's future as a Saxon warrior was entirely secure.

SUNDAY LUNCH

Our village is called Rangers' Wood. It used to be called Rangers Wood, but a couple of years ago a group of middle-class punctuation enthusiasts, including my mother, successfully lobbied the parish council to add an apostrophe. Convincing the council to do it was the easy part. The tricky bit was deciding whether to add the apostrophe before or after the *s* of "Rangers." Is it the wood of one ranger? Or are there loads of the sneaky chaps ranging about in there? I suspect the rangers who used to inhabit the village wouldn't have given a wimple one way or the other. But there are very few farming folk in the village these days—it's mostly full of middle-class refugees from London, driving pristine Range Rovers. Like my parents.

Sundays in our house can be . . . interesting. It's the same drill every week. Mum and Dad start arguing over breakfast about how best to cook the roast. You'd think that after twenty-four years of marriage they'd have come to some sort of resolution about how many times the gravy should be reduced, or at least have agreed on an uneasy truce. But no, apparently not. Dad says once is enough; Mum insists on twice, minimum. Another thing they can't agree on is whether to add water to the roasting tray before putting the meat in. Mum says that's the best way to make the gravy. Dad says the meat needs to "roast dry" in order for the sugars to caramelize.

I know. I'm boring myself even mentioning it.

It makes no difference, of course. The meat is always overdone whoever gets their way. Blossom often comes over. Both her parents are vegetarian, and this is where she gets most of her protein. She arrives around eleven a.m. We're supposed to do an hour's studying before we eat, but we usually don't. George turns up around midday, and Mum and Dad drop whatever they're doing to run outside and greet him with hugs and kisses and firm handshakes and jokey asides. Mum gets him a small lager (he'll be driving later) and they talk about the cricket scores for a bit, or rugby in winter. Never soccer. Then Dad tells him to come outside and look at his plums. George says, "I'd rather you kept your trousers on if it's all the same to you, Mr. W," and how we laugh.

It's always the same and it's always warm and comfortable. We sit down to lunch at one p.m. sharp and my mum talks nonstop. As we start to eat I wonder what sort of lunch it's going to be. Some days Mum will be relaxed and leave me alone and she'll just talk nonstop about nothing in particular. If Blossom is there she and George will have a gentle argument about politics. I'll chip in from time to time, picking my position at random. Dad will see the strengths in both sides of the argument. Mum will carry on talking regardless of anyone else and she won't seem to mind that we all ignore her. These are the best days.

Then there are the other days, when Mum is in a mood and will goad Dad until he snaps. Then she won't speak to him for the rest of the meal, just sit there tight-lipped. Dad will shake his head at her and they'll end up in the kitchen together banging plates around and having a blazing row over the dishwasher. Anyway, those days aren't so great.

"How's the studying going, girls?" Mum asked today.

Blossom and I shot a nervous glance at each other. Neither of us was particularly conscientious when it came to studying.

"Really well, Liz," Blossom lied.

"What are you working on at the moment?"

"Oh, you know. Sin, cos, tan . . . um, turds?"

"Do you mean surds?" George asked.

"That's what I said."

"Only a few more weeks before exams," Mum said, unconvinced. "Probably time to knuckle down and get your heads into the books."

"It's only first year of A-levels," I pointed out. "The important exams aren't until next year."

"All exams are important," Dad said. "And if you fall behind now, it'll be that much harder to catch up."

"I agree," Mum said. "And frankly I really don't think you should be wasting your time going to this boxing class. Your father and I talked about it last night, and we're not happy about it."

"Oh, Mum," I said. "I just want to go along once, just to see what it's like." It had been a mistake to mention it to them, I now realized.

George shook his head. "I have to agree with your parents, Fleur. Boxing is very dangerous. There's a boxing club at the college, and last year poor Toby Pitcairn-Hume had to be taken to the hospital with a concussion. Happens all the time. Even with the proper safety precautions, boxing is rough. I can tell you, more than one lad at our college has ended up needing his nose rebuilt."

I glared at Mum. As soon as George had arrived she'd rushed out to greet him and told him all about the boxing idea before he'd even gotten out of his car. I'd been planning to build up to it. I was going to start by complaining of a lack of upper-body strength, then mentioning casually that I'd heard body combat classes were all the rage, before dropping the word "boxercise" into the conversation, then rounding it all off by suggesting he pay for it.

"Oh, listen to you all," I said, rolling my eyes. "It's a sport. It's healthy. And who knows, I might learn to defend myself. A sweet right-hook might save me from some pervy sex-weirdo one day." Mum shook her head and pursed her lips, putting up the shield wall. "The question is, Mum," I went on, "why do you want me to be at risk from pervy sex-weirdos?"

George cleared his throat in an authoritative manner. "Self-defense classes are one thing. But the risk of brain damage from being repeatedly punched in the head is a genuine concern."

"If you want exercise," Mum said, "come to my Pilates class with me. You'd love Pilates, and it would be fun to do something together."

"*Would* I love it, though?" I asked.

"What do you think, Blossom?" Dad said. "You're usually not short of an opinion."

"I don't think it's a great idea either," Blossom said after a pause.

I gasped.

Blossom looked over at me apologetically. "Sorry, Fleur, but boxing is a patriarchal, exploitative sport," she said. "And while I admire your resolve in seeking to infiltrate a male-dominated organization, I don't accept that boxing is a legitimate pastime. It glorifies violence and aggressive resolution to conflict."

"See? Arguments on both sides," Dad said.

"*Et tu, Brute?*" I said to Blossom, shaking my head at this treachery. And that's when I made my mind up. I was going to do it. I'd show them.

THE BLUEBELL ROAD FILM CLUB

I love my Friday nights. Instead of going home, I go to Blossom's house, on the edge of the village, on Bluebell Road. The idea is that her parents go out so we can settle down to some serious studying and then reward ourselves with a film. But we usually don't get a lot of studying done; instead we talk about stuff or watch another film.

"How's your mum?" she asked as I made two cups of tea. "What's she obsessing over this week?"

"Meningitis," I replied. "She read an article and she's convinced I've got it. She keeps pressing tumblers to my forehead, looking for red marks. On Wednesday she shone a reading lamp into my eyes to see if I was sensitive to light."

"Were you?" she asked.

"Kinda. It nearly blinded me."

"What about your dad?"

"He's not showing any symptoms."

"No, I mean how is he? He hasn't left her yet?"

"I think he's of two minds."

Blossom and I have been friends forever, and she's been there through all the ups and downs and we're well past the stage where she feels she's not allowed to comment on my parents' personality disorders. Blossom popped a DVD in the player. It was her turn to choose tonight, and she'd gone for a Lithuanian film called *The Seventh Raven*. I was not holding out much hope.

We have a thing we call the Bluebell Road Film Club. We take it in turns to choose films and the other person isn't allowed to complain. Blossom always chooses films from Eastern Europe or China about young women leading bleak lives and holding sparse conversations in the desolate countryside. They're usually called things like *Four Yellow Stones* or *The House at the End of the Desert* or *A Hundred and Twelve Autumns*.

I tend to go for the exact opposite end of the cinematic spectrum and choose romantic comedies that Blossom tuts through and deconstructs as she watches. It might sound as though we are fatally divergent in our choices, but actually it tends to work quite well. I know Blossom secretly enjoys the rom-coms. I think that she loves that I'm not like her other friends, Magnet and the crusty Swampy types from the Socialist Action Group who are all pretty humorless. And for my part I enjoy her films because I get to catch up on sleep. I expected I probably wouldn't make it past the third raven tonight.

"How's Magnet?" I asked.

"Oh, who knows? He's at the Project," she said frostily. "No phones allowed. So I texted Pip earlier, and he's not going to Battle tomorrow. Says he's got something on, but I think he's worried Garnet will rope him into another Battle rehearsal."

"Yes," I said. "About that . . ."

"Just you and me then," she said. "Just the gals, keeping it real in a wimple."

"I'm not going to Battle either, tomorrow," I said. "I'm going to boxing."

"Oh," she said, not looking at me. "Okay."

"Pip's coming to boxing, too," I went on, wincing.

"I see," she said.

There was a long period of silence, eventually broken by Blossom, who said, "Why are you going to boxing?"

I shrugged. "Because I want to get fit?"

"Why?"

"I've decided to become a polar explorer. My training starts here."

"But I feel left out now," she said. "Saturday mornings are when we all go to Battle; now you and Pip want to do something else."

"You could come, too?" I suggested.

"NO WAY!" she cried.

"Why not?" I replied.

"How many times . . . ? Look, it's violent, it's misogynistic. It rewards aggression and strength instead of reason and equality."

"Cool shoes, though," I countered. "And at least this disproves your theory that they won't let girls join."

"Only thanks to my intervention," she pointed out.

"Well, you can't have it both ways, Blossom," I said, pressing play on the remote to end the argument. "You can't enable girls to do something then tut because you don't like what they choose to do."

EYE OF THE KITTEN

I wasn't convinced by Pip's outfit. He was wearing very long silk shorts that he said were genuine boxing shorts from the 1920s that he'd bought at Vintage Vicky's, his favorite shop. He'd come to pick me up on Saturday morning and was standing in the garden while Mum twitched the curtains.

"And are they definitely men's boxing shorts?" I asked.

"They must be. Women didn't box in those days," he said. "Women don't really box now."

"Women do box," I said. "And I only ask about the shorts because they look a bit like bloomers."

"They're not bloomers," he assured me. He wore a singlet and black high-top sneakers to complete the look. Though what the look was I really couldn't say. I wore sneakers, leggings and a Lycra T-shirt Mum had lent me when she thought I was going to Pilates. It felt a bit baggy in the front. Pip drove us into town. I still wasn't entirely sure why Pip had signed up for boxing. It can't have just been the cookies. But Pip was prone to doing odd things. It was entirely possible he'd just been looking for an excuse to buy the bloomers from Vintage Vicky's. Twenty minutes later, Pip and I stood in the Memorial Hall, looking around and waiting for the session to begin.

"That boy has an electronic tracking tag," Pip whispered.

"Shush, stop staring," I said.

"I'm a bit nervous," Pip said.

"Me too," I replied. There were a lot of people there.

And when I say "people" I mean boys. Apart from Sharon, I was the only girl in the room, and I was starting to feel uncomfortable. They mostly seemed to be in their early twenties, with short, no-nonsense hairstyles and gray or black sports clothes. No one would meet my eye.

"Do you think they'll try and hit us?" Pip asked, swallowing nervously.

"It is a boxing club," I replied. "So there's a chance."

At that point Ricky came over to greet us. He looked us up and down. I imagined his heart sinking like a stone as he saw the state of his new recruits. A tiny girl with arms like audio cables and a ginger giraffe-boy wearing a pair of frilly knickers. We told him our names.

"I never forget anyone's names," he said, clearly trying to be positive. "Can't remember my wife's birthday, but I never forget a name." He looked me in the eye as he shook my hand.

"You ever boxed before?" he asked. I shook my head. "You here to learn to box? Or just for conditioning?"

I shrugged. "Conditioning, to start. Then who knows?"

"Hmm." He nodded quickly and turned away. I'd half expected him to burst out laughing, but if he thought my ambitions amusing he managed to keep it to himself. "What about you?" he asked Pip.

"Err, same?" Pip said. Ricky pressed his lips together and nodded again before walking back to his position near the stage. I thought I heard him sigh. He picked up an iPod attached to a stereo and hit play. Awful, old man's music came out of the speakers, and Pip and I looked at each other, trying not to laugh.

We began with some warm-ups. Jogging on the spot,

swinging our hips back and forth, simple stuff. Simple, that is, for anyone with control of their limbs, but almost impossible for poor old Pip. All he had to do was jog slowly on the spot, but he looked like a newborn calf trying to moonwalk while being jabbed with a cattle-prod. I could see Joe at the side, staring in astonishment, mouth open, revealing toothless gums.

"Now race for ten seconds," Ricky cried, and we picked up the pace. "Get those knees high." I was already out of breath and could hear Pip panting beside me, gasping for air. "Now back to jogging on the spot," Ricky said. The change in pace proved too much for Pip, who collapsed in a tangle of limbs.

After that we all had to get medicine balls and thrust them up and out from our chests as fast as we could as many times as we could in a minute. It seemed easy for the first ten seconds, but then I felt the beginnings of a burning ache in my upper arms that quickly grew more and more painful. "Don't look at the clock!" Ricky growled as I did just that, seeing with dismay that only fifteen seconds had gone by.

A quick glance around showed me that everyone else in the hall was handling the exercise with ease, pumping their arms up and down like machines, hardly breaking a sweat. Somehow I got through that minute, and we had a blissful fifteen seconds of rest before the next exercise.

"Burpees!" Ricky growled, and everyone moaned.

"Come on," Ricky said. "Train hard, fight easy."

Burpees, it turns out, involve getting down in a position like a push-up, then quickly bending your knees to bring your feet up, then rising to your feet and jumping in the air. Sounds easy, and doing the first one *was* easy.

It's just like getting up off the floor. And anyone can get up off the floor once. Maybe even twice. But over and over again, leaping up into the air every time? Pip only managed one. And even that one he didn't bother with the jump, just raised his arms in the air like a half-hearted wave. The fit young boys around me were clearly not enjoying this exercise, but they kept at it, and a couple of them did twelve or more, I reckoned. I think I managed five, and some of those were feeble.

My heart was pounding and I thanked Mum for choosing a black Lycra top, because I was already sweating like a pig. Pip was flat out on the floor, groaning. There was another exercise after that, lunges, then it was back on the medicine ball. Sweat poured from me, stinging my eyes.

"This is just the warm-up, people!" Ricky growled. "If you're struggling now, you're going to hate me in a minute." Pip dragged himself to his feet and just about managed to lift the medicine ball, once. I felt like giving up—this was ridiculous, what was I doing here? Out of the corner of my eye I saw Tarik enter the hall. Sharon hugged him and he walked over to join us, catching my eye briefly. I must have looked pretty close to my best, with hair plastered to my forehead, face bright red and shining with sweat. Tarik, presumably recognizing my inner beauty, smiled briefly before grabbing a medicine ball and joining in. I redoubled my efforts and managed to lift my own ball a couple more times before the buzzer sounded. "Do one more on the buzzer," Ricky yelled, and I managed to push the ball up one last time.

After the "warm-ups" it was skipping rope for some of us, while others put gloves on and split into two groups.

Some were told to hit punching bags while the others joined Ricky in the ring. I'd thought I might be okay at the skipping. I hadn't done it since, oh, let's see, fourth grade? But I was pretty good at it back then. Also I'm light and was sure I'd read somewhere that women had proportionately better lower-body strength than men. Maybe this was where I'd hold my own.

It turned out I wasn't very good at skipping either. I could get into the rhythm okay, but it was SO HARD. Much harder than ten years ago. Who would have thought jumping up and down could be so difficult? At least I could do a few skips. Pip couldn't do it at all. He could just about flip the rope over his head, but when he'd try to jump over it he'd mistime it horribly and get the rope caught in his boots. He stumbled and fell a couple of times.

"Try it like this," one of the boys said to Pip. He demonstrated a slightly different technique where he sort of hopped over the rope, using alternate feet, rather than jumping with both feet. Pip nodded and stood on one leg like a crane before whipping the rope around and whacking himself in the ankle with a sharp crack.

"It's easier if you move forward while you skip," Helpful Boy said to Pip when he'd recovered. "Like this." The boy moved slowly across the floor as he skipped, almost like he was stepping over the rope rather than jumping over it. Pip panted and raised himself again. He stepped over the limp rope, then whirled it around, letting it come to rest on the floor again before stepping over. "Better," Helpful Boy said encouragingly. Though he was just being nice. Mercifully, it was then time to switch over, and the boy told us to put on gloves.

"The gloves will make your hands stink," he said as he helped me find some ten-ounce small gloves. "There's no way around that, I'm afraid. If you decide to come back, you might want to buy wraps for your hands. They'll protect your wrists and knuckles and stop your hands from smelling quite so bad."

"I'm left-handed," Pip said as Helpful Boy turned to assist him.

"That doesn't matter when it comes to gloves," he explained. "They're all the same." Pip and I took position on either side of a punching bag, following the lead of the boys. Our punching bag looked like it had just done twelve rounds with Mike Tyson. The stitching was frayed and whatever it was stuffed with had started to sag to the bottom, leaving it more pear-shaped than cylindrical, rather like Ian Beale might look were he to be hung from a butcher's hook. I watched the boys around us jab at their bags with the left hand, then follow with a hard right. It looked easy enough. Maybe the worst was over.

It wasn't. Punching is just about the most tiring thing you can do. You know in films where the hero gets into a fistfight with the baddies, and they just go on and on smacking each other in the jaw over and over again? Well, it turns out that's not very realistic. Unless they were superhuman, they'd be exhausted after just a couple of minutes, not to mention senseless from being hit in the head repeatedly.

"There's a reason boxing rounds only go on for three minutes," Sharon said as she came to watch us. "And there's a reason boxers have to be super-fit." Pip took a couple of swings before falling against the punching bag and clutching it like a shipwrecked sailor might hold a lifesaver. I tried to do a couple of jabs and a big right swing, or whatever it's called, but I could only do it half a dozen times before I had to stop. And when I hit the bag it hardly seemed to move at all. Some of the boys were hitting it so hard that the bracket holding it in place would creak ominously. I was hitting so weakly that I couldn't even feel the impact through the gloves. And I was tired. So tired. I looked up at the clock and groaned to see only half an hour had passed.

Pip and I kept at it as best we could, patting away gingerly while all around us young, fit boys hammered fists into the bags, pummeling them with terrifying power and intensity. I watched Helpful Boy closely and saw he sort of twisted his body and rolled into the punch when he hit with his right hand. That was how you made the bag swing, it seemed. I tried the technique for myself, and while rolling in, hit the bag as hard as I could. It juddered back sharply, thumped Pip in the chest and knocked him over. He blinked at me in surprise. "That was a good one," he said.

"Thanks," I said. "It *was* a good one, wasn't it?" I tried it again. Now I could feel it in my knuckles, through the glove.

"Drink break," Ricky yelled. "Don't drink too much too fast. After that we'll change over. Those who haven't been in the ring yet, get over here." I gave the bag one last whack. One for the buzzer! I gulped a few mouthfuls from my water bottle, resisting the temptation to drain it. Then I swallowed nervously and walked over to the ring, Pip stumbling along behind me, panting like a dog on a treadmill. We bent down and climbed through the ropes.

SWEAT ANGELS

"You two first," Ricky said, pointing to me and Pip. "I need to get your stance sorted before you do anything." He showed us how to stand, feet at shoulder width, the left slightly forward.

"Keep your fists by your cheeks. Keep them there at all times unless you're punching. Punch from the face, rolling your hips a little. As soon as you've completed the punch, bring your gloves back to your cheeks," he said. "This is the most important rule in boxing. Always keep your guard up. If you don't, someone will punch you hard in the face. Is that simple enough for you?"

We nodded.

"Okay," Ricky said to me. "Now hit my left pad with your left glove."

"You mean the opposite pad?" I asked.

"Yes, the opposite one. Hit it."

I did so. He tapped me on the left side of my head with his pad.

"What didn't you do?" he asked.

"I didn't keep my guard up," I said, annoyed with myself for forgetting so quickly.

"Hit my right pad with your right glove," he said. I did so. He tapped the right side of my head with his pad.

"What didn't you do?" he asked.

I sighed. "I didn't keep my guard up."

"It's a simple rule," he said. He proceeded to show me some basic routines, a left jab, then a right. Then a roll to the left and down as he swiped the glove over my head. One, two, roll left. One, two, roll right. All the while trying to keep my guard up and stay on my toes as instructed. There was a surprising amount to remember, and I found myself getting increasingly frustrated. At one point I just took a wild swing with my right and connected hard with his right pad, then he tapped me on the side of my head again.

"Good hit," he said, looking slightly surprised. "But you dropped your guard."

Who would have thought boxing required so much thinking?

Tapping the gloves, as Ricky called it, was my favorite part. It was hard work, like everything else, but because there was someone else involved you were too busy to think much about the physical exertion. He was there, right in front of me, waiting for me to hit him. Or his pads at least. I couldn't stop for a rest, I couldn't double over and take huge, gulping breaths. I just had to keep going, one, two, duck-roll, one, two, one, two, duck-roll.

I almost enjoyed it. Almost.

Once or twice, everything seemed to click, and I got my punch just right and felt the glove thud into Ricky's pad with a satisfying smack. He'd nod on those occasions and say "Nice." It felt good when that happened. When we'd all had a turn on the pads it was time for a warm-down. Pip and I helped each other take off our gloves.

"Oh my God, my hands stink like dead badgers," Pip said. I wrinkled my nose. The stench of stale sweat and moldy leather hit me.

"A lot of us have our own gloves," Helpful Boy said, noticing our faces. "They still stink, but at least it's your own sweat." Warm-downs sounded a little less intense, but I hadn't counted on the ab-work. There were push-ups and planks, then we had to lie on our backs and raise our feet just six inches off the ground and hold the pose for a minute, three times, or "reps." I managed about fifteen seconds on the first rep, then ten on the second and five on the third. No one was enjoying this. It was impossible not to make disturbing involuntary noises: grunts, hisses and groans.

"Winners train, losers complain," Ricky cried.

Out of the corner of my eye I could see that Pip had abandoned the exercise altogether and just lay on the floor sighing like an expiring starfish. When we got up I looked down to see I'd left a wet imprint of my body on the floor. A sweat angel.

Finally, finally, finally the hour was over and Pip and I stumbled gratefully toward the door, leaving a trail of sweat. Joe intercepted us. "Coming back?" he asked.

"No," Pip said shortly. I don't think he was being rude; he just didn't have the breath to expand on his response.

"What about you?" Joe said. The look on his face suggested that he expected the same response. I hesitated. What I'd just done had been the hardest physical thing I'd ever done in my life. And part of me felt as though it was done now. I'd come along, I'd gone through with it, and I'd even done okay. *Good hit*, Ricky had said. I didn't need to come back again. I could leave with my head held high. Mission accomplished.

"I'm so unfit," I said. I looked over to see Ricky talking animatedly with one of the boys. Not even interested enough to acknowledge us. Probably assuming this was the last he'd see of Pip or me.

"We can get you fit," Joe said. "And you've got good strength in your legs. You do a lot of running?"

"Walking," I said. He nodded. "You transfer that lower-body strength into your fists and you could be a boxer." Then he turned and walked away. Pip grabbed me by the baggy Lycra and dragged me out of the hall. We didn't talk much in the car. Pip's hands and arms were shaking violently and I had to keep leaning over to stabilize the steering wheel.

"Thanks for driving," I said as he dropped me off. He nodded and looked up at me, face still bright red and blotchy. I hoped he wasn't going to go into cardiac arrest. When I got inside, I was shattered. Even Ian Beale looked in better shape than me. He thumped his tail against the floor to greet me, then sighed and closed his eyes. I grabbed a pint glass from the kitchen, filled it from the tap, drank the whole lot down, then filled it up again and went upstairs. My mother appeared and followed me up.

"How was it?" she asked.

"Hard," I said. I really didn't feel like talking to her just now, but I knew she must have been sitting at home worried sick about me.

"You look awful," she said. "All red and puffy."

"You should see the other guy," I said. But I went into my bathroom and looked at myself in the mirror. I looked like I'd been attacked by someone carrying a paintbrush and a bucket of sweat. Some of the sweat had dried on my face, leaving little crusty, salty streaks. My hair was stuck down over my forehead and a curl had wrapped itself around my ear as if clinging to it for comfort. My face was blotchy red like Pip's had been. Suddenly I felt sick, and before I could do anything to stop it the pint of water I'd drunk came flooding back out into the sink. *Don't drink too much too fast*, Ricky had said. I looked up at Mum, expecting her to be horrified, but actually she looked relieved.

"I guess you won't be going back, then," she said.

Just at that moment, the thought of putting myself through that torture again made my skin crawl with horror. But I wasn't going to let her know that. I wiped the sick from my chin, swiped back my sweaty hair and said, "Of course I'm going back. I loved every second of it."

THE RETURN

Obviously I had no intention of going back. And neither did Pip. When Blossom asked me on Thursday if we were working at Battle on Saturday I said probably. I needed the money, and the weather was looking good.

"Only probably?" she asked. "Don't tell me you're thinking of going to boxing again?"

"I'm not. It was horrible," Pip said. "You should have seen my outfit, though. I looked amazing."

"Fleur?" she said, looking at me.

"It was okay," I said. For some reason I didn't really want to tell Blossom how difficult I'd found it. I knew how she felt about boxing and didn't want a lecture.

"You the only girl there?" she asked.

"Yes," I admitted.

"Did they make you feel welcome?" I thought of

Helpful Boy, but then remembered Ricky turning his back on me. The others refusing to meet my eye.

"I didn't go to make friends, I went to get fit. Maybe you should give it a try?"

"You don't have to get involved in a misogynistic sport to get fit," she said, ignoring my barb. "You should come on a few marches; carrying signs is great for upper-body strength."

"Hmm, I'll think about it," I said. "Anyway, I don't think boxing is misogynistic."

"It glorifies male violence and aggression," she said. "It's a brutal and dehumanizing spectacle, exploiting the most vulnerable people in society."

"Or," I said, "it encourages fitness and confidence. It teaches discipline and application to disadvantaged young people. There are two sides to the issue."

"You sound like your dad," she pointed out.

"Well, sometimes there *are* two sides to issues," I said. And we left it there.

Despite my fighting talk, I think if Mum had been able to leave the subject alone, then I might have decided to drop the boxing idea once and for all. But she just wouldn't shut up about it. Mostly I dreaded the thought of going back. But there's something about Mum that can make you want to swallow bleach rather than agree with her. So on Friday night I decided I wasn't going to Battle, but back down to Bosford Boxing Club.

With no Pip, I would have to make my own way there. The hall is at least another half a mile farther than school, and I didn't really fancy walking the whole way. So after breakfast I went into the garage and inspected my bike. It was home to a number of new species of spider, and I had to evict an extended family of earwigs who had set up a cozy home in the left handlebar grip. But once I'd dusted it off and pumped up the tires, it seemed okay. Except there was an odd scraping sound. I wheeled it around on the driveway, trying to work out where it came from, when Dad appeared and offered to help me sort it out.

"Good to see you out on the bike again," he said as he set his tools down and peered at the back wheel. I wondered if he was going to ask me to come out for a ride with him. But he didn't.

"I'm going to ride down to Bosford," I said eventually. "To boxing."

"You're serious about it, yeah?" he said without looking up. He tightened a screw on the gear mechanism, then loosened another.

"I don't know," I said. "I don't know if it's my thing, but I want to go back today."

He looked up at me with an odd mix of expressions I couldn't quite read. Though there was concern in there. "Your mother is worried sick," he said. "She asked me why you were doing it. Why choose boxing, of all things?"

"I don't really know," I said. "Maybe it's because people keep telling me I shouldn't."

"That's it? You're doing it because of what other people say? What do *you* say?"

I thought about it for a while before answering. I had a good answer. "When I hit Ricky's pad last week. When I got my balance right, and really laid into it. It felt right. I felt like I'd gotten rid of something negative."

"Do you think it's cathartic?" he asked. "That you're getting something out of your system?"

I nodded.

"I get that feeling when I'm on my bike," he said. "I can just get away, escape. And all the anger and the . . . negative feelings I have I can just . . . pour into the pedals. I'm not explaining it very well." But he was. I knew just what he meant. I waited to see if there would be more, but he just stood and said, "There, sorted. The gears were misaligned. Try it now."

I cycled up and down Badger Lane. Ian Beale had been allowed outside for once and he lumbered along behind me, wheezing in delight. I nodded to Dad as he watched.

"Thanks," I said.

"Ride safely," he said. "Do you know the way?"

"I've lived here all my life," I said, rolling my eyes. "I think I know my way around Bosford."

FEWER

I was lost. I'd foolishly decided to take a shortcut through the Malcolm Gladwell Estate, which is a bit of a maze. All the houses look the same and each one has either a mattress, a car on bricks or a caravan in the front yard. I stopped to ask a lady with a stroller the way. She seemed delighted to have been asked but gave me such a convoluted set of contradictory directions that I decided just to ignore her. I looked at my watch. I would be late if I didn't get a wriggle on. I was going to have to ask someone else. I looked around and saw a group of young men. I took a deep breath and cycled over to them. One looked up as I approached.

"All right?" I said in my best "street" voice. "Looking for the Memorial Hall, innit."

"You that Fleur," he said, "from school. Why you in Gladwell's?" I didn't recognize him. But he seemed to know me. That was odd. No one noticed me at school. The other boys wandered over. A couple of the older boys looked a little hostile. Suddenly I wondered if I'd made a big mistake. Riding through the Gladwell Estate? On my own? In Lycra?

"Never mind," I said. "I'll find it." I got back on my bike and tried to push off, but in my haste made a mess of it and nearly fell off. The boys laughed.

"Wanna push?" One of the boys walked up behind me and took hold of my bike seat. Instinctively I slapped his hand away. He looked about my age, with tattoos on his neck, and wore a baggy T-shirt. He reached forward again to grab the seat and this time his fingers touched my bum. I pushed off and pedaled away as the boys laughed. But a couple of them came running along behind me.

"You need to get fit, Fleur."

"Don't fall off, girly!" I got to a intersection and had to stop as a white van came past. The boys caught up with me, one came on my left, the other on my right. Shouts and laughter from behind told me the others were following, too. Suddenly I felt very scared. My breath caught in my throat and I lifted my hands in a defensive posture. The boy to my left laughed and imitated my posture. Then suddenly he was gone, knocked off his feet by a blur that came up from behind. I watched him go tumbling to the asphalt in front of my bike, then the boy on the right was sent the same way as someone gave him a hard shove. I turned to see who my savior was.

"Tarik?"

"Get away from her," Tarik called as the boys clambered to their feet. The rest of them had caught up now and were standing, watching. They were wary of Tarik. Maybe they knew of his skill in the ring. "You're lucky she didn't get off her bike. You didn't know she was a boxer, did you?" Tarik had the faint trace of an accent. The boys walked off, laughing in a show of bravado.

"Thanks," I said.

"No problem," he said. "It's Fleur, isn't it? What are you doing going down Belham Street?"

"That's victim blaming," I said, realizing I sounded like Blossom. "Are you saying that I shouldn't be allowed to go where I want? Because I'm a girl?"

"No," he said. "I just meant that you're going the wrong way for boxing."

"Oh," I said. He grinned and I felt my tummy do a little flip. He wore a loose hoodie but I could still make out the firm muscles in his shoulders. "Well, that's okay, then."

"Come on," he said. "Wheel your bike and we'll walk together."

I was still shaken from my experience, but Tarik's presence was reassuring. We chatted about the club and Tarik told me about Ricky's history. "He was a great boxer. Been in the ring since he was nine. Went to the

Commonwealth Games and won bronze. Would have gone to the Olympics in Athens but got injured. Sharon reckons he would have got gold. Then he went professional. Seventy-three fights."

"Wow," I said. "What's he doing in this dump?"

"Not a lot of money in boxing," Tarik said. "Not in this country. Besides, Ricky wants to give something back. He trained in a club like this. Lived on an estate, like me."

"Sorry," I said. "I didn't mean to say there's something wrong with this area." *Nice one, Fleur,* I thought. My smart mouth had gotten me into trouble again. Blossom would have told me to check my privilege, and this time she would have been right.

"Don't worry," Tarik said. "It is a crap-hole."

He reached into his bag and pulled out a bag of cashews, offering it to me. I took a handful.

"Thanks," I said.

"You should eat lots of these," he said. "Good protein, good for bulking up. Where do you live?"

"East Bosford," I said, embarrassed. "Rangers' Wood."

"Very nice," Tarik said as we walked into the club. "So what are you doing in this dump?"

"I'm here to box," I said. Inside, I saw a group of boys chatting as Ricky fiddled with the ring.

". . . So she says, 'I want you to make me feel like a real woman,'" one of the lads was saying to the others as I walked behind him. Helpful Boy coughed when he saw me, but the first lad ignored him. "So I gave her my shirt and said, 'Iron this.'" They all laughed, except Helpful Boy, who looked slightly embarrassed.

"Come on, ladies," Ricky shouted. "Let's warm up."

We were very nearly late for training and Ricky got us straight onto skipping. You had to skip for two minutes without stopping, but of course that was impossible, and every time the rope hit you on the back of the head, or got tangled in your legs, you had to drop it and do some horrible exercise, like squat jumps or alternate lunges.

"The longer you keep up the skipping the less reps you have to do," Ricky cried.

"Fewer," I mumbled automatically.

"What's that, Fleur?" Ricky asked, cupping a hand to his ear. I froze, suddenly aware that everyone was looking at me.

"Um. Fewer reps," I said. "Not less. Because you can count them."

"You got breath to correct my English, you can do ten more squat thrusts," Ricky growled. "Count those." The boys all laughed. If I wasn't already bright red from the exertion, I would have been bright red from mortification. I did the squat thrusts. When would I learn to keep my mouth shut?

"To be fair, I didn't think you'd be back," Helpful Boy said to me as we had a quick breather between reps. "I'm Dan."

"To be fair, I didn't think I'd be back either," I said. "And yet, here I am. I'm Fleur."

"We don't get many girls here," Dan said. "And those that do come usually don't last very long." That made me feel a little better. It helped to have a friendly face, and a name. As we started the next exercise, Ricky went into the spiel I'd heard a couple of times before. "Boxing is for the ring only," he began. "What you learn here in the club stays in the club. If I hear of anyone fighting outside you will be out of Bosford Boxing Club. If you see someone else struggling, you do not laugh at them, you do not mock them. You help them, you encourage them, you support them. Is that understood?"

"Yes, Coach Ricky," a few boys panted as we leaped up and down. The sweat was already starting to pour down my neck into Mum's Lycra.

"Is that understood?" he repeated.

"YES, COACH RICKY!" we screamed.

FORBIDDEN

"Don't let the dog out!" Mum cried as I came in through the kitchen door. She was at the stove, stirring a pot. Ian Beale had seen the door open and was lumbering toward me, intent on freedom. I closed it quickly, dropped my bag and dropped to my knees to give him a consolation hug.

"Crikey, Ian Beale," I said, "you stink."

"It's a side-effect of this medicine," Mum said. "It's highly unstable, which is why I have to cook it up each time I give it to him." I stood and watched her tip some crystals into a saucepan as she stirred.

"I'm pleased to hear it's just the dog's medicine," I said. "I thought for a minute I'd walked into a crack den." I poured myself a glass of water and peered at a magazine Mum had left on the table. It was called *Women's Health* and had a picture of a toned, ponytailed girl on the cover.

Maybe if I got fit I could look like that, I thought. Mum glanced over.

"You haven't forgotten about Saturday, have you?" she asked.

"What about Saturday?"

"You said you'd come along to my Pilates class with me."

I groaned. I didn't remember saying that to Mum, but it is possible I may have grunted agreement at her without really listening. Mum has been trying to get me to come to her Pilates classes for months. She says she wants us to bond, but I think she just wants to keep an eye on me.

"Pilates?" I said. "Isn't that for . . . you know, older people?"

"Not at all!" Mum replied. "You'd be surprised. It's harder than it looks, and much safer than boxing. You should come along, meet Carole, the instructor. Everyone loves Carole; she has an enveloping aura."

"Oh, sorry, Mum," I said, slightly alarmed at the thought of meeting Carole and her aura. "I've remembered I have to help Blossom with something on Saturday."

She looked disappointed. "Please tell me you're not going back to boxing."

"Well, I thought I might," I said. "Anyway, need a shower." I escaped upstairs.

"We need to talk about this, Fleur," Mum called up after me. "Please?" When I came back down, Dad was there and the table was laid. There was a steaming soup tureen on the sideboard and a bit of an atmosphere in the room. And before Mum started ladling out the soup she asked if we could have a little chat.

"It's about your boxing," Dad said.

"Is that tureen going to fit in the dishwasher?" I asked, hoping to derail the subject by triggering a dishwasher discussion. No such luck.

"Your mother and I are worried about you getting involved in such a violent sport."

"It's just a bit of skipping and hitting bags. It's not like I'm doing twelve rounds with Naseem Hamed."

"It's dangerous, Fleur," Mum said. "Can't you see I'm worried about you? I don't want to lose another daughter."

"Verity's not dead," I pointed out. "She's alive and well and living in Dunedin."

"If you're serious about it, though," Dad said, trying to be the voice of reason, "then we will allow it."

"That's good of you," I said. I could feel myself flushing with anger.

Mum took over. "But on the understanding that you only do the training. The . . . what did you call it, the conditioning? I . . . we don't want you to fight in the ring." For half a second, I thought about arguing, but managed to bring my temper under control. Because I'd just seen she'd left a slight opening in the shield wall. I could win this while avoiding confrontation.

"I have no intention of fighting in the ring, Mum," I said calmly. "I can't even hit the punching bag a dozen times without coughing up a lung. I'd be murdered."

"So you promise?" Mum said urgently. "Look at me and promise me you won't ever fight in the ring."

I sighed, but I looked at her. Part of me wanted to

shout and tell her that I could do whatever I liked, but another part of me held back. Like it always does. Mum's terror of everything was intense. I knew that. She was frustrating, but she meant well and there was no point in upsetting her more. And since the idea of me ever fighting in the ring was ridiculous, maybe it wasn't something to get upset about. "Fight, fight, fight!" Blossom would say. But Pip would tell me to choose my battles.

And on this occasion, Pip was right.

"Mum, I will never fight in the ring. I promise."

Mum nodded and smiled. She'd won the day.

THE MENINISTS

"Oh, please, come to Battle with us," Blossom said on Monday. "You've missed the last two. Pip's going to take part in the reenactment rehearsal again this week."

"Maybe," I said. I still hadn't made up my mind. On the one hand, I missed my friends and wanted to go to Battle. Not to mention the money I'd earn. On the other hand, I'd just gotten my parents to let me go to boxing. If I didn't go, they'd just think I was lacking in commitment as usual.

"Don't tell me you're thinking of going to boxing again."

"Yes. No. I don't know," I said. "I didn't absolutely hate it last week."

"Up to you," Blossom said as we went into English class. "But we missed you."

Miss Theakston was our teacher and she was encouraging us to debate stuff. She does this periodically, trying to engage us with important issues of the day, like Europe, immigration, the death penalty, etc. Somehow, though, we always end up arguing about gender issues. This is because Blossom and Bonita are both in the class, and so are William Capel and Ryan Cook. Blossom calls them the Meninists, men who think they're downtrodden and have to fight for more rights. Like someone arguing that Brighton needs more mindfulness workshops.

Today Ryan started telling us why women were inferior to men.

"Even the very fastest woman is still half a second slower than the fastest man," Ryan said smugly.

"And that's important, is it?" Blossom asked. "That half-second? That half-second is why men are paid forty percent more than women? That's why ninety-nine percent of CEOs are men? Why seventy-five percent of MPs and top civil servants are men? Because of that half-second advantage?"

"In evolutionary terms, it's vital that men get the choicest cuts of meat," William said. "Protein builds muscle and speed, and without those, next time the wildebeest gets away and we all go hungry. Why would you want the village to starve, Blossom?"

"Half a second explains why Saudi women aren't allowed to drive, does it?" Blossom went on. "That's why Malala was shot? Because she was too slow to dodge the bullet? Half a second's difference is really THAT important?"

"It might make all the difference between catching a

wildebeest or going home empty-handed," William said. "A lot can happen in half a second."

"I could kick you in the bollocks in half a second," Bonita suggested.

"Bonita!" Miss Theakston snapped. "And William, stop trying to deliberately inflame the debate."

"That's the problem with women," Ryan sighed. "They just don't get logic. They let emotion get in the way. There are some roles more suited to men than to women. That's just a fact."

"I've got another fact for you," Blossom said. "It's 2018 and girls can do whatever the hell they want. You know that there wouldn't be nearly such a mess if women were in charge of everything," she went on. "They should ban men from holding public office."

"That might work for a bit," Ryan replied. "But eventually all the women in Parliament would end up having their period at the same time. Then boom."

Bonita snorted with laughter.

A FEMINIST ISSUE

In the end I chose boxing and I was glad I did, because something strange happened at training. I got through the whole hour without once feeling like I was about to die of cardiac arrest. Don't get me wrong, it was still incredibly difficult. But I didn't want to throw up the whole time. Just most of the time. I managed to skip, without stopping, for nearly a whole minute. At one point the rope whirled so fast it actually made that whistling sound, and I was starting to think I was quite the Joe Frazier until I mistimed it and whacked myself in the back of the head.

We moved into warm-ups and Ricky turned up the awful music and told us to swing our hips and lift our knees.

"You didn't know it was a dance class, too, did you?" he called out over an awful groaning I thought might have been Phil Collins.

I found the leg drills tough. Ricky noticed me struggling. "Come on, Fleur," he called. "Train hard, fight easy."

"I am *so* unfit," I gasped, feeling everyone's eyes on me.

"Right, everyone. Drinks break. Don't drink too much, too fast," Ricky shouted.

"You should run more," Dan suggested as we went for our water bottles. "Put miles on your legs. As Ricky would say, there are no shortcuts, Fleur."

I nodded and grabbed my water, trying to just sip it, though I wanted to take the lid off and dive inside. I was grateful to Dan for coming over to chat. I'd already noticed today that the boys seemed slightly friendlier. Even so, most of them stood in little groups with their mates. Not deliberately excluding me, I don't think. Just not making a particular effort to include me. And sometimes I got the impression, when I walked close by, that the conversation would stop, or drop. Like they were uncomfortable carrying on their banter with a girl around.

"I think you're getting fitter," Dan said. "You kept up with the burpees."

"Still sweating like a pig, though," I said, looking down at the pool beneath my feet.

"Don't worry, that'll get easier," Dan said. "Just keep working. Keep pushing yourself. Oh, and watch *Rocky*."

"Eh?"

"You want to get fit? Watch *Rocky*."

"The film *Rocky*? With Sylvester Stallone?"

"That's the one."

"How can watching a film make you fitter?"

Dan grinned. "Trust me."

I wasn't sure if all this exercise was doing me much good, but it was certainly making me hungrier. During English class on Monday my stomach was growling and Blossom kept looking at me in alarm. "It's like sitting next to Chewbacca," she said. I was very grateful for the lunch bell and pretty much ran to the cafeteria, Blossom puffing to keep up.

"What's that song you've been humming all day?" she asked.

" 'The Logical Song,' by Supertramp," I said.

"The what? By the who?"

"Not the Who. Supertramp," I said as we grabbed plates and started helping ourselves to food. "Ricky is a big fan of progressive rock. He has two playlists. One is all songs that have some connection to boxing, however tenuous, and the other is prog rock classics; they get under your skin. Yesterday I had 'Moonchild' by King Crimson in my head all day."

"Is this a boxing club, or a cult?" Blossom asked.

We sat down and Blossom inspected my plate. I'd

piled it up somewhat. I had chicken nuggets and a Wiener schnitzel. Spaghetti, carrots, sweetcorn and peas. A bread roll, a chocolate mousse for dessert and a cheesecake for another dessert. I was ravenous but it still looked like a lot.

"Oh my God," Ryan Cook said as he walked past and saw my full plate. William Capel whispered something into his ear. I heard the words "going straight to her arse." They both fell about laughing.

"And another example of everyday sexism," Blossom sighed. "No one would bat an eyelid if they saw a man eating a lot of food."

"Yeah, but women do the cooking, so it's sort of our fault," I said.

"Fair point," Blossom said, and helped herself to one of my chicken nuggets. We grinned at each other as we chewed.

The grinning stopped on Friday night when I showed Blossom what I'd chosen for the Bluebell Road Film Club.

"*ROCKY*?"

"Yes, *Rocky*."

"You want me to watch a film about a stupid boxer?"

"It's a classic. Second-best sports film ever made, according to the American Film Institute," I said, reading the back of the DVD case. "Three Oscars, ten nominations."

"Fine. You go ahead," Blossom said. "I'm going to do some studying."

"You're not even going to give it a try?"

"I don't want to watch a film about oafish bullies hitting each other in the head," she said, grabbing her geography textbook and opening it.

"Well, I think that's a bit closed-minded," I said. "After all, I sat through your film last week, *The Concubine's Shoes*."

"*The Concubine's Choice*," she corrected. "And you didn't sit through it, you went to sleep."

"Fine," I said, hitting play.

"Fine," she said. She started flipping pages.

"Would you mind doing that a little more quietly?" I asked as the opening credits started to roll.

Blossom rolled her eyes. "Fine," she said again.

I forgot all about Blossom soon enough, though. Because *Rocky* is just BRILLIANT. Why had I never watched this before? It's just a great story. He's this tough prizefighter who ekes out a living between bouts by collecting debts. Then he's given the chance to fight against the heavyweight champion OF THE WORLD. He's got no hope, of course, but then this little guy agrees to train him and he gives him loads of great advice. My favorite bit is where the little guy says, "He ain't gonna kiss ya, Rocky, he's gonna KILL ya." He reminded me a bit of Joe, the old coach at Bosford Boxing Club.

There's even a love interest, too, and when they finally kissed I don't mind admitting I had to wipe my eye.

"What does she see in him?" Blossom said, tutting.

"I thought you were studying?" I asked.

"How can I study with him grunting like a warthog all over the place?" she replied. "And another thing, how come he keeps punching meat?"

"Shh," I said. "This is a good bit."

Blossom huffed and pretended to read her book, but I could tell she was watching. Of course she was watching. Rocky is the best. He's my new obsession. I decided then and there that I was going to watch every Rocky film. On my own if I had to.

ON THE BUZZER

Am I becoming accepted?

Today Coach Alex raised an eyebrow at me, which I think is his way of smiling. Jordan had offered me advice on my skipping technique. Simon with the electronic tag got me some wraps from Ricky's bag and showed me how to put them on. He told me I could pay for them next week. Probably best of all was Joe slapping me on the shoulder as he passed. It's not that they'd been rude or dismissive before, but they'd mostly ignored me.

I mentioned this to Sharon. "Yeah," she said. "Look, a lot of people come for one or two sessions, then we never see them again. The boys don't tend to start talking to you until they know you're a regular."

Wow. Was I a regular? Maybe . . . At one point, we were doing timed burpees, as many as we could do in a minute. I'd just gotten down onto my hands and knees for one when the buzzer went. I stopped and got back up.

"One more," Ricky said to me. I got down and did one more, my muscles protesting just when they'd thought they were getting a rest. "Always put one on the buzzer."

"Got it," I panted.

"Okay," Ricky said, when we were warmed up and I couldn't feel my face anymore. "So we're going to do some punching exercises, in pairs." More awful music played on the stereo. The sort of thing my parents might listen to. Genesis, ELO, some band with a flute player that Jerome told me was called Jethro Tull. Ricky explained what he wanted us to do. Facing each other, we were to do three sets of three minutes, one person wearing pads, the other wearing gloves, before swapping over.

"Any questions?" he asked.

"Yes," I said, unable to stop myself. "Who's in charge of the playlist?"

And everyone laughed. At me. No, not at me. At my joke. They didn't tell me to shut my cake-hole, or shake their heads sadly at this slip of a girl who'd invaded their space. They laughed. Not a lot. I don't want to oversell it. But I felt myself flushing with pleasure. Until Ricky replied.

"I'm in charge of the bloody playlist," he growled. "It's inspiring."

"It's . . . eclectic," I said. No one laughed that time, and I wondered if I'd overdone it. There was clearly a fine line.

"You got time for fancy words, you've got time for six more push-ups," he said. "On the floor." By the time I'd finished and found a matching pair of stink bags, everyone else had paired up. Joe was the only one left.

"Just jabs first. Three minutes," Ricky cried. "Hit from the face, bring your gloves back to your face after each punch." Joe grinned at me toothlessly and told me to keep my guard up as I started patting his pads delicately.

"Hit harder," he growled. "I'll tap in." I tried to do as he asked, but I was already tired from the warm-up exercises. "Don't go easy on me," Joe said. "I'm tougher than I look." That wouldn't be difficult, I thought, and redoubled my efforts. Left-right, left-right, roll under. The buzzer went off and I punched one more time. *Put one on the buzzer.*

"And rest," Ricky called.

"You're doing well," Joe growled as I took in great lungfuls of sweet air. I nodded gratefully, unable to speak.

"Switch to hooks," Ricky called. "Left, then right."

A hook, as I'd learned, is a slightly lower punch than the jab, one that you sort of curl in from the side, elbow out, hoping to get around your opponent's defenses. I started whacking away at Joe's gloves. "Harder," he said. "Keep going." I kept this up for about seven years before the buzzer went. Now I was starting to feel it. I was sweating and gulping deep breaths. How did boxers keep this up round after round? There is nothing harder than punching for three minutes solid.

"Uppercuts next," Ricky shouted. "Get down low, bend the knees and hit up into the pads."

Joe held the pads high and horizontally, facing down, and as the buzzer went again, I started thumping upward. After a few punches I felt a whole new set of muscles starting to protest. I'd never seen evidence that I had ANY muscles in my arms. Turns out there are dozens of the little fellas, and they were all hating on me big-time for waking them up.

"Hit harder," Joe said, leaning in closer until our faces were just a few inches apart. "Send me flying." Each punch was a huge effort. I had to brace myself, bend my knees, get into position and hit upward, which doesn't feel natural. As the time ticked down I was preparing myself for one last right when the buzzer went. "And rest," Ricky called. Remembering Ricky's earlier admonition to put one on the buzzer, I went through with the punch, giving it everything, knowing it was the last one.

But Joe, upon hearing Ricky's call to rest, had dropped the pads to his sides. My glove came up sharply and cracked him right on the jaw. He went down like someone had removed his bones. "Joe!" Ricky yelled, and raced over to him as I stood there, shocked.

"I said rest!" Ricky said, looking up at me crossly.

"Sorry," I said. "I was putting one on the buzzer."

"You put one right on my buzzer," Joe said, without lifting his head.

"Are you all right?" Sharon asked, coming over with a medical kit. Joe waved her away and, with Ricky's help, got to his feet. He stumbled over to a chair and sat down.

"I'm so sorry," I said again, mortified.

"Never mind," Ricky said to me. "It's a contact sport and these things happen. Just be more careful next time." I felt a bit better after that and tried to put the incident out of my mind. As I was leaving I checked in again with Joe.

"Are you okay?" I asked.

He grinned. "It's a long while since a woman has made me see stars like that," he said. "And I seem to remember it being more fun last time." It wasn't a joke Blossom would have approved of, but I was glad to see he seemed fine.

"I'm not sure I'm going to be the next Nicola Adams," I said. As I turned to go, he grabbed my wrist.

"We should call you Killa. You've got one hell of an uppercut," he said. I waited for him to add "For a girl."

But he didn't.

TORN

Bluebell Road Film Club had come around again, and Blossom was cuing up a film on Netflix. It was a Yemeni film called *The House of Three Deserts* and ran for nearly four hours. I sighed and went to make a cocoa, hoping it would send me off to sleep during the opening credits.

"Do you think Taylor Swift and the guy will ever get back together?" I called from the kitchen.

"What guy?"

"From the song. You know?"

"What, the song where she says 'we are never ever ever getting back together'? No, I don't."

"You don't think she's protesting a little too much?" I asked. "I mean, if she really wasn't ever going to get back with him she wouldn't keep going on about it."

"She doesn't KEEP going on about it," Blossom said as I handed her a cocoa. "The song is three and a half minutes long, and I think makes it clear she's over him."

"But IS she?" I asked. "I think there's still something there."

"That's how controlling relationships work," Blossom said.

"Controlling?! How is he controlling? They hadn't seen each other for a month when he said he needed space."

"What?"

"How is that controlling?"

"The thing about you, Fleur," Blossom said, "is that you're a romantic. You just want happy endings with couples resolving their differences and drinking cocoa together while the kids sleep upstairs."

"Kids? That escalated quickly," I said, putting my cocoa down.

"You're so binary. You always just want the guy to get the girl."

"That's not true," I said. "Sometimes I want the girl to get the guy."

She laughed and punched me on the arm. "I miss you," she said. "Feel like I haven't seen you for ages."

"I see you at school every day," I pointed out.

"Yeah, but not to hang out. You're just . . . absent lately."

"I'm right here," I said. "We're just about to watch a four-hour film about ennui together. Fun fun fun!"

"You'll be asleep in twenty minutes," Blossom complained.

"So stop choosing films where nothing happens for three and a half hours then they all die in the last ten minutes."

"PLEASE come to Battle tomorrow," Blossom pleaded. "We want to see you properly."

"I dunno," I said. "I really miss it, but I'm loving boxing at the moment. I just feel as though I need to be committed."

"That's exactly what I was thinking," Blossom said. "I was so bored last week I even texted Magnet. I actually texted my *boyfriend*, Fleur."

"Don't try and make me feel guilty," I said.

"Look," she said. "It won't hurt for you to miss one Saturday, will it?"

"Next Saturday," I said. "I promise I'll come next Saturday."

Because the thing was, as much as I missed farting about in Battle, as much as I missed spending time with Pip and Blossom—

I wanted to go to boxing more.

Mum and Dad have found something new to argue about. Yay! She's been on at him to replace the rotten old gate for ages, and he's bought a new one. The only thing is they can't agree on which way round it should go. "You know I hate the fact that the old gate opened outward," Mum said. "The new one should open in. Gates should open in; everyone knows that."

"If it opens in, it'll bash into the camellia," Dad pointed out.

"So move the camellia."

"I can't. It's established."

"Oh, so you'd rather it opened out again, into the road? What if it swings open and a car hits it?"

"That never happened to the old one. We get maybe three cars a month going past; it's not the M25. It's Badger Lane."

"It's dangerous," Mum said.

Anyway, Dad's refusing to back down. The situation

is ongoing, and very, very tense. I've taken to referring to the issue as Gate-gate.

No one laughs.

So it was a blessed relief to escape on Saturday. I'd decided to run to the club. In my head I had this idea that I'd have a nice, gentle jog down the hill, with birds chirruping at me as I passed, and perhaps friendly waves from handsome farm boys. It didn't quite turn out like that. I was exhausted by the time I got to the church. Farmer Palmer nodded at me as I puffed past, my legs aching, my lungs straining. I didn't hear any birds chirruping, but I did see a murder of crows pecking at the carcass of a fox in the middle of the road. So that was nearly as good. Nor were there any handsome farm boys. Just a carful of teenagers in a tiny Nissan Micra on their way home from clubbing. One stuck his head out and barked something at me, making me jump.

Also, I realized halfway there that I hadn't brought any water. *Keep hydrated*, Ricky's voice shouted at me.

I managed to get to the Memorial Hall without further difficulty. Luckily there was a long wait at the lights on the bypass, which enabled me to get my heart-rate under control. Even so, I was pretty shattered when I got there. As we began going through the warm-ups I could see Ricky watching me struggle. When we stopped for drinks, he came over to me. "What's up?" he asked.

"I ran here," I said. "Trying to strengthen my legs."

"You do any other exercise?" he asked. "During the week?" I shook my head as I guzzled more water.

"You see these other lads?" He indicated the boys. "They come twice a week. They're all here every Wednesday night. Even Simon, who has to race to get here after seeing his probation officer in Hastings. He makes the effort because he knows it's important. Once a week isn't enough, you see?"

"I can't do Wednesdays," I said. "It's Date Night." Wednesdays would probably stay as Date Night right up until George's dying breath.

"Well," Ricky said. "Maybe you could do something on another night. Tuesday? Try and do some cardio, something to build up your stamina."

"I'll try," I said, thinking of all the studying I had to do. Wondering when I was going to be able to spend time with Blossom and Pip. Ricky made to go, but then stopped and turned back.

"Also, did you eat breakfast?"

"Yes," I said.

"What did you have?" he asked.

I shrugged, trying to remember. "Toast, a banana, cup of tea."

He shook his head. "It's not enough. What do you put in your car when it's empty?"

"I don't have a car."

"Fuel is the answer," he said patiently. "You want to box, you need fuel in the belly, and flesh on your bones."

"Well, what should I eat?"

"You need protein. Calories."

"So like a whey protein shake?" I asked, thinking of Mum's stack of health magazines. "Some goji berries? Skinless chicken and brown rice?" He looked at me as if I was mad.

"Ever heard of bacon and eggs?" he said. "It's not rocket science, Fleur. Eat some food, get some pounds on."

DATE NIGHT

Date Night that Wednesday was at a pop-up hipster restaurant near Hastings, close to the abattoir. I hadn't even known hipsters had their own food, but it turned out to be normal food, just described in a pretentious way. Hipsters especially liked bacon, it turned out. There was a bewildering variety of bacon-related dishes. Mac and cheese with bacon, bacon-wrapped meatloaf with homemade pickles, twenty-four-day-hung blue beef burgers, with bacon. Crusty sourdough with bacon jam. And it wasn't just ordinary bacon either. It was maple syrup–coated, hickory-smoked, hand-cut back bacon. From free-range, hand-fed, massaged pigs who'd had Belle and Sebastian played to them every day on a wind-up gramophone. There were maple-bacon doughnuts for dessert, of course.

There also seemed to be a lot of offal. Lardo, crudo, broiled bone marrow, haggis and sweetbreads. Most dishes came with foam of some description. I felt a bit sick just reading the menu. George was taking it all very seriously, of course. A man with a magnificent beard approached. George ordered a Diet Coke for me and a Pabst Blue Ribbon for himself, which is apparently the beer that all hipsters drink. He swallowed as we read through the menu.

"I'm not sure the hipster movement is going to last very long," I said. "They're clearly all going to die of heart disease in a few years."

"Oh, come on," he replied. "Where's your sense of adventure?"

"Stuffing doughnuts with hickory-smoked crudo isn't adventurous," I said. "It's carcinogenic."

"Sometimes you just have to try something a little different," he said as the bearded waiter came back and asked us if we'd like to look at the bread menu.

"Could you please tell us what you have?" I asked.

"We have sourdough, gypsy bread, arugula stone-baked tortilla-bread. Twisted poppy-seed, wood-fired brioche and glazed artisan."

"No bacon bread?" I asked.

"Err, no."

"Never mind, never mind," I said. "What about spleen loaf?"

"I haven't heard of that."

"It's very big in San Francisco," I said. "But forget it. We'll just have a French stick."

George ordered the trout with bacon foam. I ordered the pork belly with polenta. "That'll be quite heavy," he said.

"I'm starving," I said. "I've been exercising a lot lately."

"Maybe you need to cut down a little on the exercise," he said. I blinked at him. Has anyone ever said that to anyone in the world before? "I just don't think you need it. You're in great shape, and you don't want to get all . . . muscly."

"Have you been talking to my mother?" I asked.

"It's great that you want to keep fit," he said. "But you shouldn't overdo it. I knew a chap at college in first year who became obsessed with physical fitness. Always pushing himself. It didn't end well."

"What happened to him?"

"He's in jail for possession of illegal drugs."

"See," I said, triumphant. "I knew you naval academy boys were all off your faces the whole time."

He shook his head. "Okay. First, no, we aren't. It isn't like that at all. And second, they were illegal steroids he had. You know, for bodybuilding?"

"Hmm," I said doubtfully.

"Anyway," George went on. "You'll get to see for yourself soon enough what all my naval officer friends are like. I'd like to invite you to the Mess Ball later in the year."

"What, at the college?" I asked, a flutter of excitement in my tummy.

"Oh yes. You'll have to wear a gown, is that okay?"

"Yes, of course," I said. "And how would I get back afterward? Or would I . . . stay over?"

"We'll sort something out," George said, flushing slightly. "Just put the date in your diary for now. Nineteenth July."

"Actually, while we've got our calendars out," I said, "I was wondering about changing Date Night to Tuesdays. Or Thursdays. It's just that boxing is on Wednesday nights and I'd quite like to go to those sessions, too."

He gave me a look of shock and disbelief. As though I'd just suggested we slaughter a hyena and eat its still-beating heart with bacon jam.

"Change Date Night?" he said quietly. "But I thought you liked Date Night?"

"I love Date Night," I said. "Even this one. I'm just saying we could maybe do it on a different night. Maybe even a Friday, or a Saturday. So you don't have to rush back to Hove afterward . . ." The waiter arrived with our food at that point, the end of his beard dangerously close to the top of my pork belly.

"I'll think about it," George said unhappily. I hadn't meant to make him sad. I didn't see why it was such a big deal. But I suppose George loves his traditions, and his nice, safe routines. I speared a red pickle on my fork and held it up.

"Remember, George," I said. "Sometimes you just have to try something a little different." I put the pickle in my mouth and began chewing as he watched me thoughtfully.

Then I spat the pickle out.

"Oh God, that's disgusting."

GIRLS CAN'T HIT

While I waited for George to ponder the weighty issue of whether or not we could change Date Night, I decided it was time to take matters into my own hands and do some extra form of exercise, if only to burn off all the polenta. Ricky was right; once a week wasn't enough. There was no point going to a boxing class if I was too tired to punch a bag after the warm-ups. After my experience jogging to the class, I wasn't anxious to do another long run during the week. I decided it was time to do something extraordinary.

"Dad," I said on Thursday, after he'd gotten back from work. "Can we go for a ride?"

"Oh, Fleur," he said, sighing. "I really don't want to get back in the car."

"No, not in the car," I said. "On our bikes. Can we go for a bike ride together?"

He looked up at me as if I'd just offered him a set of his-and-hers dishwashers.

"Yes," he said, nodding and grinning like a Muppet. "Yes, of course." He raced into the house and came out a few minutes later looking resplendent in his cycle jersey and shades.

"You look like Peter Andre in those sunglasses," I said.

His face lit up. "Thanks," he said.

"Hang on, I don't mean Peter Andre, do I?" I said. "Peter . . . Capaldi."

"Oh," Dad said.

We went out to the garage together, Dad almost running in case I changed my mind. A quarter of an hour later, we were out on the road. I possibly didn't look quite so professional as he did, puffing and panting behind, trying to keep up, wearing baggy Lycra stretched tight over my trunk. But we were both out, on our bikes, sort of together. Father and daughter. And scoff if you like, but it felt like quite an important moment. We didn't go far on that first night. And we didn't talk much. I was too puffed to talk and also about five hundred yards behind him most of the time, but I think Dad liked that I was there. And maybe I didn't hate it so much.

"Look at this punch," I said, showing Pip the phone. Pip squinted and watched Nicola Adams thump Michaela Walsh hard in the side of the head. We were in the library, supposedly studying, along with the rest of our tutor group, but almost everyone was watching YouTube, except for Blossom, who was making notes in the margins of a book by Naomi Klein. Michaela Walsh's legs buckled on the tiny screen and she only just managed to keep upright. Adams pressed home the advantage and came after her retreating opponent, dancing lightly. She got two more punches in before the bell rang before the end of the round.

"Wow," I said. "Look at the power." Blossom pretended she wasn't interested, but I suspected the idea of a female boxer achieving something astonishing in a patriarchal society must have been pressing one or two of her buttons really quite hard. I looked over at her, sitting in what looked like an uncomfortable splayed-kneeling position, her bottom resting on her heels. She never sits with her feet on the floor, Blossom. She'll be in the lotus position, or sitting Japanese-style, or with an ankle wrapped around her neck or some other such position of karmic harmony.

"She doesn't look like a boxer," Pip said. "I saw her on *The One Show*. She seemed really lovely. I think of boxers as being the sort of people who never smile and who go around thumping animal carcasses."

"She is lovely," I said. "I watched an interview with her. She smiled a lot and didn't thump any meat that I saw. She's my new hero. She won gold at the 2012 and 2016 Olympics." Blossom looked up at this.

"They have women's boxing at the Olympics?" she asked.

"Come on, Dory, do you really not remember?" I sighed. "They have three weight divisions, flyweight, lightweight and middleweight." I'd weighed in at boxing on Saturday and Tarik had told me I was actually in the upper range of lightweight, which I'd been surprised about. "Tarik thinks I should bulk up and become a middleweight, but that would mean putting on fifteen pounds, which is a lot of cashews."

"Wait," Blossom said, closing her eyes to try to process this information. "You're telling me a man is asking you to put on weight? Without impregnating you first?"

"Blossom!" I said, feeling myself blush as an unexpected and not entirely unpleasant image involving Tarik popped into my head. I shoved it back down where it belonged. "Look, women's boxing is a real thing. There are clubs all over the country. Thousands of women are members of boxing clubs."

"Really?"

"Yes, really, though most of them don't spar. They just go to classes, you know, boxercise and that."

Blossom grinned and raised an eyebrow. "Ladies' Night?"

"Sure, but plenty do proper sparring as well."

She reached over and grabbed my phone so she could have a look. "Is that Nicola Adams?"

"Yes."

"She's black!"

"Yes, of course she's black!"

"But that . . . but that's amazing. A woman, and black . . . achieving all that."

I wondered if I should let Blossom know that Nicola Adams is also gay but thought that might send her over the edge. We watched the postfight interview with Clare Balding and I turned up the volume a little to hear Nicola speak.

"Oh my God," Blossom said. "She's just so intersectional."

"I know," I said. "So many things to overcome. She's black, she's a woman, she's . . . from Yorkshire."

"So she does this for a living?"

"She's just gone pro, but there are other professional women boxers in the UK," I said.

"How many?"

I hesitated before answering. "Three," I said.

"Three," she replied. "And how many male professional boxers?"

"One hundred and thirty-six," I replied reluctantly. Blossom nodded, as though pleased to discover yet more evidence of the patriarchy.

"One hundred and thirty-six to three," she said. "That sounds about right."

"Well, who knows," I said, suddenly feeling more confident than I had in ages. "Maybe I can make it one hundred and thirty-six to four."

PART TWO

ON THE
ROPES

ROUTINE

The next few weeks passed quickly as I settled into my new routine. Sunday of course meant lunch and an argument between my parents, or sometimes between George and Blossom. I'd try to stay out of the arguments and just concentrate on the lunch side of things. I'd found my appetite had continued to increase and I'd just sit and plow my way through two or three helpings of chicken and mashed potato, peas and carrots, sweetcorn and gravy while Blossom waved her fork at George and explained how she thought that the armed forces should be disbanded and the money spent on wind farms.

I noticed George stealing glances at me at these lunches, clearly astonished by how much I was eating. But muscle burns a lot of calories. Fuel in the belly and all that. And I felt great.

Monday and Tuesday I went straight home and got the books out for studying. Wednesday of course was Date Night, for now at least, usually at a slightly disappointing restaurant where I'd have to make my own fun. Thursday evenings I went out for a ride with Dad. The days were long now and we'd sometimes stay out until nine thirty p.m., going farther and farther every time. It was amazing how quickly you improve on the bike. The first couple of times I could hardly get up Badger Hill, but after three weeks I was going up in high gear. I could even keep up with Dad for a lot of the time: I caught him on the hills but he rocketed off ahead of me downhill, where his extra weight was a bonus. On the flat he was usually a dozen feet ahead, pushing me. I don't remember us talking much. On the few occasions when he'd stop for a drink and a snack, I'd be gasping and breathless, gulping water from my bottle.

Once he realized I was serious, he took me to the cycle shop. I'd never been in before. What I saw astonished me.

"HOW much is that bike?" I said, pointing to a bicycle that looked almost identical to the one next to it but was six thousand pounds more expensive.

"It's carbon fiber," Dad said, shrugging, presumably unaware that six thousand pounds was more than some people earned in a year.

"HOW much is this helmet?" I asked, pointing at a helmet that looked like the other helmets on the rack but which had a price tag of £799.

"It's Italian," Dad said.

"So is pasta. And that doesn't cost £799. Even from Ocado."

"Fleur, come on," Dad said. "We're not looking at helmets."

Dad bought me some more Lycra, including a rainproof coat. "I'm not going out when it's raining," I said. But I was glad of the Lycra. I could wear it for boxing. He also got me some special wraparound shades that I had to admit were pretty cool. I looked at the price tag and raised an eyebrow. They were expensive. Not Italian helmet expensive. But expensive enough. One thing's for sure: boxing is a lot cheaper than cycling.

It didn't end there, though. We bought an overpriced water bottle with the SKY logo on it. Then the metal rack to attach it to the bike, then an overpriced puncture repair kit, some energy drink tablets and a pack of ruinously expensive protein bars that looked like the sort of thing Bear Grylls might pretend to eat when the cameras were on him before sloping off to the local Chickos. Dad also bought me a tube of cream.

"What's this?" I asked.

"You see, on the bike, when you ride for a long time . . . bits rub against other bits."

"Like the gears?"

"Not on the bike," Dad said, looking away. "On you. It's for chafing."

"What, behind my knees?"

"Um, maybe there, too."

The penny dropped. "You mean this is for . . . ?" Dad nodded, unable to speak. He was bright red. "You use this?"

"Yes, obviously in slightly different . . . areas. And you might find there are extra . . . areas you might want to use it on."

I looked at Dad and waited until I had his full attention before I spoke. "Thank you for this. On your advice I will take the cream. But let us never have this conversation again. Or anything like it."

"Agreed," Dad said, seemingly relieved he'd fulfilled his fatherly duties, at least until my wedding when he'd walk me down the aisle, which, presumably, he'd do very smoothly and without discomfort. The last thing Dad got me were some special pedals. The sort you clip your shoes into. He said it would improve my performance. "Why go to so much effort and spend so much money to make it easier?" I said. "If you want easy then just drive." Dad ignored me and picked up a pair of the shoes with clips. I looked at the price tag.

"HOW much are these shoes?"

Friday nights meant film club with Blossom. Without our regular visits to Battle, I didn't see a lot of Pip. And Blossom told me he would often not go either, disappearing at the weekends with some vague excuse. She became quite curious about what he was up to. I invited them both over one Friday in early June so we could hang out together and ~~study~~ watch films, but in the end Blossom had to pull out due to some crisis with Magnet and the Socialist Action Group, so it turned out to be just me and Pip.

I'd discovered there were a lot of movies about boxing on Netflix. We ended up having a bit of a marathon. We saw *Rocky II*. Then we watched *Million Dollar Baby*, *Raging Bull* and *Rumble in the Jungle*, which turned out not to be a movie, but a documentary about a boxing match between Muhammad Ali and Joe Frazier. I really liked Ali's boots.

There was one thing all these films had in common. At some point, each protagonist is on the ropes. Down on their luck. Everything set against them, when suddenly they come back and triumph against the odds. All except *Million Dollar Baby*, that is. Hilary Swank's character achieves amazing success, then gets paralyzed and dies. The only boxing film with a female protagonist, and they kill her off.

As the credits rolled, I looked over at Pip, who'd been very quiet. I assumed he'd dropped off, but he was wide awake and crying.

"Oh, Pip," I said, leaning over to give him a hug.

"Sorry," he said. "Not sure why I'm crying so much. I've just felt a bit down. The battle rehearsals aren't going well. I try to stand my ground, but when they come charging up I just have this mad panic and next thing I know I'm in the woods and people are calling out my name telling me everything's okay."

"Do you want me to come next week?" I asked.

"You've got boxing," he said.

"I can skip it," I said. "I'll build a hovel and watch you hacking at Norman scum."

He smiled and nodded. "I'd like that."

Poor Pip. It's tough to get off the ropes once you're there. I suppose in real life people don't beat the odds very often, however hard they fight.

BATTLE

I kept my promise to Pip and went to Battle the next day, although I won't pretend I wasn't a bit disappointed not to be going to boxing. Particularly when Blossom and I were just hanging around in the hovel and waiting for things to get started.

"Can you look after my sword and shield while I go

to the loo?" Pip asked. "I might be a while. Prebattle nerves."

"Okay," I said.

"Don't tell Garnet," he said, looking around nervously. "We're not supposed to let civilians touch our weapons. But they're too heavy to take all the way to the Portaloos."

Blossom tried to pick up the shield. "Oof," she said. "That *is* heavy. You're stronger than you look, Pip." He stalked off, leaving us alone in the hovel. It had been drizzling most of the day and there weren't many people about. Blossom had done a couple of lackluster ghost walks and I'd whittled another wooden willy-spoon. A brief burst of sunlight swept across the scene but then another dark cloud loomed overhead and more rain spattered down on the mud outside the door. The hovel wasn't entirely waterproof, and I was glad of the wimple. I shivered.

"See," Blossom said. "Isn't this better than boxing?"

"Hmm," I said. I wondered what exercise they'd be doing right now, and how much I'd feel it next week. Missing a session made a big difference to your fitness, and Ricky always pushed you harder the next time as a punishment. I heard footsteps approaching, quickly, someone coming to escape the rain perhaps. Two figures burst in through the door.

"Good morn, Lords Thane . . . Oh crap, not you two," Blossom said. The newcomers squinted at us, their eyes adjusting to the gloomy interior. Then they both laughed explosively. It was the Meninists, of course. Ryan whipped out his phone and took a picture. I gave him the finger.

"Don't remember seeing anyone doing that on the Bayeux Tapestry," he said.

"You ladies look . . . AMAZING," William said. "This is just the best thing ever."

"Oh, why don't you just bog off," Blossom sighed.

"Isn't this just what we've been saying?" William said, grinning from ear to ear. "The menfolk are out there, fighting battles for the future of the country, and you're in here, cooking, cleaning . . . whittling," he said, double-taking at the wooden object I held in my hand.

"We could fight if we wanted," Blossom said. "Isn't that right, Fleur?"

"Yeah, we could take those Normans down," I said.

"What are you going to fight with?" Ryan asked. "You're going to throw a cooking pot at them?"

"How about this!" Blossom said, bending to pick up Pip's sword. She held it aloft, whacking the thatched ceiling above and releasing a shower of dust and spiders. I could sense she was really straining to hold it, but her determination, and her placard-wielding muscles, betrayed nothing.

The Meninists took a step back. "Careful," William said. "That looks sharp."

"Come on, Fleur," Blossom said. "Let's repulse the invaders." She nodded to the shield. I shrugged and stepped over to grab it. It was heavy. Very heavy. But the hours in the gym had paid off. I lifted it and stood beside Blossom. I had no sword, but I did still have the wooden willy. I thrust it out at the Meninists, who were looking increasingly nervous.

"I think we should advance," Blossom said.

"Fleur can hardly lift that shield," William said, "let alone walk with it."

"There was another woman they underestimated," Blossom said, narrowing her eyes. "A humble woman who shunned glamour and was mocked for it. A woman who said what she thought needed to be said, even though it lost her millions of votes and cost her the ultimate prize."

"She means Susan Boyle," I said.

"I mean Hillary Clinton," Blossom corrected.

"Ah, Hillary Clinton's a loser," Ryan sneered.

I was suddenly filled with a wave of anger. I lifted the shield, my shoulder muscles burning with the effort, then I screamed.

"YOU'RE THE LOSER!" I sprang forward, brandishing the willy. Blossom stumbled forward beside me, waving the sword. Our enemies' eyes bulged and they turned to flee. Out into the rain we went, chasing the Meninists down the concourse. A few bewildered tourists stopped to watch us charge by, most of them grinning, assuming it was all part of the show.

But it wasn't part of the show, it was deadly serious. We chased them all the way to the gift shop and they scrambled inside to safety. We stopped outside, not wanting to be seen. We were given a lot of leeway at Battle, but I thought English Heritage might draw the line at chasing paying visitors with wooden dildos.

"Oh hell," Blossom hissed. "Garnet!"

I stopped and turned to see Garnet descending the steps from the tearoom. He hadn't seen us. "Quick, in here!" I yelled, ushering Blossom toward a row of Portaloos. Two were occupied but the middle one was free. With some difficulty, we managed to cram ourselves and our weapons in and shut the door until the danger had passed.

Drunk with our triumph of repulsing the invading Meninist army, we settled down to watch Pip take part in his second battle. We saw him drag his sword and shield with difficulty over to his place in the shield wall. Once more we saw the Normans come charging up the hill. Once more we heard Pip's shriek of terror and watched him sprinting for the trees, which Blossom and I had taken to calling Pip's Wood.

As we walked to the parking lot later we commiserated with Pip.

"Never mind," I said. "I bet loads of soldiers ran off in terror."

"No, they didn't," Pip said. "That's the thing about the Saxon shield wall. It held; no one ran off. I don't think I'm cut out to be a Saxon."

"It's not real, Pip," Blossom reminded him as we reached the car. The rain had mostly stopped now but there was still the occasional spot. "You do know you're not going to have your skull cleaved in twain?"

"I just don't feel like I fit in," he said glumly as he folded himself into the car. "I'm not right for it." We went to Chickos to cheer Pip up and he did an impression of Garnet that made me laugh so much Coke came out of my nose. I liked my dinner-dates with George, playing at being an adult. But sometimes it was fun to hang out with people my own age and just relax and laugh and shriek and make stupid jokes.

FLEUR "BROKEN" WATERS

"Oi, Killa, you pregnant?" Simon yelled across the gym as I rested, chest heaving after just completing about three hundred burpees.

"What? No!"

"Because it looks like your water broke," he said. I looked down to see a large pool of sweat had collected beneath me. Everyone laughed.

"What's your excuse?" I said, pointing to his own sweat puddle. "Weak pelvic floor?" Everyone laughed again and Simon winked at me.

"It's not a bloody biology lesson," Ricky yelled as the buzzer went. "Alternate lunges, two minutes, go!"

I was still finding the training hard, so hard it made me feel sick. As Ricky often said, "It doesn't get easier, you can just push yourself more." But after each session I felt exhilarated. I was clearly getting fitter, with the boxing, the cycling and the running, but I could also see my body was changing. I had proper definition in my arms and shoulders now. My tummy was flat and showing the first, faint signs of a six-pack, thanks to all the sit-ups Ricky made us do. ("It's called an abdomen, not a flabdomen!") The biggest improvement was in my punching, which I could tell was getting much more powerful. We did a lot of exercises where we all had to stand face-to-face with a partner and punch the other's pads while moving backward and then changing when you hit the wall and doing the same thing walking forward.

I was generally partnered with Helpful Dan, or Joe,

because they were the smallest men, and as time went on I got more and more comments like "Good power," "Nice one," "Oof," and so on. The key was always rolling into the punch, getting what weight I had behind it.

My big problem was my guard. I could punch hard, particularly with my right backhand, and I had a good uppercut, as Joe had discovered, but I'd always drop my left glove while I was doing it. It just felt unnatural to keep the glove up against my face. But every time I dropped it, my partner would tap me on my left temple to point out my error. It drove me crazy and I spent hours at home, in front of the mirror, trying to correct the fault, trying to make the muscles remember.

When he had time, Ricky would try to teach me drills to help.

"It's all about footwork," he said more than once. "Once you can get into the right position with your feet, everything else will follow."

"Even my guard?"

"Even your guard," he said. "I wish you'd come on Wednesday nights. I'd have more time to help you. There are less people here on Wednesday."

"Fewer people," I said automatically.

"Is that right? Well, I suggest you give me fewer back chat and more push-ups. On the floor." I sighed and dropped to my hands and knees. When was I going to learn to keep my mouth shut? But it felt good being able to banter. I felt comfortable there now. One of the team. Everyone had gotten used to me. Jordan, who wasn't the brightest, seemed to think I was a cross between Stephen Fry and Mariella Frostrup and would ask me advice on an enormous range of topics, from removing unwanted apps from his phone to what he should say to a girl on a first date. The thing I liked the best was that Joe's nickname for me seemed to have stuck. Everyone was now calling me Killa. I think it was ironic. But I liked it anyway.

I did some pad work with Coach Alex, too, who didn't say much, communicating mostly through his eyebrows. He'd twitch his right one when it was time for you to hit the pads and twitch his left when it was time to stop. If you got in a good hit he'd raise both of them. I found Tarik was very helpful, always nearby with a soft word of encouragement or a piece of advice. He told me I had to eat more and one Saturday he presented me with a big tub of whey protein.

"You Syrian men know how to treat a girl," I said.

"Drink it in milk shakes," he said. "Good for building muscle." I took it home, made myself my first protein shake and stared at it for a while, thinking. Wondering how serious I was. Then I took a sip.

"Oh my God, that's disgusting," I said, and went off to find some honey.

GIRLS' DAY OUT

June went on. Exam time. Not the big, important exams. Just A1s. But any sort of exam made me wake in a cold sweat. I needed to focus. I stopped the bike rides with Dad, and I stopped Date Night, too, much as I missed the shaved Armenian artichokes with lingonberry mousse. But I kept up the Saturday boxing sessions—I needed the release, and I didn't want to risk losing what little muscle tone I'd managed to develop. Actually, I think my fitness helped me with the exams. I was usually exhausted during exam time, tired the whole month and yet unable to sleep for more than a few hours. But this time round I felt much more alert.

On the first Saturday of July, after boxing, Mum took me to Brighton to buy a dress for the Mess Ball. "We'll make a day of it," she said. "Just us girls. Frock-shopping."

"I don't think they sell frocks in Brighton," I said. "Dresses perhaps?" But it turned out I was wrong. They did have frocks in Brighton and Mum knew just where to find them. When most people go to Brighton to buy clothes they'll either go to the Lanes to find something unusual or exclusive, maybe vintage. Or else they'll go to one of the big department stores. But Mum had other ideas. She took me to a street where there was a row of horrible shops selling horrible dresses. Frocks, in fact. And they weren't cheap either.

"HOW much?" I spluttered, examining the price tag on a turquoise nightmare she'd thrust at me. "Is there a worldwide shortage of chiffon?"

"It's a special occasion," Mum said, handing me a mound of cotton candy that turned out to be a gown. "You need a very special dress."

I looked at the price tag. "Just give me this much money. I'll buy something spectacular and have enough left over for an Italian cycle helmet."

The sales assistant came back and Mum made me spin around so they could both inspect me. They pursed their lips. I pursed mine right back. The dress was hideous and I didn't really care anymore. I knew it was important that I made an effort for the ball, for George, for Mum. But I felt like a fraud: playing dress-up just wasn't me.

We were in there for two hours, but we didn't buy anything. Mum took me to lunch on the seafront afterward even though I'd offended her by not wanting to dress up like a crinoline puffball. I tried to wind her up by ordering the most expensive thing on the menu.

"You are not having the lobster," she said flatly.

"We could share?"

She sighed.

"I'm sorry we couldn't find anything, Mum," I said. "I do appreciate you bringing me. I'm just not the sort of girl who wears dresses like that."

She shook her head. "I'm trying to do you a favor, Fleur," she said. "You know all the other girls at the ball will be dressed beautifully and expensively. It's all very well being different, but there's a time and a place for that. Sometimes you need to go along with what everyone else does. That's what it is to be an adult."

"I thought being an adult was all about making your own choices," I said.

"If that were the case," she said, "you'd be having the lobster."

134 – ~~NIL~~ 1!

Something incredible happened today. I scored a goal. Not metaphorically. An actual goal, in field hockey. Before the game started, as usual, Holly came up to me and asked me to stay back and defend. "If the ball comes to you," she said, "don't try to dribble it past the players on the other team, just hit it as hard as you can up to the far end and we'll take it from there." I knew that when she said "we," she meant "girls who can actually play field hockey."

Luckily, Holly and Georgie and Sophie are pretty good and I didn't have to do too much except chat to Emily, the goalkeeper. She was all padded up and wore a helmet, so it was a bit like talking to the Michelin Man. I told her I'd been boxing and she asked me if I was going to have an actual fight in the ring.

"No," I said. "I'm not even going to spar. I'm not very good. You have to be really fit to box properly." I didn't want to say that my mother wouldn't let me, but it struck me that there was no end to the list of excuses I could make about why I shouldn't get in the ring.

"I wondered if you'd been doing some exercise," Emily said. "You look fitter than you did, and you stand straighter than you used to."

"Really?" I asked, turning around, now self-consciously stiffening my back.

"Yeah, you used to slump about all the time. But now you stand straight. Like you've got more confidence and that."

"Thanks," I said, grinning.

"Now watch out," Emily said. "Here comes Destiny." She didn't mean in a metaphorical way, either. I turned to see Destiny Abbot come charging toward us, tapping the ball along delicately as she ran. Maybe it was the unexpected compliment from Emily, maybe it was my newfound energy and discipline, but something made me run out toward her. Usually I'd just wait there and try to dive out of the way at the last minute. But today I didn't. Today I challenged her.

Destiny seemed surprised to see me there. She tried to correct her trajectory but over-hit the ball slightly, losing control. I stuck out my stick toward it and, amazingly, made contact, tapping it back the other way. But Destiny was still coming toward me, unable to stop so quickly. My feet took over, Ricky's drills coming back to me.

Left, left, forward and right.

I dodged past Destiny and raced after the ball, picking it up again before looking for someone to pass to. I could hear Destiny turn and charge up behind. Meanwhile, ahead, I saw three green jerseys enclosing me. There was no way to get the ball through. One of the girls was a little ahead of the others and sprinted toward me. I shaped up to take a big swing at the ball, and she paused, ready to try and block the shot. But I didn't take it. Instead, I tapped it lightly to the right of her and ran past. She twisted to follow but stumbled and I was away. Another defender beaten.

"Pass!" I heard Holly scream from the far side. The other two green jerseys were closing on me. I didn't have much time. I stopped and swiped the ball as hard as I could in Holly's direction. But I mishit it and it zoomed off in the wrong direction, slicing off forward instead of to the side. *Dammit*, I thought.

"RUN!" Holly screamed.

"RUN, FLEUR!" Sophie screamed. I realized there was still a chance I could get the ball back. I darted after it, a green jersey racing me for the prize. With a lurch of dread, I realized it was Bonita. She was going to beat me, surely? Even if we got there at the same time, she'd just knock me over. What was the point? Time to give up.

But strangely, I didn't give up. In fact I found I was still running. And I tell you something even stranger. I was absolutely flying.

"GO, FLEUR!" Holly screamed. "WIN IT!"

I got to the ball first, tapping it on a little, just as Bonita arrived. She slammed into me, all seventy-something kilograms of her. I stumbled, the shock juddering through my frame. But my legs held. All those squat thrusts had paid off. I carried on as Bonita stumbled and fell behind. Now it was just me and the goalie. I'd never been this close to the opposition goal before; it was a strange experience. I looked for someone to pass to. Two pink jerseys were racing into position, but they'd be too late.

"Strike, strike!" Holly cried.

So I did; I took up the position and just whacked it. Right through the astonished goalkeeper's legs. No one was more surprised than me when the ball clunked into the back of the goal. Or maybe they were. There was a moment of silent bemusement around the field as everyone tried to get their heads around the fact that Fleur had scored a goal. Then my team erupted into cheers. They rushed over to pat me on the back. Holly gave me a huge hug and lifted me off the ground in her enthusiasm. I think I was pretty cool about the whole thing, just leaping about, shrieking and waving my stick for three or four minutes, five, tops. I passed Bonita on the way back, wondering if she'd congratulate me. But she didn't. She just barged me aside, her face red and furious.

STRUCTURAL
MENINISM

The euphoria didn't last long, and it was a rubbish day at school on Friday. Blossom didn't come in, and we had a stupid argument in health class. Chief Meninists William Capel and Ryan Cook were going on again about how there would never be complete equality because girls and boys were built differently and designed to fulfil different tasks. "It's just basic biology," Ryan Cook kept saying.

"Women are designed to bear our children," William added.

"Good luck with that," Bonita snarled. I hate health class. Especially when Blossom isn't there. There were just the Meninists and Bonita. Bonita got really cross and said that women could do everything that men could. Or at least SOME women.

"Some men are good at sports, some men aren't," she said. "Some women are good at sports. Some women aren't." She looked at me. I ignored her. I tended not to speak up in these situations. Blossom would have owned them. She would have run rings around Bonita and chopped the Meninists up into tiny bits. But I just let them talk their nonsense. What did I care what those idiots thought anyway? It wasn't worth the fight.

On the way home I ran into Blossom just outside Tesco.

"Are we still on for the Bluebell Road Film Club tonight?" I asked.

"Rom-com, I suppose."

"Maybe."

She shrugged. "All right then."

"Could have done with you in health today," I told her. "The Meninists are back, and still awful. Going on again about men being physically superior."

She snorted. "Why is it always the worst men who are so certain of their gender's superiority?"

"I feel like I let you down," I said. "You would have bashed them and boshed them but I just sat there and said nothing."

"Don't worry," she said. "I'll bide my time, then slit their throats when they least expect it."

"I should have said something," I said. "You must think I'm a terrible feminist."

"Of course I don't think that!"

"But I am. Remember that time we were doing Structural Feminism and I didn't know what it was and wrote an essay about Naomi Klein's house? And at first I didn't even know who Naomi Klein was."

"You thought she was the blond one from Little Mix," Blossom said, chewing her lip.

"I did," I admitted.

"You're not a bad feminist," she reassured me. "At least you're doing something."

Blossom arrived at my house two hours later and was horrified to see *Rocky V* already loaded onto the TV.

"*Rocky V?*" Blossom exclaimed. "I thought he retired at the end of *Rocky IV.*"

"You're so naive."

"How many *Rocky* films are there?"

"Loads," I said.

"So that's it now? Just *Rocky* films, no more rom-coms?"

"I thought you hated rom-coms," I said as I made the tea. "Each Reese Witherspoon film a brick in the patriarchal edifice?"

". . . ish," she said, looking supremely disappointed. "They can also be empowering, life-affirming expressions of what it means to be a young woman in the twenty-first century."

"So is *Rocky*."

"But five, though," she whined. "I haven't even seen three. Or two for that matter."

"You don't need to," I said.

"Why, are they all the same?" she asked, settling herself down onto the sofa.

"How dare you?" I retorted. "I mean that each film is a masterpiece in its own right. Look, we can always skip the film and do some studying instead?"

"Fine, we'll watch the film," she sighed, and hit play.

And wow. I mean, wow! That was just the best *Rocky* yet. A Russian opponent this time, Ivan Drago. Bred and trained under laboratory conditions, specifically to defeat All-American hero Rocky Balboa. But all their technology came to naught in the end. All the bio-kinetic training machines in the world can't beat punching a side of beef in a cold room behind a restaurant in Philadelphia. All the nutritional supplements and science pills on the planet can't beat a bowl of Italian-American pasta sauce. All the skeletomuscular training regimes in the universe can't beat running up some museum steps, raising your arms and shouting in a croaky voice.

As we watched, I kept stealing glances at Blossom. She started off with a sour expression, checking her phone from time to time. But as the film went on I could see she was gradually getting into it. She put her phone down when Apollo Creed died. She let her tea grow cold as Rocky went through his final preparations for the fight of his life. And when Drago finally slumps to his knees, defeated, Blossom the pacifist internationalist leaped from her seat and screamed, "IN YOUR FACE, IVAN."

I nodded in smug satisfaction. No one can resist the appeal of Rocky.

Ultimately of course, it's all about heart. Passion. That's how Rocky wins. Human desire, love, will defeat the robotic, joyless Russian science. There was one thing the scientists couldn't design. The love of a good, slightly insipid, improbably named woman like Adrian.

That night I dreamed about fighting a Russian girl who looked a bit like Bonita but also a bit like Cara Delevingne. It was all a bit odd and confusing at one point when we ended up in a clinch and she tried to kiss me. But ultimately I beat her.

APPRAISAL

"Why did the woman cross the road?" Jordan asked a gaggle of boys before training started on Saturday. He had his back to me and the rest of them were furiously signaling with their eyes. Dan was cutting his throat frantically.

"Who cares," he went on. "The important question is, how did she get out of the kitchen?"

There was a deathly silence.

"Fleur's behind me, isn't she?" Jordan asked sheepishly.

He turned to me. "Sorry, Killa," he said. "Just a little joke."

"You need to be careful about locking women in the kitchen." I smiled sweetly. "That's where the knives are kept."

They laughed at that.

"What is this awful music?" I asked as I stretched.

Ricky stared at me in shocked surprise. "This? It's the Beatles, only the most successful band there has ever been. That's John Lennon singing."

"No wonder they shot him," I said.

"Right, for that, you can give me twenty, down on the floor." But I could see him trying to hide a grin as I dropped down.

"You trained well today," he told me later as I was taking the wraps off. I was breathing hard and I could feel the sweat steaming off my hot skin. But I felt good. Ricky didn't hand out praise lightly, and he was right, I had trained well today. He turned to go and I called out.

"Ricky."

"Yeah?"

"I was watching a video of Nicola Adams," I said. This was true, I had watched a lot of videos of Nicola Adams, but more videos of Rocky. And *Million Dollar Baby* again.

"Nicola Adams. Yeah, fantastic, isn't she?"

"She is. And Hilary Swank."

"Eh?"

"Anyway, the point is that . . . I'm only asking. I don't really think I . . . I mean I'm not really sure, but what do you think about me maybe . . . sparring sometime?"

He narrowed his eyes.

"You?"

"Well, why not? Because I'm a girl?"

"No," he said quickly. "Because . . . well, there's not much to you."

"Have you not seen my guns?" I asked, incredulous.

"You're a bit fitter than you were," he said. "But you're not ready to spar."

I breathed in sharply. "Is this because I don't like the Beatles?"

"Not just that. I don't think you're fit enough. Or heavy enough. I don't know who to pair you up with."

I paused for a moment and thought of Bonita and the awful Meninists. I wanted to stop feeling helpless and weak. I wanted to know that I could succeed at something difficult. Something that none of them could do.

"Well?" I asked. "What do I need to do?"

"You'd need to train more often."

"What?! I'm cycling, I'm jogging. I'm doing weights . . ."

"You need another session here once a week," he said. "Then I can spend a bit more time with you on technique, with the pads. Come on Wednesdays."

"Wednesday is Date Night," I told him. He shrugged.

"Then you need to choose what's more important to you," he said. "Boxing or Date Night."

SPLINTERED PARMESAN

On the next Date Night after exams George took me to a restaurant called period. Or at least that was my joke, which George disapproved of. The restaurant was actually called dot. On the sign at the front there was literally just a dot. It was angrily modern and situated on the B3576 between the squash courts and the Volvo garage. I read the menu with alarm. This restaurant was so happening it had moved right beyond shaved parmesan and had started splintering it. It also crushed fennel, bruised beef and ripped herbs. Even the vegetarian option was split lentils and came served with worried spinach. I'd be worried, too, in that kitchen.

"Bruised beef," George said thoughtfully. "I think that's steak. There's also flattened spatchcock hen, pulped chickpea curry, whipped egg . . ."

"You had me at steak," I said.

"Hammered pork, shredded pork, twisted pork . . ."

"Why are you still talking?" I asked. "They have steak."

"Have you gotten your dress yet for the ball?" George asked, putting away the menu.

"No," I said, wincing at the memory.

"I thought your mum took you to Brighton with her credit card," he said.

"She did."

"But you came back empty-handed?"

"No," I said. "I came back with some twelve-ounce ProHit sparring gloves."

"And that's all?"

"No, that's not all," I said defensively. "I also bought a mouth guard."

The waiter sidled up and asked if we were ready to order. I noticed he wasn't carrying a pad. I was in a slightly naughty mood.

"Mademoiselle?" he said.

"Madame," I replied haughtily. "We were married three weeks ago in Grenoble." The waiter glanced down at my hand.

"The ring was accidentally swallowed by my dog, Ian Beale," I added. "We're awaiting its return."

"The dog really is called Ian Beale," George said apologetically.

The waiter waited patiently. "Anyway," I said. "I'd like a starter of pounded chickpeas."

"You mean the hummus?"

"Yes, that's right, but please ask Chef to really smash those chickpeas good. I want them properly violated."

"Yes, Madame," he said, and I felt I detected a slightly irritated tone. No one seemed to enjoy the Wednesday-evening shift in this town, for some inexplicable reason. George was watching me carefully, presumably wondering if I was going to embarrass him again tonight. Or more likely HOW I was going to embarrass him.

"And for a main course, I'd like the steak, please."

"The bruised beef?"

"Yes, but I want it really hammered hard. Knock it silly."

"Yes, Madame," the waiter said before turning to George gratefully. "And for you, sir?"

George paused for a moment.

"I'd like the pulverized *petits pois*," he said.

The waiter looked confused for a moment. "Do you mean the pea soup, sir?"

"Yeah, but totally squash those little guys," George said, looking straight at me. "Sit on them if you have to." I tried not to laugh. The game would be ruined if we acknowledged it. My tummy flipped gently as I remembered just why I liked this ridiculous boy.

"And for your main?" the waiter asked.

"I'll have the beef, too."

"Bruised, sir?"

"Bruised and battered," said George, handing the waiter his menu. "Hit it with everything you've got."

"So," he said, grinning as soon as the waiter had gone. "How did the exams go?"

"Surprisingly well," I said. "Blossom and I temporarily suspended our Friday night study sessions so we could get some actual studying done instead of just watching Rocky films. I think it paid off."

"Glad to hear it," he said.

"Speaking of changes to schedules," I said. "Could I . . . could we, talk about something?"

"Sure," he said. I hesitated. I really wasn't sure how he'd react.

"Well?" he said. "I'm on tenterhooks."

"Um," I said, thinking quickly. "Look, I know you don't want to, but the thing is . . . I wonder if we could reconsider and switch Date Night to Thursdays from now on."

He looked at me with a furrowed brow. "But Wednesday is Date Night. We've talked about this."

"We didn't, really," I said. "I suggested it, and you

hemmed and hawed, and we just left it. But boxing is important, and it's summer soon in any case, so maybe this is a good time to adjust the schedules so they work better for both of us."

"This is so you can go and hit punching bags?" he asked, checking his phone.

"Basically, yeah. This matters to me." He looked up, perhaps taken aback by how assertive I was being.

The waiter brought our abused starters at that point. "Let me think about it," George said after a while. "I'll have a look at my schedules and see what I can do." Then he lapsed into silence. I could tell he wasn't happy. And I felt bad because we'd been having such a lovely time and he'd been playing along with the food-smashing thing. As I tasted my pounded chickpeas, I contemplated taking it back. Telling him it didn't matter. That Wednesday was fine for Date Night.

But I'm glad I didn't. It was time to stand my ground.

FAIRY GODBROTHER

I pulled the curtain aside and stepped out into the shop feeling about as vulnerable as a fox at a Downton Abbey hunt ball. I was wearing lipstick and had my hair up in the way I was intending to have it for the event. The dress was black and had lacy sleeves. It was the seventh dress I'd tried on, and Pip had insisted it would suit me.

Pip shook his head. "No," he said, "you look like an Italian widow." In theory I should have been suspicious of fashion advice from someone who dressed like Pip.

Today, for example, he was wearing a sort of long, flowing raincoat with a floppy hoodie that made him look a little like a Dementor. I've never seen anyone or anything else wear an outfit that looked even remotely similar. Apart from the Dementors themselves, of course. But then again I don't get down to Brighton club nights as often as I'd like. Dementor-chic was quite possibly all the rage down there. But Pip gives off such an air of expert confidence when it comes to other people's clothes that I knew he was right. And Mediterranean mourning clothes are clearly not my thing. Pip handed me another dress, this time ice-blue satin. I sighed and went back into the changing room.

"Hi, Elsa," Blossom said, grinning at me as soon as I came out. "Have you seen my friend Fleur?" I looked at myself in the mirror and groaned.

"Why is it that it's only when you try to make yourself pretty that you realize how awful you look?" I said.

"You don't look awful," Pip said. "Just . . . weird."

"That's it, though. When I'm dressed normally I don't care how I look," I said. "I don't even think about it. As soon as I make an effort to look nice I just go weird and awkward. I hunch my shoulders. I forget how to walk properly. I don't know where to put my hands. I'm just not a ball-gown kind of girl."

"Nonsense," Pip said. "Every girl looks good in a ball gown; the problem is finding the right one for you." Then his face lit up and he snapped his fingers. "I know where we'll try next. Vintage Vicky's."

"That's all corsets and halters. I am not going to the naval college ball dressed like a Victorian prostitute," I said.

"Trust me," he replied.

And he turned out to be right, of course. Vintage Vicky's is a treasure-trove of unusual items, not just clothes, but all sorts of things from the past. Record players, old steamer trunks and suitcases with faded stickers. There are accessories jostling with old kettles and fascinators racked next to a row of antique Singer sewing machines. There's an entire room given over to buttons. Pip showed me where he'd found his bloomers, in a tiny cupboard-like room right at the back where the sporting goods were. There were old tennis rackets, an oar from a rowboat, an antique croquet set, and right down at the bottom, under a pile of random shoes, I caught a glimpse of something that made me look again. I knelt down and pulled the item out. It was a boot. A style I recognized, the sort of high, tightly laced boot that Ricky wore. It was a boxing boot, black and cream. I rummaged around until I found the other boot and checked the size. Not perfect, but close enough.

But then Pip called my name. He'd found me a dress. Simple and cream with minimum lace. I put it on and looked at myself in the mirror. It wasn't the dress so much; it suited me well. But more than that, I could see the shadowed contours in my upper arms and shoulders. I looked toned. Healthy. I was definitely bigger than I had been, and the scales confirmed this. I'd put on nine pounds and it worked on me. I got into my stance and threw a few shadow punches, rolling my waist, twisting my hips into the punch.

When I came out of the changing room Pip nodded and came over to give me a Groot hug. "Thank the stars," he said. Over his shoulder Blossom smiled at me.

HERE COME
THE GIRLS

Have I mentioned how much I hate skipping? Gradually, as I'd gotten fitter, most exercises got easier and less horrific. But not skipping. Something I was so good at as a kid, and used to love, was now a form of torture. I dreaded the words "Find yourselves a rope."

"Why do boxers skip so much?" I asked Tarik that Saturday.

"Most important thing for a boxer is fitness. Second most important is strong legs."

"What about discipline?" I asked. "Ricky says discipline is important."

"Discipline is important, too," Tarik conceded. "But fitness and legs are more important. You have good legs."

"Err. Thank you," I said. He grinned at me. He must have meant I had strong legs.

My legs *were* stronger, it was true. I'd been working hard. Even though there was one more week of school, exams had ended, so I had time. I ran every morning and did weights. And I ate chicken. A lot of chicken.

"Hi, Sharon," I said when she turned up that Saturday, carrying a big cardboard box. "How's it going?"

"Oh, okay," she sighed. "But we're a bit worried about numbers. Unless we get some more people to come we might have to call it a day."

"What? You can't close us down!"

"We're not quite breaking even," Sharon explained.

"Can't you raise the fees?" I asked.

Sharon shook her head. "A lot of the boys can hardly afford to pay as it is. There's not a lot of money around here. In fact, Ricky lets a couple of them train for free." That was sobering. And things didn't improve when Ricky told me I wouldn't be able to spar that night because Joe was in hospital.

"Oh no, what's wrong?"

"He's having his corns shaved off. He'll miss a few weeks."

"Isn't there someone else I can spar with?"

Ricky shook his head. "They're too young, too big, too fit. And most of all, too inexperienced. They can't control themselves, you see."

"I'm not sure I do see," I said.

"They won't hold back," Ricky said.

"I don't want them to hold back," I replied, bristling. "I can handle it."

"It's about safety," Ricky said. "I wouldn't let a fly-weight spar with a heavyweight, male or female. And I won't let you spar with them." He pointed to the ring, where Chris was dancing around Jerome. As if to illustrate Ricky's point, Chris dropped his guard and Jerome hit him hard in the side of the head, sending him into the ropes.

As there were only five more days of school, I didn't have much time. I typed up a flyer, went in early next morning and stuck it up on every noticeboard. You're supposed to ask permission, but nobody does. There are a lot of posters advertising for death metal guitarists (no time waisters plze) and flyers advertising Reiki treatments.

My flyer had a large photo of Nicola Adams, and the text underneath read as follows:

Ladies!

Bosford Boxing Club needs YOU!
Whether you're looking to fight in the ring.
spar or just get fit. boxing is for you.
Call Sharon at: 01233 555 6739

It was nearly time for class to begin, and as I was putting the last one up, I noticed a small crowd had formed behind me.

"Isn't that a bit sexist?" Ryan Cook asked. "What about men?"

"Oh, shut up, Ryan," I sighed. "I'm not in the mood."

"Don't you no-platform me," Ryan said. "I will have my say."

"Men are welcome, too," I said. "But this recruitment drive is aimed at women. The numbers are unbalanced at the moment."

"I suppose it's all okay to attack men, isn't it, Fleur?" Ryan said, shaking his head. "Men are the only minority you're allowed to oppress these days." Like a shark sniffing a white male oppression situation, Blossom turned up at that point, jaws agape.

"Right, first of all, men are not some oppressed minority," she began, jabbing a finger at him. "Secondly, affirmative action is a legitimate tactic used to rebalance a gender disparity. No one is stopping you doing anything. Fleur is just trying to do her bit to bring down the patriarchy."

"That's right," I said. "Though it's more that I need someone to spar against."

"Whatever," Ryan said, walking off. Blossom folded her arms in victory. She is amazing. As the crowd dispersed, I saw one person left behind. Someone who'd been standing at the back, watching the whole thing.

Bonita.

JAR JAR BINKS

The day of George's Mess Ball came around at last and I couldn't quite decide if I was excited or terrified. Maybe both. As I straightened my bangs and looked in the mirror, I breathed a quick prayer of thanks to Pip. At least the dress was right. And my choice of footwear made me feel like me—even if I was a bit glossier than usual.

George smiled in approval when he saw me, and I grinned back in relief. We hurried into the main hall and he steered me through the maze of tables and men in uniform and women in posh frocks. We reached our table and I blinked in surprise as everyone looked up.

"And this gang of reprobates," George announced, "are my so-called friends."

I glanced round uneasily. It wasn't the guys I was concerned with, but the girlfriends. They were blond. All five of them. Not only that, they all had bangs, just like mine. It was like *Being John Malkovich*. As one they smiled and waved and I waved timidly back.

"That's Fadge and Hattie," George said, indicating

the couple to our left. "Then there's Big Hal and Molly, Humpy and Caz, Jar Jar Binks and Eva, and these two here are Pete and Sal." They waved as George pointed at them. "Everyone, this is Fleur."

"Hello," they chorused. I blinked, still reeling from the bizarre introductions.

"I like your dress," Sal said.

"Thanks," I replied, "but check out the shoes." I lifted the hem of the dress a few inches to show my boots off.

"Wow!" Sal said.

"Extraordinary," Fadge added.

George's eyes looked like they were going to pop out of their sockets. "What are you wearing?" he hissed.

"Vintage boxing boots," I said. "On trend in Bosford."

"I think they're . . . amazing," Sal said. George didn't look like he was going to agree, so I decided to change the subject.

"Did you say someone's called Jar Jar Binks?" I asked. George nodded at me and pointed to poor Jar Jar's lips, which were ever so slightly elongated.

"And why doesn't Pete get a nickname?" I asked.

"Pete IS his nickname," George said.

"My real name's Dave," said Pete. "It's sort of a joke, that I have dull name so get a dull nickname."

"What's your nickname?" I asked George.

"Welly," he said, looking slightly embarrassed, but not as embarrassed as he should have in my opinion. "Because I like to give it some power."

"That remains to be seen," I said. George showed me to my seat between Humpy and Pete, who both smiled but didn't say anything. There was wine but I decided to stick to water. I hadn't eaten and there was the small matter of still being underage. Anyway, I was in training.

The boys all drank quite a bit; I'd never seen George drink much before. The girls sipped their wine demurely. It was a slightly odd arrangement because the guys sat back in the seats shouting across the table, bantering, trash-talking one another, while the girls leaned forward so they could chat. I didn't have much to say and felt slightly trapped between these two large men. So I kept quiet and just listened in, hoping they'd bring the food soon.

When the starter arrived I was slightly disappointed. Not with the dish: I like goat cheese and sun-dried tomato tart as much as the next girl. I was disappointed with the size. It was tiny. I inhaled it quickly, almost before anyone else had taken their first mouthful, and wondered if it would be uncouth to also eat the radish carved into a flower shape.

Humpy had started talking very loudly about an officer called Trumper, though whether this was his real name or a nickname, I couldn't guess. I should have eaten before I came. I bet the other girls all had. I looked around at them; a couple had taken a mouthful or two of their tarts but then had abandoned them. Sal and Molly hadn't even touched their food. I caught Sal's eye.

"Not hungry?" I asked.

She shook her head. "I'm wheat-intolerant. And egg-sensitive."

"Oh, sorry to hear that," I said, hoping she'd offer her tart to a wheat-tolerant, egg-starved Fleur. But she didn't. Listening in to the girls' conversation I realized they were all a little older than me, about the same age as the boys. It turned out they were all at university in Brighton and were mostly chatting about the lecturers. I was the baby, the only one still in high school. I sat and listened for a while, then ate the radish.

Finally, the main course arrived. Again, it looked tasty, but there just wasn't enough of it. A small chicken breast wrapped in Parma ham. A few boiled potatoes and carrots and another carved radish. A thousand calories at most, even with the creamy sauce. I tried to eat slowly, chewing each mouthful twenty times, but I still managed to finish before anyone else. I could see George watching me with slightly pursed lips. I glared back at him. *Don't judge me; can't you see I'm hungry?*

Sal didn't eat much of her food. Or at least, she ate the vegetables but hardly any of the chicken. "Are you poultry-intolerant?" I asked her, trying to make a joke but realizing as I did that it was possibly the most sarcastic thing anyone has ever said. Sal peered at my plate.

"Would you like my chicken?" she asked. I'm sure I should have refused, that there was almost certainly some obscure naval tradition that you only ever passed your leftover Parma-ham–wrapped chicken breast to the left. But I nodded eagerly as Sal gave me her plate and I scraped it off. The boys on either side of me watched this with interest and I could feel George's eyes burning into me.

I felt slightly more human after that, but still found myself hoping dessert was rather more substantial. A sticky toffee pudding, for example, rather than a sorbet. The men's conversation had moved on to rugby. It turns out Pete/Dave was Welsh and Wales had lost an important game against England earlier in the year. They were being quite mean to Pete/Dave, and although he laughed along I sensed he wasn't really enjoying being called Taffy. The girls were talking about how difficult it was to find a good flat-share in Brighton these days. I had nothing to add and wondered if I should ask if anyone had seen *Rocky IV* lately.

Dessert came without fanfare. It *was* sticky toffee pudding, but it was TINY. I frowned and scoffed it in three seconds flat before looking hopefully over at Sal. She had a couple of spoonfuls of hers, then made a "do you want this?" face. I nodded, deciding that I quite liked her after all.

"Fleur," George said as Sal passed me her plate. "Are you sure?"

He was right, I suppose. I was probably being a bit full-on. I should have just waited and got George to get me a cheese toastie from room service later on at the hotel. But it seemed silly to waste all this good food. And I was hungry right now! Also, George and I embarrassing each other at the dinner table . . . well, that was our thing. So I took the plate from Sal and I got the biggest spoonful I could manage and ostentatiously shoveled it into my mouth while everyone watched.

I immediately realized I'd put too much in, but there was no turning back. I chewed and chewed, the toffee suddenly seeming slightly too sticky. Everyone carried on watching me, the rugby talk forgotten, no one caring about rent increases in Hove. It took a surprisingly long time, but eventually I finished the mouthful and slammed my spoon down on the table, lifting my arms in victory like Nicola Adams. Sal clapped and I got a grudging nod of admiration from Jar Jar Binks, but the rest of them just stared at me. Except George, who was looking away, toying with his wineglass. I sighed. So far the evening wasn't quite meeting my expectations.

After dinner there was dancing to a swing band. Most of the men seemed to know a few steps, and the girls were all pretty good. I had no clue, of course. George took control, seizing my right hand and putting an arm around my waist.

"Follow my lead," he said, and yanked me away onto the dance floor. I had no idea what to do with my feet, so just trotted off after him like a puppy. He quickly got frustrated. "Try to follow what I'm doing with my feet," he kept saying. "Feel the rhythm."

I remembered the foot drills Ricky had showed me and as we broke apart I practiced what I'd learned. *Forward, back, two-step, swivel. Right jab, left jab* . . . George stopped. "What are you doing?" he asked.

"Dancing like a butterfly," I replied, spinning around and punching imaginary attackers.

I sat out the rest of the swing dancing. George took turns dancing with the other girls and the admiral's wife. Sal came and sat with me for a bit. "Are you okay?" she asked.

"I think George is cross with me," I said. "I ate too much. And I've lost confidence in these boots."

"I'm sure he's not," she replied. "I wish I had your metabolism. You're so slim, how do you manage it?"

"I'm in training," I said. "I'm actually trying to put on weight." I told her about the boxing and she seemed surprised at first but then nodded.

"Good for you."

"I'm not sure George agrees," I said.

"No, I think he probably doesn't," Sal said. "He's like Dave. They're all the same type. They need things a certain way. They like to be in control. They don't like change and they certainly don't like girls who eat a lot and punch people."

"I've never actually punched anyone," I explained. "Except an octogenarian, and that was an accident." Sal and I carried on chatting for a while. It turned out she had practiced jujitsu when she was younger and we compared notes. Eventually George reappeared. The swing band had finished and the DJ was just starting up.

"Shall we try again?" he asked. He seemed happier now, and I went out with him onto the dance floor. Familiar, cheesy tunes played and I felt a lot more comfortable dancing to these, not being led, free to mix my boxing drills into the dance, feeling fit and strong. We danced in a group, roaring along with the music, the men grabbing the girls' hands and spinning them around. I closed my eyes and lost myself in the music and the rhythms like I did at the club, step step, back back, pivot and jab. Duck roll duck roll, keep up your guard . . .

Then Jar Jar Binks was in front of me, throwing a punch, and with lightning speed I batted his hand away before lurching backward. I tripped over someone else's feet and went sprawling across the floor. George rushed over to help me up.

"What did you do that for?" he asked.

"I was protecting myself," I protested. "He tried to punch me!"

"He wasn't trying to punch you," George said. "He was trying to take your hand. To spin you around?"

"Oh," I said. I looked over at Jar Jar Binks, who was looking at me suspiciously and rubbing his wrist gingerly. I had smacked him pretty hard. "Sorry," I told him. George shook his head and gave me a look. But secretly I was delighted.

I'd kept my guard up.

HOME RUN

George and I stood on the sidewalk in front of my hotel. "Do you want to come up?" I asked, my stomach churning. I was starting to wish I hadn't eaten the second Scotch egg I'd bought from the bar.

"I would," George said, looking into my eyes. He'd been very quiet in the taxi on the ride back from the college. There was clearly something on his mind, and I had a feeling I knew what it was. Our first night together. No parents. No rules. Just us. And I trusted George. I trusted him completely.

Up in the room I lowered the lights a little and looked in the minibar. George stood by the bed, looking nervous. "There's some wine in here," I said. "Or a beer."

"No thanks," George said. "Look, come and sit on the bed."

"There's no hurry," I said, suddenly feeling nervous. "What about a shower?"

"Fleur," he said gently, taking my hand as I sat on the bed. "I've been thinking. A lot. About us." I could smell wine on his breath, but it wasn't unpleasant. I wanted him to lean in and kiss me. "I've been thinking about the future."

"Stop talking," I said, leaning closer. "I know what you want."

"No, this is important, Fleur," he said. "I'm . . . well, I . . . think we should break up."

It took a moment.

"What?"

"We should split up, Fleur," he said, more assertively this time.

"Is it because of the boots?" I asked, before realizing he wasn't joking. This was serious. There's a bit near the end of *Rocky III* where it all goes slow-motion and you just see Rocky standing there as Mr. T sinks slowly down onto his knees, a look of astonishment on his face, unable to believe what has just happened. It's quite simple, really: Rocky has just punched him very hard in the face, which shouldn't be that surprising for a boxer. But I guess it's the way it happened that caused the surprise, when it was least expected.

I don't remember exactly what George and I said to each other after he said those words, though I remember us talking for a long time and voices getting louder and louder until someone in the next room banged on the wall.

"This is about the boxing, isn't it?" I asked him more than once. "Because I'm eating a lot." He said it wasn't, but I remembered the look on his face when I hoovered up Sal's leftover food at the dinner table. I suppose I should have known that the moment he stopped playing along with my dinner table games, it was all over. When he finally left, it was 2:47 a.m. and I was a state. He kept asking me if I was going to be okay, and I kept telling him I'd be fine but in a way that made it clear that I wouldn't be fine at all.

I took the first train the next morning. He had texted. A brief message saying he was sorry and checking how I was. I wrote about a hundred texts, each one longer than the last, deleting them all before eventually just replying with

Fine, thx.

Blossom had texted, too, asking how things had gone. I messaged back suggesting we hang out on Sunday. I didn't want to talk about it on the train. I walked up from the station and slunk into the house through the kitchen door. Ian Beale thumped his tail when he saw me but didn't get up. Too much effort. Mum appeared and took one look at me before rushing over to give me a hug.

"He broke up with me," I said, and then the tears came. The thing was that in my head I knew it was the right thing to break up. But sometimes the rightest thing in the world can feel so wrong. I missed him already. I missed his face, his voice, the way he'd look at me exasperated when I did something stupid. I missed Date Night and the idiotic things we'd get up to. I missed the feeling that there was someone who liked me despite my flaws. But it had all been an illusion. He didn't like me for me. He'd liked me because he thought I fit into a neat girlfriend-shaped hole in his life.

And it turned out I didn't fit that hole, not properly. I wasn't neat. I was the wrong shape, inside and out.

FISH AND BICYCLES

"I never did get a weekend away," I said to Mum the next day. "He told me there'd be weekends in Hove."

"Oh, Fleur," Mum said softly. "I know it's hard, but there are plenty more fish in the sea." She waved an arm toward the English Channel, which was looking decidedly murky.

"Loads of turds, too," I told her. We were lunching, as my mother put it, at the Grand Hotel. Not the proper restaurant, of course; calm down. We were in the bistro with a view of the esplanade on one side and a family of five at the next table who were spoiling the mood, but only a bit. One of the children was throwing peas at me, but I didn't really mind.

"Now, then," Mum said cheerily. "Would you like a glass of wine?"

"I'm in training," I said.

"What for?"

I opened my mouth but had no answer. Good question. What was I training for? What was the point of any of it anymore?

"Nothing," I said.

"Well, let's look at this menu," she said. "Ooh, baked shrimp."

I really didn't feel like choosing. My head was swirling. Fragments of the conversation, the shouting from last night. Trying to stop myself from pulling out my phone and checking to see if he'd texted.

"What are you going to have?" Mum asked.

Ricky would tell me to have the mixed grill. Four

different kinds of protein. But then I remembered the scenes at the dinner table last night. Me scoffing everything in sight while the other girls ate like birds and nursed their wine. For the first time in months, I wasn't hungry.

"The salad looks nice," I murmured.

Blossom had been texting me all day, asking me how things had gone, so I went over when I got back from Brighton to give her the news.

"That bastard," she said. "Oh God, I hate men."

I shrugged. "He was actually quite considerate about the whole thing. Very mature, as usual. Thoughtful. And I guess I knew it was coming, deep down. That we weren't really right for each other."

"He's still a bastard," Blossom said. "Leading you on like that, then changing his mind."

"No," I said. "I'm the one who changed. He didn't sign up to be a boxer's boyfriend."

"He doesn't get to tell you what you can and can't do, Fleur," Blossom pointed out.

"No," I agreed. "But he doesn't have to hang around if he doesn't like it, either. And maybe he's got a point. What am I doing drinking whey protein, punching bags, and wearing boots to a Mess Ball."

"I hope you're not thinking of giving up boxing because of some stupid boy," she said. "Rocky wouldn't have given up."

"What are you talking about? He gives up in every film."

"But he always changes his mind," she pointed out. "And comes back for one last fight."

"Well, maybe now I'm changing *my* mind," I said. "Anyway, I thought you'd be pleased. You've been trying to get me to abandon boxing since day one."

"Well, if you and Rocky can change your minds, then so can I," she said. "I can see you love it."

"Boxing's the reason I got dumped," I said.

"No," she said. "Boxing is helping you understand who you really are. And it showed George who you are, too. If he didn't like that then you're better off without him."

"I'm not sure if this is who I really am, though," I said. Though I didn't expect Blossom to know the answer to that question any more than I did. "I don't even feel like myself."

"You don't have to be yourself," she said, giving me a hug. "You can be anything you want. Even a boxer."

The upside to getting dumped was that I didn't have to have Sunday lunch at home anymore. Instead, we went to Battle. There was a special event on, a procession around the battlefield that we could join in with. Blossom and I were even allowed to carry pennants. It was to mark the 1050th anniversary of the battle between Harold and Harald Hardrada at Stamford Bridge. Harold won, then he turned south to meet the Norman forces. This was an important day. Good times for Team Harold.

We held our pennants proudly; we both had strong shoulders. We were secretly pleased to see a lot of the men dropping their flags for a rest from time to time. Blossom and I held ours firmly for the whole lap. Pip was up ahead, marching with the soldiers, waving his broadsword. Blossom and I chatted as we walked. She was being very patient with me, just letting me talk it all out.

"The thing about George was that he made me feel safe," I said. "You know? He always seemed so much older, and in charge. I never felt there was anything even vaguely threatening about him."

"I would think that's the bare minimum you should want from a boyfriend," Blossom said. "You can't give them extra points because they don't knock you about."

We passed a group of cheering visitors and waved our pennants at them.

"That's not what I mean," I said. "I'm not explaining this well. I just think that maybe some boys make you feel . . . like there's a little danger there. You know? There's a sort of thrill you get, because they're . . . unpredictable? Some boys have this thing about them that makes you a bit scared, and that's sort of sexy."

"Hmmm, and George didn't have this?"

"Not at all," I said.

"So who does make you feel scared sexy?"

"Oh . . . no one!"

"There must be someone. Or else you wouldn't have mentioned it."

"There's no one," I lied, feeling grateful that however perceptive Blossom might be, she couldn't read minds.

NORMAN WISDOM

We decided to cancel film night on Friday and go to Brighton with Pip. To a cosplay club he often went to. It was Time Travel night and Pip insisted we all dress up. Any costume from any period.

"As long as I don't have to be a bloody Saxon," Blossom said.

"No one is going as a Saxon," Pip said.

"What are you going as?" I asked him.

"You'll see," he said, a twinkle in his eye. "You have to be patient, though; it's a surprise."

On Thursday he took us down to Vintage Vicky's to find some suitable gear. Now was the time to dress like a Victorian prostitute. I bought a long velvet dress with a frilled bodice. Blossom decided she would go as a World War I infantry soldier. Pip found a cane and a top hat for me. Blossom wore a peaked cap and carried a realistic-looking rifle made from plastic.

Then we went back to Pip's house to try on our new gear. Pip promised to reveal his outfit first. He ushered us into the sitting room, where his gran nodded enthusiastically and said she'd go off to make a pot of tea. Pip's gran is lovely but not the most switched-on person I have ever met. She looks a bit like Mrs. Doubtfire.

"Okay, so just wait there . . ." Pip said. "And close your eyes. I just need to go and . . . make some preparations." While we waited, Blossom was literally on the edge of her seat, legs akimbo. She was quite excited and slid off the sofa at one point. Pip's gran came in from time to time.

"You're Pip's friends," she said.

"Hello, Mrs. Harwood," we said.

"I've seen you before."

"Yes, we've met loads of times," Blossom said.

She stood there for a while, beaming at us. We smiled back.

"I'll get the tea," she said eventually.

"So what do you think it's going to be?" Blossom asked as Pip's gran disappeared back into the kitchen.

"Not sure," I said. "Earl Grey? Assam?"

"No, I mean Pip's outfit."

"I don't know," I sighed. "But it had better be good after all this buildup."

"CLOSE YOUR EYES NOW!" Pip yelled from just outside the door. There was a crash of teacups from the kitchen. I closed my eyes and waited. Then I heard a clunking noise as Pip came in. "I expect it won't be as exciting as you think," he said. "Okay. You can open them now."

I did so, and gasped. Pip had undergone a transformation. He had been a nervous, gangling youth in a gabardine. Now, on the carpet in front of us stood a knight in the shiniest armor you could ever see. He wore chain mail, with a gleaming steel breastplate and greaves. He carried a long sword. But the most arresting feature was the familiar conical helmet. A helmet I'd seen recently, in Vintage Vicky's. I couldn't believe what I was witnessing.

"You're a Norman?" Blossom asked breathlessly.

He nodded. "I'm a Norman," he whispered. He turned slowly.

"But . . . but . . . you're not a Norman," I said, disbelieving. "You're a Saxon, like us."

He didn't reply, just kept on turning. Showing us.

"Well, I think this is amazing," Blossom said eventually. "You look brilliant, doesn't he, Fleur? Fleur?" I shook my head, still trying to process the momentous news. Pip looked at me anxiously.

"I'm sorry I didn't tell you before," he said. "But I wasn't sure how you'd take it."

"You can't be a Norman," I repeated, my mind reeling. "You're a Saxon. We're all Saxons."

"I can be both," Pip said.

"You can't be both!" I cried. "I've never heard anything so ridiculous. You're either a Norman or a Saxon, and that's all there is to it!"

"Don't be so binary," Blossom hissed. "Pip, you can be whatever you want to be."

"I'm sorry, Fleur," Pip said, his voice firm. "I knew you would be upset. But I've been feeling for a long time that I just don't fit in as a Saxon. The last reenactment was the final straw. I don't want to be part of the shield wall anymore. I'm just not happy there."

I took a deep breath, stood and walked toward him, fighting the urge to reach out and knock his helmet off. I could see him shaking in his armor. I stared into his eyes, looking for the Pip I knew. And he was there. Just the same. I swallowed, leaned forward and gave him a hug. The armor felt cool to the touch and I pressed my cheek to the breastplate. I was wrong. Blossom was right. There are more than two types of people in the world. There are more than two schools of thought.

"I'm sorry," I said. "You can be whatever you want to be. And whatever you are, you'll always be my Pip."

We looked amazing, though it was a tight squeeze getting all those accessories into the Clio. Being a Norman seemed to make Pip drive even more erratically than usual, but still just as slowly. Like Mr. Toad on Ambien. We quickly ended up with a long procession of cars behind us, unable to pass because of the narrowness of the roads and because Pip was weaving left to right. Blossom and I whooped and shrieked in the back, convinced that our costumes would protect us from anything.

We had to wait in line for forty-five minutes outside the club, but that was fine because it was great fun just watching the mad folk of Brighton dressed as Victorian vampires or Edwardian cyborg chimney sweeps. There was one chap in military regalia with a working gramophone strapped to his back, blaring out marching tunes.

Inside, things were even crazier. Huge remote-controlled airships sailed lazily around the dance floor; a lady wandered around blowing enormous bubbles from a blunderbuss; I saw cave people and a Victorian Ghostbusters team, robots from the future, dinosaurs, pith helmets and lots and lots of Anne Boleyns. There was a band playing on the stage, a combined brass band/electronica fusion combo.

"Isn't it marvelous?" Pip asked us, his eyes shining.

It *was* marvelous. And insane. Everyone looked ridiculous, and that was the point; no one else cared if you didn't fit in because nobody fit in. You didn't have to dress in historical gear, it seemed—there were quite a few Stormtroopers and I saw at least one zombie. It didn't matter. Everyone was welcome here. Past, present or future. Gay, lesbian, bi, trans, queer, intersex, asexual, cis, steampunk, Stormtrooper, zombie, Saxon and Norman. And whatever the hell else.

"This is amazing," I shouted into Blossom's ear. "Why haven't we come here before?" She grinned and the three of us headed to the dance floor to join the other weirdos. It didn't matter that I couldn't dance. I didn't have to remember the steps. We just leaped about, crashing into Tsarist soldiers and World War I flying aces. Professor Elemental came on later and he was hilarious with his monkey butler and enormous trousers. It was over all too soon. Pip heard from some of his friends that there was an after-party, and I was tempted for a moment before remembering I had boxing in the morning.

"You guys go," I said. "I can get Dad to come and collect me."

"No, we're staying together," Pip said. "I'm knackered anyway." I was pleased to hear that, and we headed back through the lanes to where Pip had left his car. It was late, but Brighton never properly goes to sleep, so there were a few people around.

"Did you see that chap with the TARDIS on his back?" Pip asked as we walked. "Pure genius."

"I liked the airship race," Blossom said. "Especially when one crashed into the chandelier."

I smiled contentedly and was about to reply when we were interrupted by a shout. "Hey, freaks!"

"Drunks," Pip muttered. "Ignore them."

"Hey, you freaks!" came another shout, followed by the unwelcome sound of boots running toward us. Brighton is a great town, but there are idiots here, too. I turned to face them. There were four boys. They stopped a few feet away and looked us up and down. Suddenly I wished my dress was even longer.

"How much, Blondie?" one asked, looking right at my legs.

"Show us your gun," another called to Blossom. A third whispered into his ear and the two of them fell about laughing.

"Come on, Fleur," Pip said, tugging at my sleeve. "Let's just keep walking."

"I like that dress," the first one said, pointing at me. He wore a black jacket and had clearly spent a lot of time on his hair. They couldn't have been much older than fifteen.

"It might suit you," I replied. "It's designed to accommodate a giant arse." I felt strong. I was invulnerable. I wasn't going to let these idiots ruin our night.

The leader sneered and stepped forward. Instinctively I lifted the cane, but he snatched it from me and raised it high, threatening to bring it down on my head. Time slowed. I saw his other hand held a mobile phone, down by his side. He'd left himself completely unguarded. For half a second I hesitated.

Then Blossom squealed, and the next thing I knew the boy was on the ground coughing and gasping for breath.

I'd hit him in the solar plexus: he wouldn't be getting up for a while. I was exhilarated as I looked at the other boys. I shuffled my feet and found myself taking up my stance, bringing my fists up. They watched me closely. I raised an eyebrow. One of the boys took a step forward, and I felt a flash of alarm. I couldn't fight all three of them. But, without once taking his eyes off me, he leaned down and helped his friend to his feet.

"Come on," he said to his mates. And they shuffled away, dragging their injured companion off down the street.

"That's right," Blossom shouted after them. "You think girls can't hit? You're wrong."

"Shut up, Blossom," I said, beginning to shake as the adrenaline started to ebb. "Let's get out of here."

PUNCH-DRUNK

"Boom, crack, smash. You biffed him and boshed him!" Blossom cried from the backseat. "Take that, rapist!"

"Blossom, it's not cool. I just hit someone!"

"It was self-defense, Fleur. Isn't that right, Pip?"

"Yep, saw it all," Pip confirmed.

Was it that simple, though? I was in a daze, shivering and scared by what I'd done. But at the same time I felt excited. I hadn't actually *enjoyed* the act of hitting another person, even if he deserved it, but I loved the sense of power. It was new for me. Where had that punch even come from? In the club, tapping away at big heavy bags, my punches felt weak and meaningless. But out on the street, I was suddenly Wonder Woman, Poison Ivy and Black Widow rolled into one.

While I was sitting there, my mind and body buzzing, Blossom was busy in the backseat texting people about what had happed. No one from school, of course, just

Magnet and her mates from the Socialist Action Group. But Bosford is a small town, and word gets around. When I checked my Twitter before I went to bed I had forty-three notifications, all about the incident in Brighton. The story seemed to have been improved in the telling, though. Someone had gotten the idea that I'd been attacked by a rapist and fought him off. Most of the chatter seemed to be on the lines of *Fleur? Fleur Waters punched someone? How is that even possible?* Verity texted me from New Zealand to tell me I rocked. I even got a DM from George asking if I was okay.

I was woken on Saturday morning by my phone ringing. I peered at the time blearily. Who would call at 7:53 a.m. on a Saturday? Who is even up at that time? It's like the middle of the night. It was an unknown number, but I answered anyway.

"Hello?"

"Fleur? It's Ricky."

"Oh, hi . . ."

"Did you punch someone last night?"

"You heard about that?"

"Yeah, I heard about that."

My brain scrambled to decipher his tone. I guessed he'd be impressed, but something about his voice felt a bit off.

"I know what you're thinking," I told him.

"What's that?"

"That I'm ready to spar with the boys now."

"That's not what I'm thinking," he said quietly.

"Oh?"

"I'm thinking I should kick you out of the club," he said.

I sat up in bed, my heart sinking. I couldn't believe I was hearing this.

"You know the rules," he went on. "What you learn in the club stays in the club. No one fights on the street."

"But this was different. I mean, what's the point of me learning to box if I can't use it to defend myself?"

"You're not the Karate Kid. It's a sport; you're supposed to do it in the ring. You could have seriously hurt that boy," Ricky said. "What if he fell and cracked his head?"

"That wasn't going to happen!"

"I've seen it!" he snapped. "I've seen it happen, Fleur. I'm sorry, but I don't think I have any choice. You're out of the club." And then he hung up.

BOXING CLEVER

"On the bright side," Mum said over breakfast, "this means you can come to Pilates with me."

"Great," I said, unable to hide my sarcasm. Mum, to her credit, was trying extremely hard to not beam with delight at the thought of me not boxing anymore.

"I'll call Carole," she went on. "See if she can squeeze you in to today's session."

"Marvelous," I said as she went off to find her phone. I sat at the table facing the window, looking out over the fields, toying with my cornflakes.

I still couldn't understand it. Surely I was allowed to use my skills to defend myself? It's not as if I was going around brawling in nightclubs. I'd been protecting myself and my friends from a potentially dangerous situation. Mum came back after a few minutes.

"Carole says you're in," she said, grinning like a loon.

"Brilliant news," I replied. I gently slid the bowl of cornflakes to one side, then let my head fall with a thump down onto the heavy oak.

"Come on, Fleur," Mum said. "Give it a try; you never know, you might enjoy it.'

I looked up at her and forced a smile. It wasn't her fault; she was doing her best.

"Thanks, Mum," I managed.

"And one more thing," she added cheerfully. "At least this way all your Lycra won't go to waste."

Speaking of Lycra, I hadn't realized there was so much of the stuff in the world. There were literally acres of wobbly middle-aged flesh for it to cling to at Mum's Pilates class. There was some weird Bolivian panpipe music playing over the PA. Mum introduced me to Carole of the Enveloping Aura before heading off to chat with her friends.

"So pleased to meet you," Carole said, putting her head to one side and staring at me intensely, her ice-blue eyes burning into my soul. Suddenly I felt very stiff. "Your mother has told me so much about you."

"Has she?"

"Yes, she tells me you've been stressed about life recently."

"Did she?" I said in surprise.

"You broke up with your soul mate?"

"I wouldn't call him my soul mate, but yes . . ."

"Also that you have some issues to work through."

"*She* said that about *me*?"

"You'll find Pilates will help you work through your stresses. It's not just a physical discipline, but a holistic approach to your whole life."

"And it's great for your core, isn't it?" I said, trying to steer her away from my emotional problems and back into the real world.

"Yes," she said, leaning forward until her face was very close to mine. She pressed her hand against my abdomen, and I shivered involuntarily. "Your *core*." Then she was gone, leaving me with a sense that something had just happened.

Mum wandered back over.

"Isn't she wonderful!" she said, her eyes shining. "So in tune."

"Wish I could say the same about the music," I said.

I can't say I found Pilates THE most fun I've ever had. It's very slow-moving and just seems to involve putting yourself into awkward and slightly uncomfortable positions. Everyone was creaking and sighing so much. And at one point someone farted. But Carole kept telling us our cores were being worked and our auras cleansed. And frankly, by that stage she had us wrapped around her little finger.

So I didn't hate Pilates.

But it wasn't nearly as good as boxing.

THEY SAY IT'S YOUR BIRTHDAY

I think I possibly had the most underwhelming seventeenth birthday ever. My birthdays have always been low-key. Being born slap bang in the middle of the summer means that either I am away for the day in question or everyone else is. It didn't help that I was in a foul mood the morning before. Mum had tried to enthuse me, to no avail.

"What day is it tomorrow?" she'd asked as I was eating breakfast.

"Friday," I replied.

"But what's the date?"

"Thirteenth of August."

"And what does that mean?"

"It means this milk is past its use-by date," I said, pointing to the carton.

"No. I mean, is there anything else significant about tomorrow?"

I took out my phone and checked the calendar. "Yes, it is significant," I told her through a mouthful of Shredded Wheat. "It's International Left-handers Day."

"And your seventeenth birthday!" Mum replied.

"Whatever." I shrugged.

"Honestly, Fleur," Mum said, sighing. "I do my best for you. I really do."

Later, Blossom tried her luck and asked me to come on a march with her and the SAG group. It was about equal pay for women. "Come on, Fleur," she said. "If you don't come I'll have to walk with Magnet. You wouldn't make me do that, would you?"

"He's your boyfriend," I said.

"Exactly."

"Sorry, Blossom. I just don't feel like it," I said. "I'm sorry to let you down, but right now I don't feel like doing anything except lying on my bed reading."

She waited a while, and then she forced a smile. "Okay, Fleur," she said. "Maybe see you tomorrow?"

"Yeah, maybe."

I knew I was acting like an idiot. But I was feeling miserable and the last thing I wanted was for Mum or Blossom to be all chirpy and snap me out of it. It's like the more people try to make me think or feel a certain thing, the harder I fight against it. I certainly didn't feel like celebrating, that was for sure. I got up early and went for a long cycle ride instead. At that moment I wasn't sure what I wanted except that I needed to get away for a while, by myself. The air was still and mild and I had to keep my mouth shut or else I'd have swallowed a thousand bugs. Maybe that was one way to increase my protein intake.

I started out tense, angry and morose. Thinking about George and Mum and being thrown out of the club. I pushed hard, going up the hills in high gear, straining my thighs. But as I ticked off the miles, as my muscles loosened and my lungs started to burn, I found myself gradually sloughing off the mood. Breathing deeply, calming myself, working away the tension. I did fifty miles in a little less than four hours and was knackered when I got back but felt a lot clearer about what I was going to do.

I had to go back and fight for my place at the club. I couldn't just give up. Tomorrow morning I was going to march down there and demand that Ricky let me back in.

I also had some bridges to mend. So when I got back to the house just before noon I was pleased to see Pip's Clio pull up in the driveway with Blossom in the front passenger seat, gripping the dashboard for dear life. They got out and stood on the grass as I put away my bike.

"How far did you go?" Blossom asked as Pip threw a tennis ball for a wheezing Ian Beale.

"Fifty miles," I said.

"Wow," she said. "You're amazing."

"I'm not amazing," I said, unclipping my helmet and tuning to look at her. "I'm a terrible person, a bad friend, a rubbish daughter. And an awful feminist."

She raised her eyebrows. "None of those things are true. Why do you think you're an awful feminist?"

"Because I don't go on marches like you," I replied. "I don't deconstruct things. I make stupid jokes instead of being supportive. And I muted Emma Watson on Twitter."

Blossom looked at me and shook her head. "This is what the patriarchy does," she said slowly. "It makes us doubt ourselves and argue with each other. Fleur, you are an excellent feminist. You've just taken a different route than me. Or anyone else. But that's okay. There are thousands of different ways to be a feminist. And the great thing is, you get to choose which way works for you."

As I stood and looked at my lovely friend, I burst into tears. It had been an emotional few weeks. The stress of exams, the breakup with George, being thrown out of the club, the tensions with Mum. Blossom walked forward and gave me a big hug.

"You act like you don't care," she whispered. "You act like you want to avoid confrontation, like you're terrified all the time. But I know how tough you are, Fleur."

"I am terrified, though," I said.

"That's okay, too," she replied, squeezing me harder.

Afterward we went for lunch in Brighton. Blossom paid. Then we sat on the beach for a while. But it clouded over in the early afternoon and so we went to the cinema. There was nothing we hadn't already seen except for a Pixar thing, so we went into that along with about a million tiny children and their tired-looking parents. It's always like this in the summer. But I don't mind.

When we got back to Bosford, Blossom asked me if I wanted to go to Chickos.

"Nah," I said. "I need to spend some time with Mum. I think she's cooking me something special. Crystal meth, possibly."

"Wanna come over and watch a film later?" she asked. "Rocky marathon?"

"Maybe just one," I said. "Or two. I've got boxing tomorrow."

She looked delighted and did a little dance.

"What's that brilliant *Rocky* quote?" she asked. "About how hard you hit?"

"It ain't about how hard ya hit," I replied. "It's about how hard ya can *get* hit. And keep moving forward."

"That's how winning is done," she finished in triumph.

SHOWDOWN

I found Tarik outside the club. He was early, like me, and sitting with his back to the wall, in a sunny patch, reading an Enid Blyton novel. I sat down next to him and waited until he'd gotten to the end of the chapter before saying good morning.

Sharon turned up to open the doors and we went in and helped get everything set up. Laying out the skipping ropes, lifting the bags onto the wall brackets. Joe hobbled in, soon after. "All right, Killa?" he said to me. Ricky arrived a few minutes later and started assembling the ring. I went over to him, wanting to get this out of the way.

"Ricky," I said, trying to stay really calm. "I'm sorry about punching that boy even though it was self-defense. But I love boxing. And I think I'm getting better at it. I think I'm fitter, and stronger, and more confident and happier, and I think I am a boxer even if you don't think I'm ready for sparring yet."

Ricky stopped tightening the bolt he'd been working on and looked up at me, his customary grimace on his face. "I'm very pleased to hear all that, Fleur," he said. "And I'm glad you're getting something out of this club. We get out what we put in. But one thing I didn't hear you say you'd taken away from this club is the one thing I've been trying to teach you since you first arrived."

My mind was blank. What did he mean?

"Starts with a *D*?"

"Dancing?"

"Discipline! You want to be a boxer? Well, learn some bloody discipline." I could hear Tarik, Joe and Sharon shuffling about at the other end of the hall, chatting quietly, pretending they couldn't hear us. Ricky glared at me. "That's why you hit that bloke. Because you couldn't control yourself. That's why you keep dropping your guard. Because you've got no discipline."

I swallowed. He was right. Discipline has never been my strong point. Or dancing, for that matter.

"Two things," Ricky said. "If I ever see or hear of you fighting outside the club again, you're out for good, straightaway." I nodded. He turned away and got back to tightening the bolt.

"What's the other thing?" I asked.

"You can spar. If you still want to."

"What?"

"You're ready. Or you will be soon, if you work hard enough and do what I tell you."

I suddenly felt swamped with emotions. Relief that I had been let back into the club. Surprise at this unexpected turn of events, abject terror at the thought of actually throwing punches in the ring. Or more likely, being punched in the ring. "Okay. Just tell me what I need to do."

ONE OF THE BOYS

I was nervous. Tonight was my first time in the ring. It was September; I'd come twice a week for the last three weeks and Ricky had finally agreed to let me in the ring for a "taster," as he put it. Ricky had paired me up with Joe, who had said he wouldn't hit me. But I wasn't quite sure I believed him. For all I knew, he wanted to get revenge for the time I'd put one on his buzzer. I stood with my gloves on, waiting for our turn, watching Jerome and Chris dance and jab as Ricky shouted encouragement or technical advice. Some of them looked terrifyingly strong, and so, so quick. Dan sidled up to me. "Erm, so no big deal but I'm getting married in a couple of months," he said. "I'm gonna organize a bachelor party. Just a few beers. Nothing special."

"Oh, cool," I said, wondering why he was telling me. "Have a good one."

"So do you wanna come?"

I paused. "You want me to come to your stag do?"

"Yeah, only if you've got nothing on."

"Okay. Why not?"

"Killa!" Ricky snapped. I looked around. "You're up." He held the ropes for me and I climbed into the ring. Joe climbed in behind me. We faced each other, both wearing head guards, mouth guards and twelve-ounce gloves. A bit heavy for me, a bit light for Joe, but Ricky was trying to even us up as much as possible. Joe and I were about the same height, but he was wiry and muscled. I think the word often used for men like Joe is "spry."

My stomach churned like a cement mixer, though that might have been partly because of the second massive portion of porridge I'd had for breakfast. Is this how the Anglo-Saxons had felt on the eve of the battle? They probably weren't wearing fetching black-and-cream boots with new pink sparkly laces, but apart from that I felt a real kinship with those brave warriors.

The boys were pretending not to watch, just carrying

on with their skipping or their bag work. But I could feel the sideways glances as I lifted my gloves and took up my stance. "Right," Ricky said. "Now, take it easy and keep your guard up. I don't want anyone knocked senseless."

"Don't worry," Joe growled.

"Not talking to you," Ricky said. "She's already laid you out once." I laughed. Ricky was very good at making jokes to keep us buoyed. Joe stepped forward and jabbed once, softly. I blocked the punch. Then he jabbed with his right. I blocked that, too.

"That's it," Ricky cried. "Just like the drills." I carried on blocking, moving backward and circling around as Joe kept up the jabs. It was hard work even without throwing any punches myself. But Joe couldn't get through my defenses.

"Stop," Ricky called. Joe backed away from me. "What are you doing?" Ricky asked.

"What? I'm doing what you always tell me. Keeping my guard up."

"You have to try and hit him back," Ricky said. "It's called boxing, not defending."

"But how can I hit him when he's throwing punches?"

"Block his jab, return his jab. Go again." This time I tried to do what Ricky had asked. I'd wait for Joe to jab once, I'd block it, then try to jab back. But by that time he was following up with a right and I had to block that, too. My punches weren't getting close to him. I couldn't keep up my guard and reach out far enough to hit him at the same time. "Can you stop punching me for a sec and let me hit back?" I panted.

"I'm not falling for that again," Joe replied, and jabbed once more. Gradually, I grew more and more frustrated. Eventually I decided enough was enough and took a wild swing with my right.

"Are you all right?" Ricky said, looking down at me. I seemed to be lying flat on my back.

"Sorry," Joe called from somewhere nearby.

"What happened?" I asked.

"You dropped your guard," Ricky said. "Big swing, no ding. You missed Joe completely and dropped your left hand. Joe tapped the side of your head and you went down."

"That was a tap?"

"Afraid so."

Ricky helped me to my feet and out of the ring. I sat down for a bit and Sharon brought me a cup of water. "How do you feel?" Ricky asked after a few minutes. I blinked a couple of times and shook my head, testing it to make sure it wouldn't fall off.

"A bit shaken," I said. "But not as bad as I'd thought I might be."

"The first time is the worst," Ricky said. "After a while you stop feeling it. When you've got no brain left. Maybe we should concentrate on defending for now. We can work on your guard a bit more before we get you attacking the next time."

"Next time?" I asked.

"Next time sparring. If you want to, that is."

SURPRISE!

"Three new members!" Sharon said as I arrived at training on Wednesday night. "All girls. It's your posters that did it."

"That's brilliant!" I said, delighted. I walked into the hall and looked around for the newcomers. But when I saw them, my heart sank.

Destiny.

Taylor.

Bonita.

The Iceni.

"So, err . . . how come you're here?" I asked, trying hard to sound friendly while warning bells went off inside my skull.

"You put flyers up," Bonita said. "Remember? We need something to do to keep ourselves off the streets."

"Great," I said, trying to sound like I meant it. *But why does it have to be boxing?* I thought. *Why can't they go and raid nearby villages instead?*

"Sharon said you'd been looking for someone to spar against," Bonita said. "So here I am." She laughed and Taylor and Destiny joined in like they were her evil henchmen.

"You'll need to come to a few sessions first," I said. "Ricky won't let you get straight into the ring."

"Won't take long," Bonita said. She aimed a few air punches in my direction.

Ricky gave us the parish news as we warmed up. "Don't forget about the tournament. There'll be fighters from Hastings and Rye and Battle. All those interested in fighting, let me know and we can talk about weights."

"When is it?" Bonita asked.

"December eighth," Ricky said.

"And girls can join in?"

Ricky hesitated a moment, and I saw his eyes flicker over to me. "Possibly. But I'm not letting anyone fight who's not ready."

"I'll be ready," Bonita said. She winked at me and I found myself swallowing.

Needless to say, the Iceni didn't find their first training session nearly as difficult as I had. They were all pretty fit anyway. I sized them up as we jogged on the spot, wondering which of them I might be prepared to spar with. Taylor was the smallest, not much taller than me. But she was quick and strong and possibly the fittest of them all.

Destiny was a few inches taller than me but probably in the worst shape. She didn't seem to be pushing herself as hard as the other two. If I had to spar against one of them, she was the one I'd feel least threatened by. But even so, looking at these tough, sporty girls, suddenly the prospect of sparring didn't seem quite so enticing. I reminded myself of what Ricky had said. *No one has to fight if they don't want to. If you just want to do the conditioning that's absolutely fine.* I didn't have to fight any of them. Maybe I should just stick to the exercise, play it safe.

"Work hard," Ricky yelled as we did about a million squats. "If you take one on the chin, the first thing to go will be your legs. They need to be stronger than oak trees."

The one thing the new girls did find difficult was the ab-work and leg raises. No amount of field hockey and netball could prepare you for that special brand of torture. We had to lie on our backs and raise our feet six inches into the air and hold them there. Everyone found it tough; there was so much hissing and puffing it sounded like an episode of *Thomas the Tank Engine*.

"Shouldn't have had those Pringles," Jerome panted.

"I dunno what you've been telling your fiancée, Dan, but that's not six inches," Ricky called. Bonita laughed out loud briefly.

"You can tell the new ones," Sharon said. "They haven't heard all Ricky's jokes yet."

As we were leaving, Bonita appeared next to me and punched me on the shoulder. "See you on Saturday, Petal," she said.

"Ow," I said, my heart sinking. "You're coming Saturday, too?"

"Yep, loved it." She winked at me and walked out, Taylor and Destiny trailing behind her.

THE TON

"Come on, Dad," I called from the top of the hill. I stretched and took a swig from the world's most expensive water bottle. The day was hot and I was enjoying the faint breeze coming at me from the South Downs. We were about halfway through the hundred-mile ride and I felt good. This was a planned stop, at a picnic area on top of Jump Hill. You could see a long way from here.

We'd taken it in turns to be in the lead, benefitting from each other's slipstream, not talking much, just listening to the hiss of the tires on the road and the sound of the wind and the wildlife in the hedgerows. In the last mile or so we'd hit some "bumps," as Dad called them, or "huge bloody-great mountains," as I called them. But surprisingly, and before I'd realized it, I'd pulled away from him until he was about half a mile behind.

Dad arrived, puffing and panting. He unclipped his pedals and got off his bike, looking at me suspiciously. "When did you get so fit?" he asked.

I slapped my legs. "Pure muscle," I said. "Also I'm thirty years younger than you."

He took his drink and went to sit on a bench. "It's the boxing, isn't it?" he said as his breath returned.

"Yeah, and all the protein I've been eating," I said. "I'm up to a hundred thirty pounds now." I ripped open a pack of jerky and offered it to Dad. He shook his head and pulled out a banana from the pocket at the back of his cycle jersey.

"That won't do you any good," I said. "You need proper food. Here, have a pork pie."

"Your mother's worried about you," he said.

"She's always worried." I shrugged. "She doesn't even like me going to Costco because she thinks those big shopping carts are dangerous."

"They can build up a lot of momentum when they're full of mega-tubs of dog food," Dad said loyally. "Anyway, she thinks you're going to end up fighting in the ring. She's been researching boxing deaths down at the library. Turns out being punched in the head a lot can be quite bad for you."

I sighed. "Lots of things are bad for you. Would you rather I was in Brighton with my peers, getting drunk and stoned all summer?"

"I'm not the one you need to convince," Dad said. "She brought home a printout yesterday about a young man who became a paraplegic after a boxing match. He'll be in a wheelchair for the rest of his life."

"Look, I get it, okay?" I said. "The reason Mum is so . . ."

"Protective?" he suggested.

". . . irritating," I said, "is because Verity abandoned her and went to live in New Zealand. She doesn't want to lose another daughter."

"It's not just that," Dad said.

He paused and stared out at the view, his graying hair ruffling in the breeze. He looked tired. I waited until he seemed to make a decision and spoke again.

"You know your mother and I struggled to have children."

"Yeah," I said. "Mum had a couple of miscarriages before Verity."

"And one after," Dad said. "In fact . . . it wasn't a miscarriage. You had a brother. For a day." The breeze turned a little stiffer, dragging reluctant clouds across the sky. I sat there, stunned, trying to process this information. Why had they never told me?

"You mother didn't want to tell you," Dad said, as if reading my mind. "But I think it's important you know."

"Does Verity know?" I said.

"Yes," Dad said, before sighing heavily. "It came up during an argument. Not the right time."

"Did he have a name?"

"Ben," Dad said. "We knew he wasn't going to make it. We were prepared. As much as you can be. Problem with his heart. Poor little fella." I saw a tear trickle down Dad's cheek, and I didn't know what to do. I put an arm around him awkwardly, but it didn't feel like much. "He fought hard. Lived a whole day. Which was longer than they thought he was going to," Dad said. "Bit like you. Stubborn."

"You think I'm stubborn?"

"When you find something you care about. Anyway, that's why she's . . . the way she is. Partly, at least. She was a little like that before, but she got much worse after Ben. So just go easy on her, won't you?"

I nodded, not trusting myself to speak. Thinking of my brother all those years ago. We sat there for a long time, not speaking. A few cars drove by, people staring at us curiously, a girl in Lycra with her arm around her father, neither of them moving.

After what seemed like an age, I finally spoke.

"He fought hard, did he?" I asked.

"He did," Dad replied.

"I bet he would have been a good boxer," I said.

Dad nodded. "I bet that, too."

PART THREE

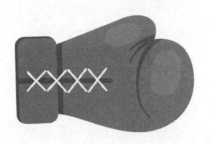

DOWN FOR
THE COUNT

FLOAT LIKE A BUTTERFLY. STING LIKE A BUTTERFLY.

Destiny jabbed.
    I blocked.
Destiny jabbed.
I blocked.

This went on for a while. I'd been seriously nervous before getting in the ring, knowing that today was the day. My first proper sparring match. Ricky had said he wanted me to concentrate on keeping up my guard and not worrying too much about offense.

Destiny jabbed with her right.

I blocked.

"Very good, Fleur," Ricky yelled. "Keep up that guard."

"Hit her, Destiny," Joe croaked. Joe was Destiny's second. Ricky was mine.

Destiny jabbed with her left.

I blocked.

"I like it," Ricky said. "You're getting it now." Destiny jabbed again three times and I blocked again, three times. This wasn't so bad. As long as I was in the right position, and kept my gloves up, it was actually pretty hard for Destiny to do any damage.

Destiny stepped back and dropped her gloves. "Aren't you going to try and hit me back?"

"What?"

"We're supposed to be sparring; you haven't tried punching me yet."

"Ricky said I had to work on my guard."

"Just hit me," Destiny said, rolling her eyes.

I stepped in and took a swing with my right.

"Guard!" Ricky yelled, but it was too late. Destiny leaned back, avoiding my punch, and brought her own right glove around to whack me on the side of the head. I'd dropped my guard again. As soon as I swung with the right, the left glove automatically dropped. Every time.

"You okay?" Ricky called. I nodded.

My head was spinning and I stepped back, trying to get away from Destiny. She followed, trying to press home her advantage. She jabbed. I blocked. She jabbed again, I blocked.

She swung a big clunking fist.

I blocked.

"Fleur," Ricky said, beckoning me over at the end of the session. *Here we go*, I thought, *he's going to yell at me again for dropping my guard*. "So what do you think?"

"About what?"

"About the tournament."

"I thought I wasn't ready?"

He shrugged. "You're not ready for Bonita, no. But Destiny? Maybe."

I frowned at him doubtfully.

"Look, Fleur, my main priority is the safety of my fighters. I don't let anyone box against someone much better; I don't let anyone box against someone much smaller or lighter. Remember, you can punch up, you can punch out, but never punch down."

"And I'm ready? I didn't land one punch on Destiny."

"I didn't want you to land a punch on her," Ricky said. "I just wanted you to keep your guard up. I just wanted to make sure you could protect yourself."

"But what's the point of a boxing match if one of the boxers doesn't punch?"

"It's a demonstration match," Ricky said. "Three rounds of three. I want to encourage more young women to pick up the sport."

"What? You've changed your tune," I said.

He shrugged. "I'll train anyone if they show commitment. I hadn't found many girls who had what it takes. Until you started."

I didn't know what to say to that. "The papers are going to be there," Ricky went on. "I want the crowd to see that women's boxing is a good form of exercise, and that it's safe."

"Right, so you want me to box because I'm not likely to knock anyone out?"

"Basically," Ricky said. "Think about it, yeah?" He walked off, and I went to find Tarik. Bonita was all over him, asking him questions about technique. I hovered for a bit but then gave up and walked home by myself, skirting the Gladwell Estate.

SUNDAY PUNCH

On the last weekend in September, we decided not to go to Battle, and I invited Blossom and Pip over for Sunday lunch. I wanted to keep Mum happy but was worried that without George it could all get a bit dull, and I thought Pip might liven things up. Unfortunately, I'd totally forgotten that Pip is cripplingly shy in situations like this. He was even scared of Ian Beale, who he's met loads of times.

"Is he dangerous?" Pip asked me nervously.

"He won't bite," I said. "Though you might catch something from him." Ian Beale lay in his basket, wearing a cone of shame and groaning softly. One of his legs was shaved where the vet had had to give him a shot.

"Just don't let him out, whatever you do," Mum said, coming into the room with a bowl of mashed potatoes. Pip's met my parents dozens of times, too, but still can't look them in the eye. He spent most of the meal either staring down at his plate or knocking things over with his long arms before apologizing profusely. He also ate his whole meal with a teaspoon, which is an odd thing to do even by his standards.

Today's pointless argument turned out to be about pronouns, specifically the use of "they" to denote someone of indeterminate sex. Mum was against. She doesn't like change. Blossom Esquire led the case for the defense and I hurried out to the kitchen as soon as I could.

"Do you think wooden spoons can go in the dishwasher?" I wavered.

"Yes. No. I don't know," replied Pip, who was "helping."

I decided to be a rebel and put it in.

"How's the boxing going?" he asked.

"Fine, apart from Bonita!" I snapped. "It was my *thing*, you know? My release. The one thing I was better at than her."

"I thought you weren't competitive," Pip said.

"I'm not. I just don't want her to be better than me," I said, jamming a fistful of forks willy-nilly into the cutlery section.

"So can't you box her and knock her down? You said you had a good right hoof?"

"*Hook*. Right hook."

"That too. So what's the problem? I saw you knock the rapist down."

"The problem is that Bonita is taller and heavier than me," I said. "She can reach farther with her fists and hit harder. That's why they have different divisions in boxing."

"She ain't gonna kiss ya, Rocky," Pip said, in his worst Burgess Meredith voice. "She's gonna kill ya."

"Exactly," I said. "If I want to fight her, then I have to put on weight."

"So put on weight," he said, shrugging. I looked up at him as he scraped crumble out of a bowl into the trash. Some people really like to overcomplicate things, but not Pip. To him it was simple.

"Do dessert bowls go in the top or bottom?" he asked.

"It doesn't matter," I told him. "Just plonk it in and risk getting it wrong."

"Fourteen, fifteen, sixteen," I puffed, doing push-ups. My morning run was roughly three miles and about half-way I cut through Bosford Park. I always stopped at the bridge over the duck pond and did some push-ups, squats and burpees, just to mix it up. As I completed push-up number twenty, a pair of green sneakers appeared in front of me.

I lifted my head and squinted against the sunshine to see the smirking face of Bonita. She held out a hand, and after a moment, I grabbed it and she pulled me up. She was also wearing Lycra. Hers was green. Mine was pink.

"So you gonna fight in this tournament?" she asked. I shook my head.

"I'm a lover, not a fighter," I said with a winning smile.

"Yes, that explains why you joined a boxing club. Oh, wait a minute, no, it doesn't."

"It's just for fitness," I said.

"I overheard what Ricky said," she went on. "He said you were ready."

"I'm sure he's right," I said. "Still not going to happen, though. And why do you care, anyway?"

"Why don't *you* care?" Bonita asked, pointing at me. "What kind of girl are you, anyway?" I felt myself blush. I knew she was deliberately goading me. Trying to find the right buttons to push.

"Look, just because you're strong and fast and good at sports doesn't make you better than me," I said. "Girls don't *need* to be sporty any more than they *need* to be princesses. You don't get to decide what I should be."

"So what are you?" she asked. "What exactly *are* you?"

It was time to go.

"See ya, Bonita," I said, but as I jogged slowly away from the confrontation, I found myself wondering about Bonita's question.

And I wasn't at all sure I knew the answer.

HOLD THE FRONT PAGE

Sweat dripped from the end of my nose. Today's session had been tough, and we weren't even out of the warm-ups yet.

"I'm gonna show you a new exercise," Ricky said. He placed a medicine ball carefully on the floor and got down painfully. His back was clearly bothering him. But once down, he showed his fitness by resting his feet on the medicine ball and performing ten quick push-ups, while drawing alternate knees up and to the side. "Spider-Man push-ups. Did everyone see that?" he asked as people lay around, expiring. Everyone nodded, and Ricky clambered to his feet, grunting with the effort.

"No," I said. "I wasn't watching. Can you do it again?"

Ricky sighed and started to get down again. "Just kidding," I said. Everyone laughed except Ricky.

"If you've got breath to make jokes, you can do three extra reps," Ricky said. Everyone laughed except me. As I was working on a bag with Destiny later on, I saw a man with a satchel walk into the club and look around curiously. Ricky rushed over to him and they shook hands before going off to one of the trestle tables. The man pulled a notebook out of his satchel.

"Who's that?" I asked Sharon as she passed.

"He's from the paper," she explained. "They're going to do a story about the club, and the tournament." As she said this, Ricky turned and pointed to me and Destiny, then Bonita and Taylor on the other side of the hall. The reporter nodded and scribbled something down in his book.

After the session I looked for Tarik, wondering if he might walk me back to the bypass. I found him in the kitchen with Bonita and Taylor. They were laughing at something he was saying. I caught his eye and waved good-bye before turning away. I tried not to be annoyed. Why shouldn't Tarik and Bonita be friends? It's not as if I had some claim on him. But once again, it seemed Bonita had muscled her way in on my life.

I was a hundred yards down the street when I heard someone running behind me. My heart leaped and I turned quickly. It was Tarik.

"Hey! You didn't wait," he said, falling into step beside me.

"Sorry," I said. "You seemed . . . busy."

"She's funny, Bonita," he said.

I pulled a face that he wasn't supposed to see but did.

"Don't you like her?"

"I don't know. I don't think she and I are . . . similar people. She's a fighter. I'm not."

"Yes, you are," he said.

I stopped dead. He walked on a couple more paces

and turned to me, his deep, dark eyes peering at me curiously. "You think I'm a fighter?" I asked.

"Sure. You keep coming back, week after week; you push yourself. You always look to improve. You listen, you think. Ricky threw you out of the club; you came back with a face like a storm."

"But I've never actually fought against someone else," I pointed out.

"Who said you had to fight against someone else?" Tarik said. He tapped his temple. "Sometimes the toughest opponent is in here."

When I got home my exam results were waiting for me. Mum was dancing around like a flyweight, nervously waiting for me to arrive and open the envelope.

"They're not important," I said as I pulled out the sheet inside. "It's next year's results that really count." It was easy enough to tell myself that, not so easy to believe it, though. My stomach was churning. Because if I'd screwed it up . . . then what? It was not going to be easy to make up the ground in the final year.

I looked at the sheet. Taking it in. I swallowed.

"Well?" Mum said, her voice quivering. "Well?"

"Bloody hell," I said.

"Oh God," she said, and sank down onto a chair. "It's bad, isn't it? I knew it. All that boxing business has been a distraction."

"No, Mum," I said. "Actually, I nailed it. Four As."

She snatched the paper from me and read it in astonishment. I practiced a few shadow punches in her direction, bouncing on my toes. She looked up at me and her face broke into a huge grin. She leaped up and grabbed me in a great bear hug, squeezing tightly. "Oh, Fleur, I am so relieved. All this exercise, all this pushing yourself. I've been really worried."

"I know you have, Mum," I said, hugging back. "But you know what they say."

"No. What's that?"

"*Mens sana in corpore sano.* A healthy mind in a healthy body."

SCHOOL (AND JERKY)

"People, we are running out of time," Ricky shouted. "We have ten weeks, and I'm seeing too much flab, too much fat, too many breaks. I need you as sleek as racehorses. Do you get it?"

A few people mumbled a yes.

"DO YOU GET IT?" Ricky screamed.

"YES, COACH RICKY," we yelled back. It was all part of the theater. But I loved the feeling of being part of a team. Like a unit in the army.

"Now, we have five fights set up. Four boys' matches and one girls' match."

"Why only one girls' match?" Jerome asked. "We've got four girls."

"We only have three girls ready to fight," Ricky said. "Remember. No one has to fight if they don't want to. There's no pressure." But as Bonita, Destiny and Taylor turned their heads to look at me, arching their eyebrows,

I did feel the pressure. I knew I was letting them down. "Now, those who are fighting in December," Ricky went on. "I want you over in the ring."

People started moving. I stayed still.

"The rest of you," Ricky finished, "find yourselves a skipping rope."

"How's attendance?" I asked Sharon after the session. I could see Bonita, Destiny and Taylor still in the ring, clustered around Tarik, laughing and chatting.

"Not great," Sharon sighed. "We have plenty for the Saturday and Wednesday sessions, even if some of them aren't paying. It's the Thursday sessions that are the problem; we only had three last time."

"Ladies' Night?" I asked, surprised. "I thought women's boxing was much more popular now?"

"It is, but boxing's still dominated by men. And the problem is, the women we do have tend to be from around here. Which is brilliant, but I know Ricky was hoping we'd get more from East Bosford. You know, women with time on their hands, trying to keep in shape."

Ricky wandered over at this point to join in the discussion.

"You mean the Yummy Mummies?" I asked. "They're all at the posh gym."

"The thing is," Ricky said, "a lot of women still think boxing is dangerous. And so they decide it's not for them."

"Do you want me to put some more flyers up?" I asked, slightly dreading the thought of running into the Meninists again.

"That would be great," Sharon said. "Also, I thought we could put more pictures of girls up on the website. You know, on the tournament page?"

"That's a good idea," I said.

"So would you mind if we took some pictures of you?"

"Me? I'm not even fighting in the tournament. I'm not exactly a success story."

"I disagree," Ricky said. "You've worked hard and you've really come on. When you got here you could hardly lift your fist, let alone punch. Now you're looking like a real boxer. I'd say you are a success story, Fleur."

"Thanks," I said, blushing. I was always ridiculously pleased when Ricky gave me a compliment.

"So you'll do the shoot?" Sharon persisted, not letting me off the hook. "Tarik's already agreed to it, but it would be so good to have a girl."

Tarik was doing it? "Well. I suppose if it's to help out the club . . ."

"And if you did want to fight in the tournament," Ricky added, "you'd be ready. And that way we could have two women's matches."

I paused for a moment before answering. Ricky and Sharon were serious about promoting the club to women. What would Blossom say? Despite her opposition to the patriarchy, she'd tell me to do it, for the sisterhood. Mum would have a fit. Dad would say there are two ways of looking at it. Pip would tell me to do what my heart said. My heart didn't know. The truth was, I was scared.

"I'll think about it," I promised.

GIVE ME ANGRY

On Saturday, Sharon texted and asked me to come early, for the photo shoot.

When?

Err. Now?

I rushed into the bathroom, slapped on some makeup and pulled on my best Lycra. I was a little worried about doing the shoot. Not because I thought I might look ridiculous—that was a given. But because Mum might see the photos. She'd never believe I wasn't fighting in the ring if she saw photos of me promoting a boxing tournament. Just as well she never went online.

I took my bike, not just for speed, but because I'd be less sweaty when I arrived. You can freewheel most of the way into town anyway. The photographer was already there when I arrived. So was Tarik. He was wearing his loose top that showed off his trapezius muscles. Since I'd been doing weights I'd become familiar with the Latin names of the major muscle groups. There's something about the word trapezius that makes me go a bit wobbly. And bicep. Gluteus maximus, maybe not so much.

I realized a little late that I'd forgotten my chest protector, which meant my boobs were a bit more noticeable than they should have been. The photographer took a few standard shots first, head and shoulders. Smiling at the camera, then glowering. She asked us to stare into each other's eyes and look mean, and that's when I got the giggles. I was a bit nervous anyway, and Tarik just couldn't do mean. He has such a naturally friendly face. He doesn't smile a lot, not with his mouth. But his eyes are always bright and warm.

"Look angry," the photographer said. Tarik narrowed his eyes and stuck his bottom jaw out toward me.

"You look like you need the loo." I grinned.

"I do need the loo," he said. "I've been drinking isotonic fluid all morning."

"Channel the discomfort," I said. "Work it."

"Grr," he said, and then he fell about laughing, too. The photographer looked up at the ceiling and sighed.

I met up with Blossom and Pip at Chickos that night. They'd been to Battle and Pip was feeling glum.

"He ran off again," Blossom said.

"Back to his wood?"

"Back to his wood."

"I thought everything would be different as a Norman," Pip said. "The helmet, the armor, the sword. But I'm still just as scared."

"Oh, Pip," I said. "I'm sorry. Would you like some chips . . . Not too many!"

"He's thinking about giving up altogether," Blossom said.

"Maybe I'm not a Saxon OR a Norman," Pip said dejectedly.

"Or maybe you're both," Blossom suggested.

"Is it just the battle itself?" I asked. "Or are you not very sure about the dressing up?"

"I LOVE the dressing up," Pip said. "But when I charge up that hill and see all those stern Saxons facing me down . . . their shields so strong and solid . . . I just panic. I think, how can I ever burst through that wall, just me, on my own? Then someone takes a swing at me and then suddenly it all goes fuzzy and I'm clutching a yew tree."

"Poor Pip," I said.

"Maybe I should pull out of the reenactment," Pip said sadly, and took a slurp of his Coke. "I think there's a vacancy in the gift shop."

"The big one is coming up, though," I pointed out. "The anniversary of the battle itself. Thirteenth of October."

"Fourteenth of October," Blossom corrected me. "Thirteenth is World Thrombosis Day."

"Either way," I argued. "It would be a shame to miss it."

PUNCH UP

That Wednesday we did a lot of pad work. Ricky was holding his pads up high, and I had to stretch right up to hit them.

"Why have you got them so high?" I asked afterward.

"Always punch up," he said. "It works the shoulder muscles. Good for fitness. But also, remember you're aiming for your opponent's head, which is a little higher than your shoulders. And if your opponent is taller than you then you'll be ready."

"What if your opponent is shorter than you?" I asked.

"Then punch out. You can punch up, or out, but never down. Never punch down."

"Good rule for life in general," I said.

"Sure is," Ricky agreed. As I climbed out of the ring, a song started up on the stereo. It was a song I'd come to know quite well during the time I'd been with the club, and it was possibly the worst song ever recorded. It was "Black Dog" by Led Zeppelin, and I hated it more than I hate skipping.

And I really hate skipping.

I leaned back over the ropes as Ricky prepared for the next pad session, with Jerome. "Ricky," I said, "would you mind if I put something else on?"

"Eh?"

"The music, Ricky, this god-awful music. Please let me put something else on. Radio 1? Radio 2, if you absolutely must, just not Led Zeppelin again . . . ?"

He glared at me. "No one touches the playlist," he growled. "It's scientifically designed to help you reach your top performance."

"It's scientifically making me want to top myself," I said.

"Use that anger," he advised, then turned away.

As I was leaving training I looked for Tarik. I went into the little kitchen area but there was no sign of him, just Bonita and Destiny. They spun round as I came in.

"Did you see the paper?" Bonita asked.

"What paper?"

"This one," she said, and showed me a copy of the *Bosford Gazette*, turned to page five. There was a picture of me, gloves raised, smiling and looking like I was about to laugh. There was no sign of Tarik. Underneath it was an article about the club and the tournament.

"Funny that they chose to illustrate a story about the

tournament with a picture of someone who's not even in it," she said. "Oh, hang on, no it isn't, because she's blond."

"The story isn't just about the tournament," I said. "It's about the club. We're trying to encourage more girls to join."

"I'm a girl," Bonita said. "I'm in the club, and I'm in the tournament. No one asked me to be in the photos." She walked off. I stood for a moment, staring at the picture, then I dropped the paper on the table and ran out after Bonita. I caught up with her outside the hall.

"Hey," I called. She stopped and turned, glowering at me.

"I didn't realize they were only going to take photos of me and Tarik," I said. "I thought they would include photos of us all."

"Sure," she said, and started to go. I trotted after her. "Will you stop?"

She turned once more.

"Look, I'm sorry, okay?" I said. "It should have been you in those photos. All I want to do is train and get fit. I was just trying to help the club. I don't want to fight with you."

She watched me closely, then seemed to soften slightly and nodded. "Look, it's fine," she said. "I know I'm big and ugly."

"You're not ugly," I said.

"I am, but thanks," she said. "I'll see you Saturday, yeah?"

I nodded. "See you Saturday."

My stomach was flipping as I jogged home. I'd thought the photos were just going to be on the website. That was fine, because Mum never looked online. But she got the *Bosford Gazette* most weeks and read it cover to cover. No story about the litter problem in Gostrey Park or the closure of another coffee shop on the high street was too parochial for her, and since the paper was full of crime reports it reinforced her negative view of the outside world. My only hope was that she hadn't got around to reading it yet and I could tear out the offending story. But as I came in my heart sank. She was sitting at the dining table, the paper open in front of her.

"So," she said as I sat down opposite her. "Would you like to explain?"

"I'm not in the tournament," I said, looking down at the table. "They just used my photo."

"But you are sparring," Mum said. "It says in the article that the reporter watched you sparring. You told me you were only boxing for fitness."

"Sparring isn't dangerous, Mum," I said.

"You lied to me," Mum whispered.

"Well, you were being ridiculous . . ." I began.

"Was I?" Mum asked. "Was I really? Trying to keep my child safe is ridiculous, is it? Expecting my daughter to keep her promises to me is ridiculous?" She glared across the table at me, her nostrils flared and her cheeks pink with anger.

The tension was punctured somewhat by the sound of a long and whining fart from Ian Beale in the corner. "Look, I'm sorry I didn't tell you," I said. "I should have. But I knew you'd overreact. It's not a big deal. And it didn't affect my exam results, did it?"

"It's going too far, Fleur," she replied. "I see you eating whey protein and kissing your biceps. I see you out-cycling your father and clanking weights at all hours. I see you wearing boxing boots to a Mess Ball."

"Is that what this is about?!" I snapped back, my heart pounding with anger. "It's about George. Because you lost him. You think I should have stayed as I was, all flimsy and pathetic. Well, I've changed, Mum. And you'll just have to live with it."

"I don't have to live with anything," she said, glaring at me. "This is my house."

"I see," I said. "So that's the way you want it? Fine." I stood quickly, knocking my chair over as I ran to the stairs.

"Fleur!" Mum shouted, but I ignored her.

I ran up to my room and flopped onto the bed. My head was spinning with all the things I wished I'd said and all the things I was glad I hadn't.

Then I grabbed my phone and texted Ricky. Just two words.

I'll fight.

DESTINY CALLS

"I'm not fighting Bonita."

"No, you're not fighting Bonita, she'd kill you." I was tapping into Ricky's gloves in the ring on Saturday. He'd asked me to stay behind after everyone else had gone so we could talk about the tournament. I hit the pads four times, then rolled under the punch.

"You don't have to do this, you know," Ricky said. "If you don't feel ready. You don't have to prove anything to me."

"I know," I said. "It's more about proving it to myself. I'll fight Taylor, or Destiny."

"You're fighting Destiny. She's heavier than you and stronger, but she won't kill you."

One-two-three-four duck.

"What's the number one thing I need to do to beat her?" I panted.

"Put on twenty pounds."

"What's the number two thing I need to do to beat her?"

"Don't worry about beating her. This is just a demonstration. The important thing is that everyone sees how safe boxing is. How it teaches discipline, strength and confidence. We don't want anyone knocked out."

One-two-three-four duck.

"So you just want me to defend myself for three rounds?"

"Exactly," he said, tapping me on the side of the head. "Keep your guard up, Fleur."

"But that's not going to make for a very exciting bout," I said. "You don't want me to even try to win?"

"Hey," Ricky said, stepping backward. "Did Rocky beat Apollo Creed the first time they fought?"

"No," I said instantly. "He lost on points. But he lasted the full fifteen rounds."

"So did he step out of that ring a winner, or a loser?"

"A winner," I said.

"Yep." He held up the pads again.

"Boxing certainly is complicated," I said as I started

punching again. "Do you really think I need to put on more weight?" He'd weighed me at the end of the session. One hundred twenty-seven pounds. Thirteen heavier than when I'd started.

"Destiny is one hundred forty-one pounds" he said. "That's a big difference, but she's still in lightweight class, or thereabouts. You're in the middle of lightweight. You could do to put on another couple of pounds. Lots of protein. Eggs, nuts, meat."

"Great," I said. "More bloody protein. What I wouldn't give for a bowl of chips."

"You can have a few chips, but it's protein you really need. Keep your diet balanced. You need lots of different colors in your food."

"What, like Haribo?"

"Keep your guard up!" he snapped.

"Sorry," I said, lifting my gloves again. I was exhausted. "What does Bonita weigh?"

"One hundred sixty-seven pounds," he said. "She's middleweight. You're twenty-four pounds away from that class."

"And that's why there's no danger of me being allowed in a ring with Bonita?"

"You got it," he said.

"Thank the Lord for that," I said, swinging a punch at him. He dodged it and tapped me on the side of the head.

"Keep your guard up."

TARIK

The next few weeks went by quickly. Senior year was tougher than junior year, but I felt okay about the work. I felt fit and alert. I was sleeping well, and the good exam results had given me confidence. The best thing of all was I'd dropped health class, so I didn't have a class with the Meninists anymore. I still saw them in the corridors from time to time, but they mostly stayed clear since we'd defeated them at Battle. Over the next month I stepped up the training. Dad and I moved our cycle rides to Sunday mornings because it was too dark in the evenings. We'd go out for three hours and try to do more and more each time. After training on Saturdays I'd go for a run with Tarik. It didn't take me long to get to the point where I could keep up with him, and sometimes even managed to say a few words other than "Ugh" or "Oof" or "Stop . . . I'm dying."

On Wednesday nights Ricky took us through a lot of intense pad exercises, then two by two we'd get into the ring with a sparring partner and try to look like boxers. The main problem was that I was always exhausted by this time. It is unbelievably hard to keep your gloves up for three minutes, while circling around dodging and blocking blows from a heavier opponent. Rocky made it look easy. After we'd sparred we were encouraged to watch the others in the ring. Some of them were really good. I winced once when I saw Jerome hit Dan hard right in the head. But Dan kept his feet and returned a couple of hooks to the taller Jerome's midriff. It was possible to get hit hard in the head and not go down, if your legs were strong enough. I liked watching Tarik best. He was silky smooth and always seemed to have enough time to duck a haymaker or block a series of jabs. He never stopped moving, like a shark, and would circle his opponent, waiting patiently for a mistake, then dart in and land a punch or two before backing off again.

As I climbed out of the ring on one of these nights, still panting from my bout with Destiny, Joe hobbled up to me for a little chat.

"All right, Killa?"

"All right, Joe."

"Defensively," he said, "you're doing great. But I don't think I've seen you land one punch in the last three weeks."

I stood and looked back at him, my chest heaving. "It's hard!" I said. "Just blocking is difficult enough."

"Blocking is a lot easier if the other fella's on his back."

"The problem is, every time I try to hit, I drop my guard," I said. "Ricky says I'm better off just blocking for three rounds and losing on points. It's only a demonstration."

"A demonstration of boredom," Joe growled. "You can't always be blocking."

"But Ricky said . . ."

"Forget Ricky," Joe said. "He doesn't know everything. And his first thought is always to protect his fighters. That's okay as far as it goes. But it's your job to ignore him from time to time and do something stupid, you know what I mean?"

"Not really," I said.

"Every now and again," Joe said, "you need to just drop your guard and take a wild swing."

"And risk getting knocked out?"

"Yeah, but risk knocking the other guy out, too."

CAREFUL, NOW

I noticed something odd on Tuesday at school. Or to put it another way, everyone had noticed something about me, oddly. I was used to people ignoring me in the corridors. I was used to teachers ignoring me in the classroom, for that matter. But today as I walked from the LRC down to the cafeteria, I couldn't help but notice loads of people stopped to watch me go by. Conversations dried up as I passed, people ducked out of my way.

It wasn't until I walked past the noticeboard in the lobby that I realized why. There was a large poster stuck up. At the top it read:

BOSFORD BOXING CLUB
YOUTH TOURNAMENT

DECEMBER 8

5 BOYS' BOUTS
2 GIRLS' BOUTS

"Nice work on the apostrophes," I muttered. On one half of the poster was a large photo of Tarik, looking smolderingly mean with his gloves against his chest, where they shouldn't have been. On the other side was a picture of me, trying to look mean, but I remembered when that photo had been taken and I could see the corner of my mouth just starting to twitch up.

"That Lycra is looking quite stretched," Pip said, appearing behind me, making me jump. I remembered I hadn't been wearing my chest protector, and he was right, my boobs were looking larger than I'd ever seen them look.

"Shut up," I snapped. But I looked again. Part of me was mortified, but another shallower part of me thought I actually looked pretty hot.

It was time for English, and Pip and I walked together, him chatting away about some new steampunk album he'd discovered. I wasn't really listening; I was too busy noticing how everyone was giving us a wide berth. Usually walking down a corridor Pip would get shoulder-barged or tripped up three or four times. But today, nothing.

As the weeks went by and the days grew shorter, it started to get dark on Wednesday nights by the time we left the club. Tarik would wait for me and we'd either walk or jog together to the bypass. One Wednesday, in October, he suggested we run a bit farther. "Got to get some miles in the legs," he said.

When Tarik said "a bit farther," I'd assumed he meant around the block a couple of times, but it turned out he meant running to the next town. I was puffed after the first mile, but I could just about keep up with him, as long as I didn't talk. He did all the talking, in fact, and I just grunted and panted at him from time to time to show I was still listening, and indeed still alive.

"God, I miss carbs," he said. "Whey protein, meat, nuts, beans. It all gets so boring after a while. What's your guilty carb pleasure? Pasta, roast potatoes, white bread?"

"Chex mix," I wheezed.

"Oh, Chex mix," he groaned. "I love Chex mix. And kebabs. You like kebabs?"

I grunted in a tone that suggested I loved kebabs only I was having difficulty articulating my interest just then due to being on the verge of coughing up a lung.

"Sometimes after training I walk through Morrison's car park and stop at the Kebab Shack."

"Thought that got closed down," I gasped.

"Oh, look, that happened two years ago," Tarik said, sighing. "And ever since people are all like, 'botulism this, salmonella that.' The point is they do the best lamb kebab this side of Damascus."

"Okay, sorry I mentioned it," I puffed.

"You should come with me one time. I'll buy you a kebab."

I glanced over at him, his olive skin glowing. He ran easily, on springy heels, seemingly tireless. Doner kebabs in Morrison's car park was some distance from worried spinach at the hipster restaurant. But right then it sounded irresistible, botulism and all.

"It's a date," I wheezed.

Tarik carried on talking as we ran. He seemed at ease, his feet padding regularly beside me, in contrast to the heavy, irregular slapping noise mine seemed to be making. After another mile or so I stopped and asked if we could go back. Not in so many words, of course. I mimed it, by collapsing onto the road, clutching my heart and pointing weakly back toward Bosford.

Tarik looked a little alarmed at my condition. He glanced around. "There's a shop over there. Do you need some water?"

"Yes . . . please," I managed to pant. "And . . . a defibrillator . . . if they have one."

1066 AND ALL THAT

On October 14, I missed Saturday training session for the first time in six weeks. And it took a major event to make it happen. As every schoolchild should know, October 14 is the anniversary of the Battle of Hastings, the second most important fight in this country's history, after Cassius Clay versus Henry Cooper in 1963. And my friend Pip was taking part in it. Admittedly, he was fighting on the wrong side, but some things are more important than an existential threat to your entire country. Friendship is one of those things, and for this day only, I'd be cheering for the French.

Blossom and I were in full costume, including wimples, which I was glad of because it was a chilly autumn day. The leaves on the trees in Pip's Wood were a hundred shades, from still vivid green to russet brown. We had arrived early as there was a lot of preparation. This wasn't a typical reenactment, with a couple of dozen soldiers on each side. This was the main event, with reenactment enthusiasts coming from all over the country. The battlefield was teeming with actors in full armor and

American tourists taking photos. Blossom and I made a small fortune in tips by curtsying all over the place and adopting a sort of bogus cheeky Cockney repartee, which seemed to go down well. "Bless me wimple, ma'am, I'm proper honored to be pulling yer ruby. Apples and pears and a good old knees up."

We made rush lights and baskets, whittled willy-spoons and told tales of life in the eleventh century. These were almost entirely made up and included a story about how William ate a macrobiotic diet, used to spend hours playing a primitive version of foosball, and liked to dress up as a nun on religious holidays. When it was finally time for the battle itself we were pretty shattered, but Garnet had told us we had to narrate the battle for the benefit of the tourists. A crowd of people gathered around.

"Cor blimey, guv. It was a day just like today," Blossom began. "A thousand years ago and fifty. When William came to this place, to fight for the greatest prize, the very crown of England."

As she spoke, we watched William's men form up at the bottom of the hill: there must have been well over a hundred, far more than usual, and at least twenty horses. I could make out Pip, gangling and hanging back, his height marking him out. I felt a heavy lump in my stomach. I so wanted this to work out for him. The Saxon numbers were swelled, too, maybe a hundred and fifty in the shield wall, reflecting the superior strength of Harold's troops on the day itself.

Blossom was hissing at me. "Your turn."

"And so the two sides stood a-facing each other, arr," I cried, before realizing that I'd somehow found myself talking like a Cornish pirate. But I'd started, so I had to carry on. "But who was to begin the fight? William's minstrel took that honor. A man named Taillefer, who rode alone hard at the Saxon lines, sang rude songs at them and juggled his sword, before dropping his breeches, bending over and showing them the full moon. So it be."

A little boy in the front row grinned in delight at this revelation.

"But Taillefer was soon cut down by a hail of arrows, arr."

The little boy's face crumpled.

Just then we heard Garnet cry "CHARGE!" and we turned to see the Normans come thundering up the hill. I stopped talking as my heart leaped into my mouth. There was Pip, charging: no longer at the back, he was running, sprinting almost, his shield held high, swinging his sword around his head. I fancied I could hear his roar as he came charging. It was a new Pip. A powerful, purposeful, elegant Pip who I scarcely recognized.

Closer and closer came the Normans, as the Saxons ducked down behind the shield wall. Surely they couldn't resist this onslaught?

And then with a crash and a clatter the Norman knights pounded like a wave against the Saxon wall. In an instant the charge was snuffed out, stopped, just as it had been a thousand years before. We heard the clash and clang of swords as the two opposing sides swung at each other. The little boy next to me shrieked in excitement. It looked frighteningly real, and I suddenly had a surge of fear for Pip. Where was he?

"I can't see him!" Blossom cried. I stood with her on the crate and we squinted to see.

"Come on, Pip," I shouted.

"Has he gone down?" Blossom asked. "He'll be crushed. Is he on the ground?"

"I don't know," I said. *Oh God*, I thought. *Poor Pip.*

"Oh wait," Blossom said. "There he is."

I turned to look. Pip had dropped his sword and shield and was running, stumbling toward his safe space.

"Ahem." One of the tourists coughed and suddenly I remembered we were supposed to be commentating.

"But William's shield wall held," I said. "The Saxons fought with such resolve that, err, some of the Normans turned and fled. Arr."

"They're chasing him," Blossom cried. It was true; a detachment of Saxon warriors had broken out of the shield wall and in their excitement were pursuing poor old Pip toward the woods, waving their swords excitedly. Pip turned to see them and squealed in terror. Back at the main battle, the Normans charged again, concentrating their forces on the gap in the shield wall. I could hear Harold screaming at his troops to close up the gap, but it was too late.

"They've broken through!" someone cried. And he was right. Just as in the actual battle, the shield wall had failed when overexcited Saxon churls chased after fleeing Norman soldiers. Now that the invaders had the upper ground and were surrounding the Saxons, the Normans quickly overran Harold's defenses. Harold was located and cut down by a detachment of knights, and the rest of the Saxon troops ran for the safety of the woods, or the tearoom. William had won the day.

"All thanks to the clever soldier who *pretended* to run away," Blossom explained to the cheering observers. "He tricked the Saxon defenders into breaking up the wall. And the rest is history."

"That it be!" I cried, and received a smattering of applause.

Blossom held out her pinafore and curtsied as people threw coins. And that was that. I think it all happened a bit quicker than had been anticipated; the entire battle had only lasted less than an hour, but it had started to rain and frankly everyone was ready for a Bakewell tart.

DOWN FOR THE COUNT

Next Saturday, Sharon pulled me aside. "We got LOADS of girls on Thursday night," she said excitedly. "It's all because of the newspaper story, and your photo."

"How many?" I asked.

"Twelve," Sharon said. "We turned a profit for the first time. If this keeps up, we'll be able to start paying off the loan. We won't have to close."

"That's brilliant," I said.

"And the newspaperman said he'd come along to the tournament and write a follow-up piece about it. I think he might want to ask you some questions, if that's okay?"

"Me? Why would he be interested in me?"

"Why wouldn't he be interested in you?" Sharon replied. "You've come on so well since you started. You're fitter, stronger, more disciplined. More confident. You're a role model."

"I'm a role model?" I echoed, incredulous.

"Why not?" Sharon said, laughing. "When you arrived you used to slink around like a shadow, hardly saying a word. Now you're standing straighter, asking questions, getting involved. Always in the middle of everything."

"God, I sound really annoying."

"Not at all," she laughed. "You just give as good as you get. Never mind the fight, you're already a winner, and the journalist can see that in you."

"Yeah, but will he still see that when Destiny knocks my block off?"

"That's not going to happen," Sharon said. "Ricky would never let you fight if he didn't think you were ready."

I frowned.

"You're not thinking of backing out, are you?" she asked, suddenly worried.

"No," I said. "I'm definitely in."

"And what about the interview, will you do that?"

"I will," I said. "On one condition."

"What's that?" she asked, hope in her eyes.

"That I get control of the playlist."

"What's wrong with my playlist?" Ricky asked fiercely.

"It's dire," I said. "Too slow. I mean, what's this song playing at the moment?"

"It's Simon and Garfunkel," he said. "You don't know this?"

"I know it makes me want to hang myself with my wraps."

"It's inspiring!" he said, genuinely surprised. "Uplifting. Doesn't it make your heart bleed?"

"No, it makes my ears bleed. Why did you put this on the playlist?"

"It's called 'The Boxer,'" he said. "It's about *boxing*."

"It's about a *failed* boxer," I said, mimicking his inflection. "Who's on the verge of *suicide*." He paused for a second, giving me the eye of the tiger. I stared right back. Then he cracked and grinned.

"If you fight that hard over a bloody playlist," he said, "then I wouldn't want to face you in the ring."

Tarik stayed late that night to work on some technical issue with Ricky, so I prepared to walk home on my own. I'd take the long route and avoid Gladwell's. But as I left, Bonita came barreling out and fell into step beside me.

"Good sesh," she said.

"Yeah, you trained hard," I said. "Not walking home with the other girls?"

"Nah," she said. "They're chatting up Jerome."

"Both of them?"

"Yeah, it might get ugly. I don't think he likes either of them. Not like that."

"Oh dear." I grinned. "Well, anyway." I made as if to peel off to the left. "See ya next time."

"Where you going?" Bonita said. She pointed toward the Gladwell Estate. "You'll wanna go this way to get to the bypass?"

"Yeah, I was going to . . ." I stopped. It'd be all right the two of us together. No one was going to give Bonita a hard time. "Okay, let's head this way."

Into the Valley of Death walked the two. "Great that

you're going to be fighting in the tournament," she said. "Destiny's really looking forward to it."

"Yeah, well. I guess it'll be fine. Ricky did say we should be careful not to be too aggressive."

"Sod that," Bonita said. "I'm going to hit Taylor so hard her kids'll be dizzy."

"It's just that Ricky wants us to demonstrate that boxing is a safe sport. . . ."

"No one's safe in the ring with me," Bonita said.

"You only have one setting, don't you?" I said, exasperated. "You are the most competitive person I've ever come across."

"Boxing is competitive," she said, shrugging. "Life is competitive."

"But boxing isn't a violent sport; people aren't really trying to actually hurt each other," I said. "It's actually quite cerebral, don't you think? Like chess?"

"What are you talking about?" Bonita growled. "Of course it's violent. And by the way, if you and I were playing chess, I'd pick up the board and smash you around the cerebrals with it."

I sighed. Someone shouted in the distance and I shivered. It was cold tonight and I was damp with sweat.

"My mum told me that you don't get anything if you don't fight for it," Bonita went on. "And I have three older brothers who are actual seagulls in human form. If I didn't learn how to fight I'd have starved." I glanced over at her and reflected that she must have learned to fight really well. Bonita was solid muscle. In fact I felt a little sorry for those brothers.

"Don't you think, though, that it's important to show

other women that boxing isn't necessarily dangerous? And that it can be fun?"

Bonita thought about this for a while. "No," she said. "I don't. I think women are just as good as men and we should show them that." Suddenly she stopped. "This is the one thing I don't like about you, Fleur. You think everyone can get on and be nice and not have to fight for anything. And that's fine for you, because you're clever, and you're pretty and you live in a nice area."

"That's not how I think," I said. "What would you know about me anyway?"

"I know that if I had your brains, and your looks and your opportunities," she said, "I wouldn't waste them."

Bonita didn't move an inch as we stood glaring at each other. We were in front of a grimy little house, lit by a harsh orange streetlight, with a disassembled motorbike in the front yard and a moldy pumpkin on the step. I didn't like to stop here. I could hear boys shouting in the darkness; someone went by on a bike without lights. I shivered, wanting to get the hell away from the estate.

"Come on," I said. "Let's get out of this dump."

"That's it?" she said, shaking her head. "You're not going to yell back at me? Call me names? Tell me to stick it?"

I shook my head. "No. Not everything has to be a fight. I think women should work together. Now, are you coming?"

"No," she said.

"Why not? Because I won't fight you?"

"No," she said, pointing to the horrible house behind her. "Because I live here. In this dump."

The door slammed behind her and I was left alone, in the middle of the Gladwell Estate. At night. I looked around nervously. The body heat I'd built up during training had faded now and I could feel the cold. My hoodie was damp. I heard someone shouting in the distance and I could see that the boy who'd cycled by before had stopped under a streetlight a hundred yards down the road. For a moment I considered banging on Bonita's door. I could call Dad and ask him to come and collect me.

"Come on, Fleur," I muttered to myself. "Stop being so wet. It's West Bosford, not Mogadishu." I put my hood up, wondering if I could disguise myself as a Gladwell's resident. But then I pulled it back down and took a deep breath. *Face your fears, Fleur. You are strong, you are confident, you are disciplined.*

I remembered what Sharon had said about me standing taller, and thought of how people had started to look at me in the corridors at school. Like someone you don't mess with. I walked down Carter Way, then turned onto Hutton Close and cut through onto Belham Street, which has a real reputation in Bosford. Mum calls it Bedlam Street. Someone was stabbed there last year.

I passed a few people: a couple of teenage girls who ignored me, a tired-looking mum pushing a stroller, who I thought I recognized from the junior session at the boxing club. A man walking on his own who didn't even look at me. I turned onto Queen Elizabeth Street, which took me all the way up to the bypass. I could even see the traffic lights in the distance. I was nearly there. But then, halfway down the street I saw a gang of boys hanging about a bus stop. One circled lazily on a tiny bike; another was smoking. I breathed in deeply and walked on, refusing to cross the road. They looked up as I approached and one flicked a butt, which arced past right in front of me, like the world's worst firework.

"Hey, you got a cigarette?" he called out softly. I stopped and turned.

"Sorry," I said. "Don't smoke." I walked on, my heart thumping. This was it; this was the moment they'd come running after me.

But they didn't. Maybe it was to do with the way I carried myself. With confidence. Without showing how scared I was. I didn't want to be scared anymore.

OUTLIERS

On Wednesday we were standing around, waiting for Ricky to finish fussing about with the bolts on the ring and come and start the session. I was excited because I'd finally completed the new playlist and it was cued up and ready to go.

"I'm rubbish at organizing things," Dan was moaning.

"What are you trying to organize?" I asked.

"My stag do," he said.

"But that's on Friday," I said. "You haven't organized it yet?" He shook his head. "And I thought the best man was supposed to organize the stag do?"

"Yeah, but it's Jerome," he said. We looked over at

Jerome, who was currently filling in his bicep tattoo with a red pen.

"So just go to Brighton," I said. "Start at the pier and see what happens."

"Can't go to Brighton because Simon isn't allowed to leave the Bosford area," Dan said.

"So what are you going to do?" I asked.

"Well," he said, looking at his shoes. "I wondered if you might be able to arrange something."

"Me?"

"Yeah, you're all organized and that. You know, classy."

"Oh, err," I said. "Thank you?"

"Nothing cultural," he added quickly.

"No, I wouldn't do that," I said. "Somehow I can't see Jerome enjoying a new installation at Bosford Beaux Arts Center."

"No," Dan agreed. "His idea of culture is watching French porn."

"Right, before we get started," Ricky shouted. "Quick announcement. It's Dan's stag do on Friday, and he's asked me to tell you that you're all invited. Boys and girls."

I felt a twinge of disappointment to hear that the other girls had been invited, too. I thought I was the chosen one, sneaking into the boys' tent.

"Unfortunately," Ricky went on, "I will not be able to attend. I want you all to have a good time. You've been training hard. But at the same time, don't be stupid. Don't drink too much too fast, understand?"

"Yes, Ricky."

"Understand?"

"YES, COACH RICKY."

"Don't want anyone ending up in jail," he said. "Or going back to jail," he added, glaring at Simon. "Now, let's get moving. I want you to work hard today, people. Train hard, fight easy." He reached over and hit play on the stereo. I hopped up and down in excitement as the opening minor chords of the first song of my playlist jangled out.

"Oh, I love this!" Jerome cried.

Ricky looked dumbfounded. "What is it?" he asked me.

" 'Kung Fu Fighting,' " I said.

"That's not boxing!" he cried. "Do I look like bloody Bruce Lee?"

I grinned. "My playlist, my rules." Grumpily, Ricky started the warm-ups and everyone got into it. It was good to have some lively music for a change. It made a difference, and I could see everyone was up for it tonight. We were dripping by the third song.

"Sweat is your fat crying," Ricky shouted.

"Well, then I reckon my fat's just had a messy breakup," Destiny puffed next to me.

Ricky stalked over to me after the session. "Look," he said. "Dan tells me you're in charge of this little shindig on Friday."

"Apparently so," I replied. "I thought I'd reserve some tables at Chickos? The boys can have a beer and we can all have something to eat. They've got a hot wing special."

"If you ask my advice," Ricky said, frowning, "you

should organize some kind of other activity, just so they're not drinking steadily for six hours."

"Other than hot wings?"

"Yes, other than hot wings. Can you just keep an eye on things? Make sure no one gets into trouble."

"Oh, come on, Ricky," Sharon said. "They're good lads."

"It's not the lads I'm worried about," Ricky said, looking over at Bonita and Taylor, who were wrestling each other. They crashed heavily into the old piano, which gave out a plaintive chord of protest.

"And make sure Simon gets back home for his curfew," Ricky said.

"When is it?"

"Midnight," Ricky said. "If he breaches his probation I lose one of my best boxers. If anyone gets into a fight, then I could lose my license."

"No pressure then," I said.

"I'm not expecting you to be a nursemaid," Ricky said. "Just be the voice of reason, okay?"

Hmmm. Me, the voice of reason? That was a first.

START SPREADING
THE NEWS

When I got to Chickos on Friday, I found Jerome, Simon and Dan were already there, each halfway through a pint.

"You started early," I said.

"Lot to get through," Jerome replied.

"Are you supposed to be drinking?" I asked Simon. "You know, with that." I pointed to his ankle.

"It's an electronic tag," he replied, "not a Breathalyzer. As long as I'm home by midnight, then we're cool."

"Okay, Cinderella," I said. "Tonight I'll be your fairy godmother. I'll make sure you get home in time, but in return, you have to leave when I say, all right?"

"Yeah, yeah, sure," he said, finishing his pint and waving for the drinks guy. "Who's for another?"

"I'm serious," I said. "Ricky gave me strict instructions to keep an eye on all of you, but especially you. He doesn't want to lose any fighters."

"Don't worry," Simon said, grinning at me and showing a couple of missing teeth. "I'll be a good boy."

I can't believe how much boys drink. I thought George and his mates drank a lot, but the boxing lads made them look like the Salvation Army. They were on their fourth pints and talking very loudly by the time anyone else turned up.

It didn't help that today, for some reason, we had two very attentive drinks waiters. They're like buses. They all turn up when you don't need them. They set up a sort of relay system, bringing trays full of huge foaming glasses of beer.

No one ordered hot wings. Just beer. Lots and lots and lots of beer. I thought time had slowed. It seemed to take forever before it was time to go to Tone Def karaoke. And then it took even longer to round everyone up and get them to finish their drinks. I'd get a few of them organized and with coats on, then go off and find the others. Then when I got back to the first group I'd find they'd sent the drinks waiter off again for "one last round."

But eventually, with Tarik's help, I got everyone out and down the street. Destiny and Taylor had already been a bit drunk when they arrived and they were now stumbling along behind us, shrieking loudly. It was nine p.m., and I think Tarik and I were the only sober people within twenty miles.

We all crowded into a booth. I'd booked the largest one as there were twenty-two of us. Most of the people from the boxing club, plus one or two workmates of Dan's, plus some random girl who we didn't really know, though Destiny said she thought her name was Fran.

There was another drinks service, but I had a word with the waitress. "Could you take your time bringing the drinks?" I asked. "Some of the boys have been going for it, and I want to slow things down a little if possible. Could you bring some water, too, please?"

"Water?" the waitress replied, as though I'd asked her for a bucket of spit. But she duly came in with a jug just as the opening chords to "(Is This the Way to) Amarillo?" started playing on the karaoke machine.

"Good idea bringing them to karaoke," Tarik said, appearing behind me. "They need something to focus on other than drinking."

"Are you not having a beer?" I asked him.

"I've had one or two," he said. "But I don't want to have too much. I'm in training."

"Me too," I said, and was about to ask how he was feeling about the tournament when Bonita grabbed Tarik and pulled him away to sing. I saw Destiny and Taylor on either side of Jerome, trying to persuade him to sing with them.

"I can't sing," he said. "I can't sing."

"Get him another drink," Destiny said. "Where's that waitress?" I started to feel quite pleased with myself as the session went on. The drinking must have slowed. The boys were either singing or flicking through the playlist, looking for inspiration. None of them could sing, except Dan, a bit. And Bonita, of course, who was good at everything, and seemed to know all the words to every Beyoncé song ever.

"Have a go," Bonita said, thrusting the microphone into my hand when she'd finished.

"Oh no, no," I said. "(A) I can't sing, and (B) I'm not drunk." But it was too late.

"Kill-a, Kill-a, Kill-a!" everyone chanted. My eyes flicked to the screen in a panic and I saw the song cued was Tina Turner's "Simply the Best." The intro played out and I started singing.

And you know what? I wasn't too bad. The music was loud and there was a faint backing track to help me get in key. And it's not the hardest song to sing, especially when everyone joins in on the chorus. I shut my eyes and got into it after a bit—I didn't even need the lyrics. When I opened my eyes again I saw Tarik watching me, a smile on his face. Apparently I'm not only a brilliant boxer and cyclist. I also totally rock at . . . well, rock.

Then it all went wrong, because my eyes flicked to the left and I saw Jerome holding a bottle of Jägermeister, pouring it into Simon's plastic water cup.

"You're simply the . . . WHAT THE HELL ARE YOU DOING?"

Jerome looked up, startled. "The waitress is taking forever," he shouted back as strobe lights played across his face. "We were thirsty."

The session finished at ten thirty p.m., but it took nearly twenty minutes to get everyone out of the booth and down onto the street.

"What's the plan?" Simon asked me, swaying a little.

"The others are going to Lick'd," I said. "But you're going home."

"What!" he cried. "I can't go home. It's early. It's Jerome's STAG DO! He's my best mate!"

"It's Dan's stag do," I corrected him.

"He's my best mate, too," Simon told me, less convincingly. The others were trailing off down the street, arm in arm. Dan staggering a little. Destiny and Taylor escorting Jerome. Fran tottering along behind on a pair of high heels.

"Look, by the time we queue, and you go downstairs and get a drink, it'll be time to leave," I said. I was ready to go home, too. I'd done my bit, and hanging around drunk people when you're completely sober isn't exactly the best fun in the world. "And you still have to walk home. I really think you should go now."

"No way," he shouted, and ran off down the street, his tag flashing as it reflected the streetlights.

"Simon!" I shouted. And then I ran after him.

It was very, very loud in the club. It was also dark, with vomit-green laser lights flashing back and forth and a black light somewhere that showed off everyone's dandruff. I wandered around, unable to find anyone in the crowd.

I found one of the dance floors, where some thumping drum and bass track rattled my fillings. I saw Chris dancing with Fran. And there were Alex and Jordan, and over on the other side were Destiny and Taylor with their hands all over poor Jerome.

"WANN' DANCE?" a man screamed in my ear.

"Trust me," I replied, shaking my head. "You don't want me to dance." He shrugged and walked off. Behind him I saw Tarik leaning against a brick pillar, Bonita facing him and talking. Their faces were very, very close together.

"Okay," I said, and turned away. I had far more important things to worry about than Tarik and Bonita. Then I saw him, Simon. He was across the dance floor, with one of Dan's work colleagues. Matt? Stan? Something like that. They each had a fresh pint. I darted across the floor, dodged through the swirling dancers and slid up beside Simon.

"Finish that and then we've got to go," I shouted.

"I've only just got here," he said. I showed him the time on my phone. 11:18 p.m.

"I've still got an hour," he said.

"You still have to get home," I reminded him. I looked up to see Jerome, backing away from Destiny, crash into another girl and knock her over. Instantly, the girl's dance partner leaped forward and shoved Jerome in the chest.

"Oh bollocks," I said. I was sure Jerome was going to hit the bloke. I was just about to rush forward and put myself between them when Jerome held up his hands in apology.

"Sorry, mate," I saw him mouth. He reached out a hand to help the girl up, and she nodded in thanks.

Jerome said something else, I guessed offering to buy them a drink, but the couple shook their heads and moved to the other side of the dance floor.

"I thought he was going to hit that bloke," I shouted into Simon's ear. Simon shook his head.

"Jerome wouldn't do that. None of us would. Just not worth it."

"Do you mind me asking . . ." I began, before stalling.

"How I got my tag?" he replied. "Not by fighting. Me and some mates took a car. Just a bit of fun. Got me on CCTV."

"Oh," I said, not knowing what else to say.

"I didn't even know they had CCTV in Plimpton."

"Why were you in Plimpton?" I asked.

"That's where I live," he said.

"What?! Plimpton is twelve miles away."

"I know."

"I thought you lived in Gladwell's. . . ."

He shook his head. I took his beer from him, put it down on a table and grabbed him by the lapels. He was seven inches taller than me and about thirty pounds heavier. But just at that moment he looked a bit scared.

"We have got to leave now," I said clearly. "And I mean RIGHT. NOW."

For a moment, it looked like he was going to protest, but then he looked into my eyes and apparently realized I meant business. "Okay," he said. Holding him by the arm in case he changed his mind, I marched him out of the club and up the stairs.

"It'll be all right as long as we can get a cab," I said, mostly to reassure myself.

NEED FOR SPEED

There were no cabs. "They don't like to come here," the bouncer explained. "There's usually trouble."

I walked up and down the street. "Might as well pop back in for another one," Simon said hopefully. He didn't seem concerned at all. I looked at my phone again. "We have thirty-three minutes to get you home," I said. "Or else your tag will explode, or whatever."

"Don't worry," he said, sitting down on the steps in front of Bosford Brazilian Tanning Salon and inspecting the tag. "I think I know how to disable it."

"DON'T try and disable it," I yelled.

"Well, what else are we going to do?" he said.

"Don't worry," I said. "I think I've got a plan."

Twelve minutes later a tiny white Clio chugged down South Street and slowly mounted the curb, sending Lick'd's bouncer diving for cover. It lurched to a stop in front of us. Pip grinned at me from the driver's seat. He was wearing an aviator hat and goggles.

"Get in," I said to Simon.

"A Clio?" he spat.

"Oi!" the bouncer yelled, getting to his feet and looking furious. I shoved Simon into the backseat and clambered into the front passenger seat. I put on my seat belt, then turned to look Pip in the eye.

"You have fifteen minutes to get us to Plimpton. For this one night only, you must drive as you've never driven before. Tonight, Pip, you must drive at the speed limit."

"Got it!" Pip said. As the bouncer appeared at the window, Pip gently pressed his foot down on the accelerator. The Clio bumped off the curb. I studiously ignored the bouncer, who was now tapping on the window and following as we moved sedately down the street.

Simon coughed politely in the backseat. "Do you think we could maybe, you know, speed up a bit?"

"Yes, maybe a little," I agreed as the bouncer bashed on the glass and shouted something unrepeatable. Pip swallowed nervously and sped up. The bouncer fell behind and we reached the intersection. Pip turned left.

"Why are you going this way?" I asked.

"I don't know where Plimpton is," Pip replied.

"The other way, the other way," I said. Pip spun the wheel, and the tires squeaked as we turned. Then he pressed down on the accelerator again and we were off in roughly the right direction.

"Seriously, though," I said, glancing at the clock on the dashboard. "You're going to need to speed up a little bit."

"I'm nearly at the speed limit now!" he cried, beads of sweat appearing on his forehead. But he pressed harder on the accelerator, and the needle crept up into uncharted territory. Simon did most of the navigation, asking why Pip was going so slowly from time to time. But I knew that for Pip, this was the equivalent of Jason Bourne driving a Mini the wrong way around the Périphérique. He even went through some yellow lights and actually did go the wrong way around a roundabout at Telham, though I think that was just from general confusion rather than a deliberate attempt to speed up our progress.

"Made it!" Simon cried from the back as we groaned to a stop in front of a block of flats. I got out and turned to drag Simon out as well. He gave me a massive bear hug.

"You're brilliant, Fleur," he said. "I love you."

"All right, all right," I said. "I love you, too; now get inside and sleep it off."

He bent over and leaned in through the window of the Clio to look at Pip.

"Jenson Button," he said, then belched loudly. We watched him swaying and staggering as he walked up to his door, fumbling with the keys. As he clomped inside and slammed the door closed behind him, I checked my phone. 11:58. A weight lifted from my shoulders. Mission accomplished. I got back in the car and gave Pip a squeeze.

"You're a hero," I said.

"I know. Where now?"

I really wanted to go home.

"I'd better go back to the club," I said. "Make sure no one else is in any trouble."

"You got it," Pip said.

"No hurry this time," I said. "You can stop for yellows."

THIS IS A DISASTER!

Pip parked around the corner from Lick'd and said he'd wait. Luckily, the bouncer he'd nearly killed wasn't on duty anymore. It was another bloke, equally huge, and he waved me in. "Has anyone punched anyone else?" I asked Tarik downstairs. I couldn't see Bonita, but Chris and Fran were snogging by the cigarette machine.

"No," he said. But just at that moment we heard a shrill scream and a crash from the dance floor. We ran. Destiny was on the back of the man who had threatened Jerome earlier. Broken glass lay glinting on the floor. The man's girlfriend grabbed hold of Destiny and pulled her off. The girls tumbled to the floor, grappling each other while Jerome stood by, looking helpless.

I rushed forward. Part of me knew I shouldn't get involved, but I was thinking maybe I could stop the fight before it got out of hand. Unfortunately, before I could get there, Taylor waded into the mess and punched the man, who went down like a sack of bricks. Destiny and the girlfriend were still on the floor, scratching and kicking. Then the bouncer from earlier appeared. He grabbed Taylor and Destiny and bundled them out.

"She started it!" Destiny roared, pointing back at the girl Taylor had punched. I saw the poor girl had a bloody nose. The bouncer ignored Destiny and dragged her and Taylor bodily up the stairs.

I groaned. This was a disaster.

"This is a disaster," Ricky said. "I just don't know what we're going to do." He looked as dispirited as Tyson Fury's PR manager. Ricky had thrown Destiny and Taylor out of the club. Or more accurately, they were "suspended pending an internal investigation," as Ricky had told the Boxing Federation people.

"This is worse than that bit in *Rocky IV* when Rocky finds out Adrian isn't going to Russia with him," I said.

"Not everything in life has a metaphor in a *Rocky* film," Tarik said.

"You're so wrong," I told him.

"Never mind all that," Ricky said. "What are we going to do? We've currently got no women's fights. Fleur and Bonita are in different classes. And the tournament is in two weeks. We've sold loads of tickets to women, and all the Thursday night ladies will be there and they want to see you girls box. I've got the newspaper guy coming, hoping to write a big story." He lowered his head into his hands and shook it, groaning softly.

"Can't you give them another chance?" I said. "You gave me a second chance when I punched the rapist."

"That was different, Fleur," he said in a muffled voice, not lifting his head. "You weren't brawling in a nightclub like a couple of badgers. You hit a bloke who was physically harassing you. It was self-defense."

"I KNOW. I believe I told you that at the time!" I said, getting cross before I remembered this wasn't actually about me.

"What about some of the Thursday ladies?" Coach Alex suggested. "Are any of them up for a fight? Shouldn't be a weight problem with that lot."

"There's no time," Ricky said. "Even if they did want to fight, it'll take at least four months to get them ready to box properly. I won't let anyone fight if they're not ready."

"What about other clubs?" I suggested. "Hastings? Brighton? Do they have women boxers?"

"I've been phoning around for the last hour," Sharon said. "No luck. The only club in Sussex that is currently training women for fighting is Lewes, and none of them are available."

"Not Brighton?" I asked. Sharon shook her head.

"None of them ready for a bout. You're a rare breed. I can keep calling clubs farther away . . ."

"No one's gonna be available at such short notice," Ricky said, shaking his head. "Especially a few weeks before Christmas. We have to bite the bullet and let everyone know the girls' matches are off. Give people refunds if they want."

"We can't afford that," Sharon said. "We need that revenue."

"We don't have a choice," Ricky said. A heavy silence fell across the group.

"Unless . . ." a voice piped up. "Unless . . . well, there might be a way." Everyone looked hopefully at the person who had spoken up. Which, rather surprisingly, turned out to be me.

"Unless . . . I fight against Bonita," I said. Ricky's shoulders slumped again and he shook his head.

"Look," I said. "This is my fault. I was supposed to keep everyone out of trouble. Now it's up to me to fix it."

"I told you, Fleur," Ricky said. "You're thirteen pounds too light. I can't allow it, even as a demonstration bout."

"We have two weeks. How much jerky would I need to eat to put on thirteen pounds in two weeks?"

"Half a cow?" Tarik suggested.

"It's not just a question of weight," Ricky said. "Bonita is taller than you. She has a longer reach."

"Are you saying I'm not good enough?"

"She's good enough," someone called. We all looked over to the door to see Joe, who'd just come in. "She could take down the big girl. They don't call her Killa for nothing."

"I don't want anyone taking anyone down," Ricky said. *Good luck explaining that to Bonita*, I thought. "Fleur, the question is, can you keep your guard up for three rounds?"

I licked my lips, which had suddenly become very dry. "Yes," I said, even though the correct answer was *probably not*. Ricky didn't say anything. He just looked at me. Judging me. *Appraising* me. He looked over at Sharon, who nodded. He looked at Tarik, who gave a thumbs-up, sending a thrill through me.

"You're going to have to train like you've never trained before," he said.

"Not a problem."

"You're going to have to focus like you've never focused before."

"Not a problem."

"You're going to have to eat like you've never eaten before."

"Definitely not a problem," I said, nodding briskly.

SHOW ME THE JERKY

Every morning my alarm went off at seven a.m. I got up, had a protein shake with fruit and did a half hour of weights. Then I ate some chicken and nuts. I know, right? For breakfast? Then I ran to school, sometimes diving into a hedge as Pip chugged by, Blossom waving at me through the rear window. I showered at school. I had a packet of cashews in my pocket and would sneak them into my mouth when the teacher wasn't looking.

I ate two lunches and snacked on jerky in the afternoon. After school I'd run back home again, eat a pork pie and get on the exercise bike in the garage. While cycling I'd listen to music on my headphones and fuel myself with slices of buttered bread.

Dinner was the big problem. I didn't want to tell Mum I was now eating as much as a juvenile orca, and she still kept giving me bird portions. I could see her watching as I inhaled the meager offerings she kept serving up and looked around hopefully for more. Because here's the thing: I was hungry ALL THE TIME. Luckily I had my stash of food in the bedroom and I spent a lot of time up there "studying"—i.e. stuffing my face with Scotch eggs.

The only let-up in the routine was Friday night and the Bluebell Road Film Club. I skipped training for the night and took some whey protein and a pack of jerky over to Blossom's, even though it was her turn to choose a film. She handed me the case when I arrived. I stared at it.

"*Creed*?"

"*Rocky VII*," she said.

"Are you sure?" I asked. "I thought you wanted to watch *Dance of the Sixth Daughter*?"

"Too long," she said.

"What about *Winds from the Red Steppes*?"

"Too boring."

"Or *Silent Women of the Jasmine River*?"

"No such film."

"Fine, then." I flashed her a smile. "*Creed* it is."

After a week I was looking pretty ripped. I was developing a proper six-pack. But I wasn't putting on enough weight. I'd only gained four pounds. I had another nine to go. I went for a weigh-in on Saturday. Ricky shook his head. "This isn't going to work."

"She needs Bulkup," Joe said, rubbing the back of his stubbled scalp.

Ricky frowned.

"What's Bulkup?" I asked.

"It's calories in a can," Ricky said. "Useful for putting on weight quickly. You'd need a lot of it, though . . ."

Oh my God! Bulkup is disgusting. Cloying, sickly sweet with just a hint of toxic sludge. I started reading through the ingredients but got scared after a few minutes. I just concentrated on the one slightly positive piece of advertising on the front of the tub, which said *New Flavor: Strawberry!* I mixed it with full-fat milk, drank a glass and felt immediately bloated. I went and looked at myself in the mirror, wiping the pink goo off my cheek. What on earth was I doing? Deliberately putting on weight, exhausting myself daily, spending all my savings, just so I could get into the ring with a girl who wanted to tear my head off and shout insults down the neck hole.

I must be absolutely crazy.

BUSTED

"Can you stay a bit later tonight?" Ricky asked me at the drinks break on Wednesday night. This would be my last day of training. Ricky had said I'd need to rest for the next couple of days and concentrate on putting on an extra four pounds. I was doubtful it was physically possible, but Ricky said he had a few tricks up his sleeve.

When the session finished, I hung around, slowly stretching, waiting for the others to leave. Bonita had cornered Tarik again in the kitchen and the two of them were laughing over something. I just wanted to get home. I was hungry and I'd only brought half a packet of jerky, which I'd nearly finished. Eventually, Bonita abandoned the kitchen and came over.

"You wanna walk back together?" she asked. Since Bonita had learned I was going to fight, she'd become slightly more human, if not exactly friendly.

"I can't, I need to talk to Ricky about something," I said. Bonita glanced suspiciously over at Ricky, then back at me. It didn't really seem fair that Ricky was giving me extra attention, but the bout couldn't go ahead if he wasn't satisfied with me. She shrugged and walked out.

"Right," Ricky said as soon as it was just me and Tarik left. "Get in the ring, you two."

"Why?" Tarik said.

"Fleur's nearly ready," Ricky said. "But there's one thing she needs. And you're going to give it to her."

"Shouldn't he buy me dinner first?" I asked.

"You got time to make jokes, you got time for ten push-ups," Ricky said. I sighed and dropped to the floor. Tarik dropped down beside me in solidarity. After I'd finished, I stood there puffing as Ricky explained what he wanted.

"There's a good chance that in the ring, Bonita will smack you one right in the chops," he said.

"Thanks for the vote of confidence," I said.

"Being hit in the head is not fun, but it happens, and you need to be ready for it. You need to know what it feels like, then you'll be able to deal with it in the fight itself."

"I've been hit before," I said. "Destiny lamped me, remember? And Joe."

"Being hit by someone your own size is one thing," Ricky said, frowning. "Being hit by someone bigger and stronger . . ."

"Wait a minute," I said. "I can see where this is heading. You want Tarik to punch me in the face."

"Yes," Ricky said. "He's about the same weight as Bonita, same height, same reach. I want you two to spar a bit, and Fleur, I want you to drop your guard and open yourself up to him."

I looked over at Tarik. Put it that way and it didn't sound too bad.

Tarik and I circled, gloves up, watching carefully, each waiting for the other to make the first move. Tarik stepped toward me and I jumped back. Then I shuffled forward and he retreated. All the while our gazes were locked together. His brown eyes were dark and endless. But this wasn't the time to be noticing things like that.

"Hit her," Ricky said.

He pushed out a glove. I gently tapped it away.

"Not like that. Thump her!"

Tarik tried a right hook, but so slowly and softly I just pulled back and let it brush past my chest harmlessly.

"All right, so he won't hit you. Fleur, you hit him. See if that gets him moving."

I swallowed and stepped forward, jabbing lightly, without properly extending. I didn't want to hit him.

"PROPERLY!" Ricky roared. I tried an uppercut,

the punch that Joe had said was my killer. But I didn't hit hard, and telegraphed it a little, giving Tarik the chance to block, which he did easily.

"She's open!" Ricky cried, and I realized he was right, I'd dropped my guard, but Tarik didn't take the bait. In fact he dropped his gloves and stepped back.

"I don't want to hit her," Tarik said. He turned and began unwrapping his gloves.

"Fine," Ricky said, grabbing his own gloves. "I'll do it!" He clambered into the ring, and my heart lurched in alarm. Ricky was twice the size of Tarik. His arms were like tree branches, his legs like trunks.

"It's all right," he said, getting into his stance. "I won't hit you hard. Now try and take a swing at me." I took a deep breath and hesitated. But then shrugged. If I was ever going to get home and eat something, I needed to get this over with. Lifting my gloves, I darted forward and let fly with my best right hook, crouching to get in low.

I think he must have been surprised that I went in for the killer blow straightaway, because I actually made decent contact with his rib cage. My glove sank into his flesh with a satisfyingly solid thump, and I was delighted with myself for exactly three nanoseconds before a medium-sized delivery truck slammed into my head and it exploded into stars. I felt myself go staggering across the canvas.

"Keep on your feet," Ricky yelled. "Don't go down, Fleur."

"Fight it!" Tarik cried. His voice was coming from a mile away. The room swam and circled with lights and punching bags and ropes and concerned faces. I staggered, keeping away from Ricky, trying to keep my gloves by my face. If that's what happened when you dropped your guard, I wanted no part of it.

But all the leg work had paid off.

I stayed on my feet.

"So let me get this straight," Blossom said. "You've fallen for a man because he told you he didn't want to punch you?"

"I didn't say I'd fallen for him. I just said he's really hot."

"And he doesn't want to punch you? You're sure about that, right?"

"Pretty sure, yes."

"He sounds like a keeper."

"I agree it sounds a bit underwhelming out of context . . ."

"It sounds demented. Who is this Tarik anyway? What's his backstory?"

"Backstory?" I said. "He's not a character from a fantasy novel." Blossom had a point, though. In hindsight, the whole evening had been a little confusing. And I wasn't sure what I thought about it. Tarik was gorgeous. There was no denying that. When he smiled at me, my tummy leaped like a salmon. And he did smile at me, in that way. I just wasn't sure I wanted to get involved with another boy right now. I didn't want to go back to Date Night.

And part of me knew it was different with Tarik. He wasn't "safe" like George had been. Safety wasn't what I thought of when I looked at him. Quite the reverse. I felt that if I didn't keep my guard up, Tarik might be someone who could really hurt me.

THE BIG FIGHT

Even though it was past midnight, Mum was still up when I got home. This time, though, there was no newspaper in front of her. This time she had her laptop open. Alarm bells started to ring.

"Hi," I said.

"Hello," she replied quietly, and I knew then something was definitely going down.

I walked past her to get a drink and glanced at what she was looking at on the screen. My heart skipped a beat as I saw she was on the Bosford Boxing Club website. At the bottom, in big black letters I saw

BONITA CLARK VS. FLEUR WATERS

"Could you come here and sit down, please," Mum said in her white-lipped voice.

"Oh crap," I muttered, under my breath. I filled a glass and brought it back, sitting opposite her.

"Is this about my Christmas list?" I asked. "I'd just like money."

"Shut up!" she snapped. "Just shut up!"

I stared at her, a little shocked by just how angry she was.

"It's always a joke with you. Or a barbed comment, or . . . or a lie."

"Well, you just overreact to everything," I said, my heart pounding. This is why I didn't fight back. It's what Blossom didn't get. The truth was, I was scared of my mother. Scared that if I started the battle, it would be a fight to the death.

"How can I have a normal conversation with you when you're just irrational?" I said.

"So I'm irrational now, am I?"

"Yes," I said. "I feel like I have to walk on eggshells around you."

"If only you would," she replied. "You lie to me. You laugh at me behind my back. You have no . . . no regard for me or how I feel."

"That's not true," I said. "Dad told me . . . he said . . ."

"He told you what?"

"Why you're always so . . . worried about me."

She narrowed her eyes. "What did he say?"

"He told me about Ben."

She sat back like I'd shot her and went white. The grandfather clock sliced the seconds off one by one as I waited for her to respond. I counted twenty-two before she spoke again.

"He had no right."

"*You* should have told me," I said. Even as I said it, I knew it was the wrong thing to say.

"I wanted to protect you," she said.

"I don't need you to protect me," I whispered. She seemed to wince. And then she looked incredibly tired.

"Don't do it, Fleur," she said. "Please. Don't take part in this fight. For me."

"I'm sorry, Mum," I replied. "I'm not doing it to hurt you. I know how you feel, and I'm sorry I haven't been truthful with you."

"So why weren't you?"

"Because I was a coward," I said. "Because I backed away from the fight. But I'm not backing down anymore. I'm fighting tomorrow." She shook her head sadly, and the clock carried on ticking.

"Well, don't expect me to be there, watching you," she said eventually. "I couldn't bear it."

"Whatever." I shrugged, not wanting her to see how upset I was. "I'll stay at Blossom's tonight."

THE COUNT

It was horribly cold when I woke. I checked the radiator, but it was off. Blossom's family didn't use the spare room very often. I'd forgotten to pack my dressing gown, of course. More important than the cold, though, was filling my aching belly with something. I went through into the kitchen. No one was up.

I ate four bowls of Shredded Wheat. Carbs were fine now, and frankly I think I'd reached peak jerky. Now it was all about weight. In eight hours or so I'd be jumping on a set of scales. If I didn't hit 143 pounds the fight would be off and everything would be for nothing. The training, the eating, the argument with Mum.

I ate another Shredded Wheat.

It was peaceful sitting there, munching my breakfast, not being attacked by my mother, not having to listen to my father explain the two different ways to clean a set of bike gears. Not smelling Ian Beale's farts. But there was another empty hole in my stomach, one that couldn't be filled. A guilty, churning hole of regret. I'd been furious, but underneath I knew it was all my fault. I had lied to her. I had betrayed her. I had hurt her. Because I'd been scared. Because I wouldn't stand up for myself. Because I backed away from the fight.

Eventually Blossom came in, looking exhausted. Blossom is not a morning person. She nodded at me and came over to the table, slumping her head onto her forearms.

"Want some coffee?" I asked.

"Yeah," she said. She opened one eye and peered at my drink. "What's that?"

"Bulkup with yogurt and blueberries," I said.

"I'll stick with coffee, please," she said. "So tell me about the fight with your mum."

"Oh God. It's all her fault," I replied. "If she wasn't so protective of me, then I wouldn't have to lie to her. I feel like she's suffocating me. Like she's trapped me with balloons and however many I pop I just can't get away."

"You and your mum are so similar," she laughed.

I stared at her. Turned to stone. "What did you say?" I asked eventually.

"You're two peas in a pod," she said. "Always have been."

"That's not true," I said. "That's the opposite of true. That's . . . false."

"You're both super-careful, you're both stubborn, you look the same, you have the same mannerisms, and you're both OBSESSED with punctuation." My jaw dropped. The words wouldn't come. I pursed my lips and shook my head. She was wrong.

I'd had about a dozen texts and missed calls from Dad since I'd turned off my phone the night before. Nothing from Mum. I'd texted him back to say I was fine and with Blossom. Midmorning Pip turned up and we drove down into Bosford to hang out, something we hadn't done for months, it seemed. Pip spent about half an hour in Vintage Vicky's; Blossom spent even longer in the feminist bookshop on South Street. Then it was my turn to choose the shop.

"Greggs?" Blossom sighed. "Do you know where the meat comes from in their pork pies?"

"No, but I know where it's going to end up," I replied, buying two. "In my belly."

"So, when's your fight start tonight?" Blossom asked as we left the shop. It was bitterly cold outside and I clutched the warm, greasy packet of food tightly.

"We're on last," I said. "So it should be around eight-thirty, maybe nine."

"If we sit in the front row, will we get splashed with blood?" Pip asked. I stopped and looked at him in surprise.

"You're coming?"

"Of course we're coming," Blossom laughed. "Wouldn't miss it for the world."

WEIGH-IN

I waddled up to the scales, feeling like a water-filled balloon. Ricky watched me nervously. He'd made me drink two liters of water a few minutes before and I was bursting for the loo. Sharon stood beside him, wringing her hands. Bonita had just been weighed, and she was at 158 pounds, just inside the middleweight category. No one was surprised that she'd hit her target. If Bonita wanted something, she just went ahead and did it. And she'd had less to lose than I'd had to gain.

I took a deep breath before I hopped onto the scale, then had a quick panic that having extra air in my lungs might make me lighter. So I breathed out again, before realizing how ridiculous that thought was. I could suck in the Goodyear Blimp and it wouldn't make any difference to my weight, so I took another great lungful.

"You're gulping like a carp," Tarik said. "Just breathe normally." I glared at him. I could see everyone peering to look, especially Bonita.

143 pounds

The room erupted into cheers. Tarik clapped me on the back. Sharon gave me a hug. Dan gave me a high five. Alex raised his eyebrows.

"Well done, Fleur," Ricky said, looking immensely relieved.

"Yes, it's all great, but can I go to the loo now?" I asked urgently.

As I rushed out I came face-to-face with Bonita, who'd watched the whole thing. She winked at me. I wondered just what I'd gotten myself into.

The hall was packed. Ricky had formed two dressing rooms up on the stage, behind the curtain, and Bonita and I watched proceedings from there. I spotted Blossom at the front, with Pip next to her. I saw the back of Dad's head, sitting on the aisle we'd be walking down in a few minutes. There was an empty seat next to him, which meant Mum wasn't there. I wasn't surprised. Bonita and I helped each other with our wraps and gloves, not really talking, avoiding each other's eyes.

"You're using ProHit gloves?" she asked.

"Yeah, why, what are you wearing?"

"RDX," she said with a smirk. "They're the best." I felt a surge of annoyance.

"It's not a competition," I said.

"It IS a competition," she replied.

The boys' bouts had all gone well. Tarik beat Jordan quite easily. Jordan was full of frantic fury for the first round, but Tarik just waited until he got tired, then finished him with a few well-aimed rights. The crowd was quiet at first but got louder as the evening went on. The hall wasn't that big really. There were a lot of people there, and Sharon was selling bottles of beer. Whenever someone received a good punch the whole place erupted with noise. I felt the hairs on the back of my neck tingle in anticipation. Soon I'd be walking out there.

Alex was Bonita's second. And Joe was mine. I'd hoped to have Tarik, but Ricky wanted someone with more experience. After the last fight, between Jerome and Simon, which Simon won on points, Ricky came to find us.

"Now, listen," he said. "This is the first proper fight for both of you. Don't go in there hell for leather, all right? It's a demonstration. Show them your skills, fair enough, but the object is not to try and murder the other fighter. We have friends and family out there." The speech was directed at the two of us, but I could see Ricky was looking mostly at Bonita.

He left, and Bonita and I caught each other's eye. I grinned awkwardly, but she just turned away. Was she nervous? She wasn't showing it. I cleared my throat.

"So this is our first fight."

"Yep," she said.

"We've got our friends and family out there . . ."

"You do," she said. "My mum couldn't make it."

"I just . . . I just wanted to make sure . . ."

"What?" she asked, turning to me. I was interrupting her preparations.

"It's just a demonstration match, yeah? We're not going to go at it tooth and nail?"

She fixed me with a glare and a wicked half-smile. "I don't know why *you're* here," she said. "But I'm here to fight."

Then the lights went down.

The crowd hushed as I heard a squeal of feedback. Ricky had brought a guitar amp and a microphone to make the announcements. I peered through a gap in the curtains to watch while Bonita shadowboxed behind me, puffing and hissing.

"Ladies and gentlemen!" his voice boomed out. Sharon rushed to turn the mic down a bit. "We have saved the best for last. Tonight, for your viewing pleasure we have the first ever women's boxing match at Bosford

Boxing Club. The fight will be three rounds of three minutes each. So without further ado, may I present to you for the very last fight of the evening: iii-ii-in the blue corner, weighing in at one hundred fifty-eight pounds, we have the 'Bosford Fist,' Bonita . . . Clark!"

Bonita shoved past me through the curtain to a brisk round of applause. She ran down the steps and down the aisle toward the ring, shadowboxing as she went. There were a few whistles and catcalls, too. I watched her climb into the ring, where she was met by Alex, who took her towel and squirted some water into her mouth.

"Aaaaaaa-and in the red corner," Ricky continued. "Weighing in at one hundred forty-three pounds, we have Fleur 'Killa' Waters!" The crowd clapped politely. I heard a few cheers and whistles. This was it. The butterflies in my tummy exploded into a frenzy of fluttering as I came out from behind the rope and trotted down the steps. I wasn't sure what I should do, but everyone was watching, expecting me to do something boxer-y, so I sideways-skipped my way down the aisle, swapping over halfway, trying to look like I knew what I was doing. I heard Pip whistling loudly and Blossom shouting out my name. Joe held the rope as I climbed into the ring and stood on the canvas, the spotlights dazzling me. My heart was thumping like the bass line at Lick'd. I turned 360 degrees, looking out at the crowd. I saw Blossom and Pip, I saw the Thursday ladies cheering like mad. I saw the boys, wraps off, fights over, watching us, clapping and stamping.

There was Dad. Smiling encouragingly.

And next to him sat Mum. I hadn't spotted her before, tiny as she was, and I'd assumed she hadn't come. But she had. I felt myself flush. On the one hand I was relieved and grateful that my mum had come to see me, even though it must have been the most terrifying thing she'd ever done, but on the other hand I now felt doubly nervous, knowing she was there. The pressure was really on.

Must not get killed, I thought to myself. *Must not get killed.*

She sat there, staring at me. White-faced, clutching a tissue. I waved a glove at her and she forced a quick smile. Dad reached over and squeezed her hand.

"Come on, Killa," Joe said. "Time to fight." He led me to my corner and held my wrist.

"Seconds out!" Ricky cried. "Touch gloves. Back to your corners, then come out fighting." I walked forward to Bonita and we touched gloves. If I'd hoped I might see some kind of mercy, or even nerves, in her eyes, I was wrong. She stared at me, emotionless. Like Drago, the Russian fighter in *Rocky IV.* I knew she wasn't going to go easy on me. That just wasn't in her blood. I swallowed nervously, my heart hammering inside my chest like it was trying to escape. We each turned and walked back to our corners.

Then Ricky rang the bell.

ROUND ONE

I don't know what I was thinking really. We'd already done the touching gloves thing. Ricky had said "come out fighting." But when I stepped forward I wasn't ready. It was as if I hadn't actually realized I was in a real fight this time, that it wasn't just sparring or drills. I walked right up to Bonita with my gloves down and she promptly hit me in the face.

The crowd gasped and I staggered back, feeling my legs go but just about managing to stay upright. There was no time to recover, either, because she was coming after me, glowering, clearly wanting to finish the fight before it had even gotten started. Bonita didn't want to just beat me, she wanted to drive me into the ground.

But I'd trained hard, too. Bonita may have thought I was some useless piece of dental floss who'd never worked hard for anything, but she was wrong. I'd run, I'd cycled, I'd lifted weights over and over until I hated the sight of the damn things. And I'd been there, doing my drills, hitting the bags, tapping the pads, working my abs, and eating. Oh, so much eating.

So I didn't go down. I stayed on my feet. And I didn't let her hit me again. I lifted my gloves and took guard. Bonita rained furious blows down on me. She was powerful and had such a long reach I knew I could never get close enough to return her blows. But I knew how to block. I was a Saxon after all. Gradually my head cleared and I remembered about moving my feet. I crabbed my way to the side and circled round her, getting away from the ropes.

Thud, thud, thud went her gloves against mine, my arms soaking up the impact. I heard someone shriek in the audience; it could have been Mum. I was on the back foot all right, but I knew if I could just get through this round, then I'd have a chance to recover, get my breath back and think about what I was doing.

Boom, boom, thud-thud. The punches kept coming, mostly jabs, from the face, but she dropped a few times to try a few hooks, one of which got me right in the left breast, causing a sharp pain. I gritted my teeth and kept up the gloves. I could hear shouts from the crowd. "Hit her. Keep going!"

"Come on, Fleur," someone cried. Maybe Blossom.

I realized I hadn't actually tried to punch Bonita yet. There hadn't been much opportunity.

Three minutes is a long time when you're being pummeled. I was forced back onto the ropes twice more but managed to slip away. I could see Bonita starting to get frustrated. That was good: in fact some of her punches were starting to look a little loose, her gloves dropping, leaving her head open. Could I perhaps . . . ?

The bell rang.

ROUND TWO

"You haven't hit her yet," Joe said as he squirted water into my mouth.

"I'm too busy trying to keep my head attached to my shoulders," I gasped.

"You missed a couple of openings," he said, wiping my chin with the towel. "She's strong, but she lacks discipline. She's all over the place."

"That's where my teeth will be if I drop my guard," I said. "All over the place."

"I thought you were going to go down when she punched you," Joe said. "What were you thinking walking out with your arms by your sides?"

"Do you have any *useful* advice?" I said, exasperated.

"Keep your gloves up and not down."

"Yeah, learned that one. Anything else?"

"Try hitting her?" Joe said. The bell rang and I hauled myself to my feet. Joe's second piece of advice might have sounded straightforward enough, but I had no intention of following it. Ricky had said to keep my guard up and I should get through the three rounds. I'd lose on points, but I wouldn't disgrace myself and it would be a good example to show the audience that women's boxing was safe.

So round two started off just as round one had finished, with me skipping around the ring, retreating from Bonita and weathering her constant attacks. Now I'd recovered from the initial blow, I felt better able to cope. Bonita was strong, but she was heavier and slower than me. I was fit and, by constantly moving, I was making it difficult for her. I could see her frustration growing, her face becoming redder and her breathing more and more labored.

When I thought I saw an opening, I jabbed once or twice, and one of my punches even got through. I think I might have scored a point but wasn't sure. My problem was that she had so much more reach than me. I had to get in very close to get a jab through her defenses. Each time I tried it she redoubled her attacks, driving me back again. Though I think I boxed much better in round two, she still outpunched me by twenty to one. As the round neared the end and I was wondering if the bell had broken, Bonita lurched forward and shoved me hard against the ropes. Ricky jumped forward to pull us apart, but not before she'd gotten in a few hard punches to my stomach. I hit back almost instinctively even though I knew I wasn't supposed to in the situation and felt my right hook connect satisfyingly. She grunted in pain.

The bell rang.

ROUND THREE

"Only one more round to go," I said, panting. "I can do this."

"Do what?" Joe said. "I haven't seen you do anything yet."

"I got in a couple of punches," I replied, slightly miffed.

"Well, I didn't see them," Joe said. "Except for that hook, but that won't count. Why don't you try that when you're not in a clinch?"

"Because that would leave me open," I said. "I can break the cavalry if I keep up the shield wall."

"What are you on about?"

"I mean I can get through the round if I can keep my guard up."

"But what's that worth?" Joe said. "What's the point of doing it at all if you're just trying to survive until the bell?"

"That's life, Joe," I said.

"No, it isn't," he replied. "Look, forget what Ricky told you. He was a great boxer, Ricky. Could have been a champion. But he was always cautious, played the percentages, you know? Sometimes the best thing to do is drop your guard and just hit the bastard."

Then the bell rang again and I hauled myself up.

Again I felt less than inclined to follow Joe's advice. If I let myself get KO'd by Bonita in front of my mother, I'd never be allowed to box again. It would be bad news for the club. Also, more important, it would really really hurt. No, the sensible, safe thing to do would be to carry on blocking and let Bonita take the win on points. There was no shame in that.

She came at me hard again and I tucked my head down behind both of my gloves, forming the shield wall. The Iceni could batter themselves against that if they liked; I wasn't going to show so much as a chink in the armor. By keeping my elbows tucked in tight, Bonita couldn't get through to my torso either, and being lighter on my feet and fit as a puma, I could keep moving, tiring her out.

As the seconds ticked down, I could feel her battering harder, hear her panting as she grew more and more frustrated. The occasional punch burst through, and she got a couple of roundhouse hooks into my sides, but nothing I couldn't handle. I was giving away points here and there, but that didn't matter.

Then once again, Bonita rushed forward and embraced me in a clinch. "Come on, Petal, fight," she hissed. "Take a bloody swing." As Ricky pulled us apart, she jabbed out at me, hitting me in the breast again. I gasped as the pain hit me and my entire right side seemed to freeze up. Shocked into immobility, I could do nothing but watch as Bonita came at me again and slammed a glove into my face. The crowd roared as I staggered back and spun, hitting the ropes hard, my head reeling.

If this were a cartoon, little birds and stars would be circling my head. If I hadn't been held up by the ropes, I would have gone down for sure. The crowd roared at the blow. In the maze of blurred faces, I saw Dad, his mouth open in an O of horror. Next to him sat Mum, looking absolutely terrified. I had to do something.

I spun back around dizzily to see Bonita coming in to finish me off. She grinned and pulled back a fist. *Keep your gloves by your cheeks*, I heard Ricky say in my head. *Punch from the face*. Bonita hadn't done this. She'd bent her arm right back, exposing her head. Her other glove was down and wide, forgotten. In her desperation to land the killer blow, she'd forgotten the lesson we learned right back at the start. She'd left herself open. Suddenly my head cleared as I was flooded with a jolt of adrenaline. I knew exactly what I had to do.

Should have listened to Ricky, I thought as I danced forward in slow motion and hit her as hard as I could with a left. Not my strong right hook. Not my killer uppercut. Just a simple, straight left, because that was the right punch for the situation.

There has never been a blow as sweet as that one. Not Ali. Not Joe Frazier. Not Rocky bloody Balboa ever put as much into a punch as I put into that left. Every mile I'd cycled, every step I'd run, every leg I'd raised, every sodding packet of jerky I'd eaten, went into that hit.

As Bonita went down it occurred to me that she'd probably never been hit before. Not like that anyway. I knew what it was like when Destiny got in a good one, and then again when Ricky "tapped" me last week. But no one had ever put one on Bonita's buzzer quite like I had. She hit the canvas hard, and to utter silence. Just like when I'd scored the goal on the field hockey pitch, it seemed no one could quite believe what I'd done.

Then Ricky darted forward to tend to the fallen Bonita, and that triggered the crowd to react with an enormous roar. I spun, confused, and saw that everyone was on their feet, clapping, cheering, whooping and whistling. Joe ducked into the ring and gave me a massive hug.

"You did it, Killa! I bloody knew you'd do it!" Then Sharon was there, and Blossom and Dad, but not Pip because he'd gotten caught in the ropes. I caught a glimpse of Mum in the crowd, sitting bolt upright, white-faced, clutching her tissue and staring right at me in astonishment. Tarik squeezed me in a great bear hug. Everyone was clapping me on the back, but all I could think about was Bonita. I pulled away from the crowd and knelt beside her. Ricky had helped her into a sitting position.

"Are you okay?" I asked. She blinked at me, trying to focus.

"Good hit," she said. "Bloody good hit." And then I was dragged away and it was time to go and celebrate.

ELEVEN BEERS. ONE COKE, FULL FAT.

We went to Chickos for the post-fight meal. We pretty much filled the whole upper floor. Sharon had reserved loads of tables. I'd wanted to ask Bonita to come, but she'd slipped off. Ricky had been a bit worried about her because she'd been so quiet after the fight, but the Saint John Ambulance lady checked her over and said she was fine. Part of me felt bad about having won. I almost felt like I'd tricked her into opening up her guard like that. That I'd won by a lucky blow. But Joe told me I'd played it perfectly.

"Sometimes your opponent beats himself," he said. "And you should let him."

"Or her," I reminded him.

"Or her. The trick is never to try and play him . . . her . . . them at his . . . her . . . their own game. Play it your way. Wait until he . . . she . . . they make the mistake."

"That's not what you said before the fight; you just kept telling me to hit her."

"And you did. Eventually," he said. "The thing about you, Killa, is that you don't like being told what to do. You do things your own way." I looked at him, wondering how he knew me so well. Either he was an experienced observer of human behavior or I was just a very transparent person. While we were waiting for the food to arrive, I went over to the next table and sat opposite my mother, who was staring at Simon's electronic tag.

Mum looked at me and breathed in. Then she smiled. "Well done," she said. I inspected her to try and get a clue as to what she was thinking. Was there a hint of pride in her expression? If so, it was heavily masked by a look of relief combined with nervous exhaustion.

"Thanks, Mum," I said. "I'm glad you came."

"I hated it all," she said. "But I wouldn't have missed it for the world."

I laughed.

"So are you going to keep it up?" she asked. I nodded.

I hadn't even asked myself the same question yet, but I already knew the answer.

"I know you think it's dangerous, Mum," I said. "And I suppose, honestly, it is a little. It's a contact sport and there's always a risk. But everything in life is risky, at least everything worth doing. And with proper training, and proper rules and a supportive group of people behind you . . . well, I think the risk is worth taking."

I was dragged away at that point by Jerome and Simon, who wanted me to come and have a beer with them. I drank some, just to be polite, but I didn't really enjoy it. Mum and Dad left soon after. I was exhausted and I headed home after an hour or so, leaving the party in full swing. As I pulled on my coat and headed out into the December chill I heard someone follow me out the door.

"Hey, you," Tarik called.

I stopped and turned. "Hey yourself," I replied. He walked over to me, in his shirtsleeves, his face lit by the Christmas lights running down the high street.

"So I guess you didn't see that coming, huh?" I said. "Me beating Bonita."

"Of course I did. I knew you had it," Tarik replied. "You were playing it cool. Waiting for the right moment." Suddenly he was standing close to me, and my tummy was feeling a little like it had just before the fight.

"I'm really not that cool," I said. "She just opened herself up and I took my chance." He stood there, not saying anything, as if he was waiting. A newspaper page flapped by, picked up by a gust of wind. Tarik shivered.

"You'd better get back inside," I said. "Before you freeze."

"I'm not cold," he said.

"Well, I am," I replied.

"I think you're amazing, Fleur," he said.

"It was just a lucky punch."

"That's not what I mean," he said. Then he leaned forward and hugged me tightly. I wrapped my arms around him, feeling his taut muscles through his thin shirt. He shivered again.

"Get inside," I ordered, pulling back. "You're in training."

"Okay, Coach," he said, grinning. Then he leaned forward, more quickly this time, and kissed my cheek. His lips lingered for a fraction of a second. A fraction of a second that said everything. He paused, his face close to mine.

"See you tomorrow?" he asked.

I nodded. "See you tomorrow."

When I came downstairs the next morning I was greeted by Mum, who gave me a huge hug. I hugged her back and we actually had a bit of a moment. Ian Beale was in high spirits and came out of his basket for a while, snuffling around my shoes. He even licked my hand, which was a nice gesture, but his saliva smells like a gangrenous sailor's leg, so I had to go and wash it with rubbing alcohol. Later on Dad and I went for a quick ride together before lunch. Roast chicken and mashed potatoes, of course. It was good to be home. Good to have things back to normal. Normal, that is, except for two things that made me feel that things were going to be better from now on.

The first thing was Mum let Dad stack the dishwasher all by himself.

And the second was that after lunch Mum took the newspaper with the article about me and cut out the photo and the accompanying story. She stuck them into her scrapbook while I made her a cup of tea. Then she took out an old photo album I'd never seen before and showed me some pictures of Ben.

I never knew I had so many tears inside me. But I got a lot of them out.

TRAFFIC LIGHTS

Bonita didn't come to training on Wednesday. After the initial elation, I'd almost started to feel bad about it. It would have been much better if I'd stuck to the original plan and let her win on points. You don't need to blow out other candles for your own to shine brightly.

It was the last session before Christmas, and we all took ages to say good-bye afterward, chatting about Christmas plans and discussing how the fights had gone on Saturday. A grinning Sharon came over in a state of great excitement to tell me that after Fight Night they had been deluged by inquiries from new people, including at least a dozen girls. Ricky was thinking of starting a Friday session to accommodate everyone.

"It's all down to you," she said.

"No, it isn't," I replied, feeling myself blush. "It's down to all of us . . . but partly me, perhaps."

Tarik sauntered up just as I gave Dan a hug.

"I need to chat with Ricky, but if you wait until I've finished I'll walk you to the traffic lights," he said.

"Sure," I replied. He grinned and slung his bag over his shoulder, revealing a tantalizing glimpse of his trapezius muscles.

We chatted about school and Christmas as we walked and I reflected on how easy things were. How different I felt with him than I had with George. For all George's safety and certainty, I had never realized how constricted I'd felt. How my life had narrowed into a safe, predictable path. I had no idea where things were going with Tarik, and that was exciting.

"So, are you going to keep fighting?" he asked after a while.

"Always," I said.

"I mean in the ring," he clarified.

"Maybe," I said. "Or maybe I should quit while I'm ahead."

"What if Bonita wants a rematch?" he teased.

"Don't even joke about it," I said. We came to an intersection and stopped. Up ahead were the traffic lights. He turned to face me.

"Are you going straight home?" Tarik asked. "If we turn right we get to Morrison's car park. And you know what they have in Morrison's car park." Right, left, straight on. Just at that moment I felt as though any direction would do, as long as he came with me. But there was something bothering me. Something important I needed to do.

"I'd love to go for a triple doner with you, Tarik," I said. "But there's someone I need to see."

"Okay," he said, looking slightly disappointed. Then he shrugged. "See you next year?"

"Or earlier," I said. "You've got my number. And you owe me a kebab." He broke into a huge smile, and I leaned forward and kissed him on the cheek, letting my lips linger for just a fraction of a second.

There's always one family on every street that goes mad for Christmas and swathes their house in hideous, flashing lights. It wasn't Bonita's house; it was the one next door. I stood there for a while, taking in the falling-snowflake lights, the illuminated sleigh and the multi-colored fiber-optic Christmas tree. My personal favorite was an animatronic Santa bending over to feed a carrot to Rudolph. Only some fun-loving local had turned Rudolph around so now it looked like jolly old Saint Nick was trying to jam the carrot in an entirely less festive orifice.

Bonita's door opened and she peered out at me suspiciously.

"Did you do that?" I asked, pointing to Rudolph. She nodded. A dog barked furiously inside her house and I heard a loud thud as it crashed into something.

"Good work," I said.

"What you doing here?" she asked.

"You didn't come to boxing. Thought I'd pop by and make sure you were okay."

"You didn't hit me *that* hard," she said.

"I know. That's not what I meant," I said.

"Wanna come in?"

"Yeah, okay. Does the dog bite?"

"Yes. I'll put him in the laundry room."

Bonita made us both a cup of tea. The kitchen was cluttered but clean. I don't know what I'd expected, but the whole house was tidy and looked-after. The only worry was the dog, whose bloodcurdling growls I could hear behind the closed door at the back of the house.

"So why didn't you come to training?" I asked as the kettle boiled.

She shrugged. The dog started scrabbling at the door and woofed a throaty bark at us. I took out the paper and showed her. "Did you see this? Sharon has had loads of people signing up for next year. Loads of women."

"Great," Bonita said. She handed me a cup of tea and led me through to the front room. The dog thudded hard into the laundry-room door. I hoped it was stronger than it looked.

"Since the London 2012 Olympics, loads of women have taken up boxing," I recited as we sat down. "But not that many of them are sparring, or taking part in tournaments." I'd been sort of preparing this and now I was worried it sounded like a lecture. I pointed to the picture again. "It's really important that this kind of positive message gets out there. To show women that boxing is safe and fun, as well as being great for fitness. I don't think you should give up just because you lost a fight."

Bonita blinked in surprise. "Who said anything about giving up?"

"Oh, it's just that . . . well, you didn't come to training . . ."

"I had to look after my brother," she said. "Mum's working. Some of us have responsibilities."

"Sorry," I said, feeling embarrassed again. The dog crashed into the door. I thought I heard splintering.

"I'll be back next year," Bonita said. "And I'm going to pound you into the dirt."

"We'll see about that," I replied, my hackles rising. But then I looked up at her and saw laughter in her eyes.

"I knew you had some fight in you," Bonita said. "I just needed to keep poking you until you poked back." I grinned and sipped my tea.

THUD. That door was definitely splintering. It was time to go. As I was leaving Bonita thanked me.

"What for?"

"For coming to see me. It's not been easy, having to move here, after Dad left. You know, we used to live in a bigger place. In East Bosford."

I shook my head. "I didn't know that."

She shrugged. "Anyway, I felt ashamed to have friends around."

"Is that what we are?" I asked in surprise. "Friends?"

Bonita shrugged again. "What would you call us?"

"How about . . . sparring partners?" I suggested.

Bonita grinned. "Works for me. See you next year."

BATTLE

"Are you ready for this?" I asked Pip. He looked at me and nodded vigorously, his helmet slipping down over his eyes.

"Are *you* ready for this?" I asked Blossom. She smiled grimly, gripping the halberd tightly.

Then the cry went up. A hundred Norman knights ran up the hill screaming with murderous intent. "Now!" I cried. From our hiding place in the bushes at the bottom of the hill, the three of us sprang out and joined the back of the charge. The unfamiliar Norman armor felt strange, awkward and heavy. But it also felt right, what I was doing, and I was fit enough to handle it.

The cavalry came charging up behind us as we ran, stumbling and panting over the rough ground. Ahead, up the hill, we saw the line of Saxon warriors standing waiting for us. Shields interlocked. I heard horses' hooves behind me and turned to see Garnet glaring at us in fury. I grinned and kept running.

"Come on, Pip," I heard Blossom call. Pip was struggling quite a bit under the weight of the armor. But Blossom seemed as strong as Bonita, she held her halberd high, placard muscles firm.

"Oh God," Pip panted as we neared the Saxon lines. "This is the part I hate."

"Onward!" I shouted, clapping him on the back, urging my friend forward. With a great clatter and a ringing of steel, the two mighty armies came together. I found myself face-to-face with Pete Thorburn, who was a regular on the Saxon side. He seemed quite surprised to see me there in Norman garb but didn't break ranks.

"Hi, Pete!" I cried cheerily, swinging my axe at him. It clanged off the shield. To my left, I heard Pip give a great wail as another Saxon waved a sword at him. He made as if to turn and run, but Blossom and I grabbed him and held firm.

"Wait!" Blossom said. "Remember what we talked

about? You have to make it look good. Put on a show. Then you can run."

Pip nodded and swallowed. "Okay," he said, lifting his sword.

"You can do this," I told him. Together, the three of us ran back at the Saxons and hacked at the shield wall. I got a couple of good hits in on poor old Pete's shield before Garnet called for the retreat. Pip dropped his sword in relief, turned and sprinted off toward his wood. We charged after him, whooping with delight.

"You did it, Pip!" Blossom yelled. "You did it!" But Pip didn't respond. Having been given permission to run, he was damn well going to.

When the battle was over, we caught up with my parents in the café for a victory Bakewell tart. They'd come along for the day. Mum was trying harder to "take an interest in my activities," as she put it. I think it was more that she wanted to keep an eye on me, but that was fine too. While Pip went to the loo, Mum and I looked through the menu, pointing out grocer's apostrophes and typos.

"Look, you can get a cup of chino," I said.

"Or something belonging to a blueberry muffin to judge by the possessive apostrophe," Mum added. "I wonder what it is?"

Blossom rolled her eyes. "So what did you think of the battle reenactment?" she asked my parents.

"I thought it was brilliant," Dad said enthusiastically. "Very convincing."

"It looked extremely violent," Mum said, shaking her head disapprovingly. "Isn't it dangerous, swinging those swords about?"

"No," Blossom and I said in unison.

"Yes," Pip called as he returned and folded himself onto a chair.

Mum groaned. "Boxing, battle reenactments. Why do you girls choose such dangerous activities?"

"Because we can, Mum," I said, pouring her a fresh cup of tea. "Because we can."

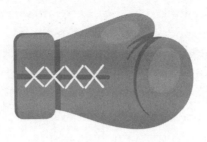

AUTHOR'S NOTE

I didn't set out to write a feminist book. It just sort of happened. I was asked to write a follow-up to my 2014 book *Boys Don't Knit*, a story about a boy taking up a nontraditional pastime (knitting, obvs). *Girls Can't Hit* just seemed like the other side of the same coin.

But of course a book about a girl who takes up boxing HAS to be a feminist novel, because there's so much to deal with. Body shape and weight. Aggression and physicality. Parental concern. Shame. I was nervous but my teenage daughters provided both inspiration and incentive to do my best. *Girls Can't Hit* is dedicated to them.

Of course my agent and editors were of enormous help. They told me where I was going wrong, they showed me where my bias or privilege was evident. Most importantly, they pointed out more than once that I needed to lighten up. In the first few drafts I was trying too hard to tackle all the issues, and poor Fleur, the main character, ended up having to take on so much that the book became far too heavy.

In the end it's a funny, and hopefully uplifting, book about an ordinary girl finding herself in an extraordinary set of circumstances. That's all. I'm not trying to destroy the Patriarchy (I would if I could), I'm not trying to mansplain feminism to the world. I'm just trying to make people laugh, to poke a bit of fun at traditional gender roles and maybe to provide a bit of inspiration for someone who wants to try something a little different.

A man writing a feminist text might be taking a risk, but as Fleur learns in the book, sometimes you just have to drop your guard and take a swing.